Silent
IS THE HEART

DIANNA ROMAN

WILD ONE
PRESS

For information address diannaromanbooks@hotmail.com

Published by Wild One Press
Cover design by Wild One Press

Editing by Jennifer Green
Proofread by Margaret Neal

ISBN: 978-1-959553-29-8 (ebook)
ISBN: 978-1-959553-30-4 (Trade paperback)
ISBN: 978-1-959553-31-1 (Hardcover)

CONTENT ADVISORY

This work is not intended for those under the age of eighteen. Please read at your discretion. It contains the following topics:

- Loss of a loved one/parent
- Descriptions of domestic abuse and death
- Feelings of despair and grief
- Feelings of low self-worth
- A self-deprecating vocal impairment term used by a vocally impaired MC
- Descriptions of queerphobic speech used by an antagonist
- Secret infatuation of an adult by a seventeen-year-old
- Criminal plot elements
- Explicit adult language
- Explicit consensual sexual content

NOTE TO READERS

Several characters within this work use American Sign Language (ASL). While there are multiple citation suggestions to write ASL dialogue, for the purpose of this work, ASL is written in italics.

Silent
IS THE HEART

to our younger selves
who had no idea
what we were capable of enduring

SPECIAL THANKS

Thank you to my Alpha reader, Beta readers, and my ARC team for your enthusiasm and support in helping me prepare this story for publication and release. To Marlene Trabal Lebron and Stephanie Henigin--thank you for all of your emails and messages back and forth with me on your speech pathology backgrounds. And to H. Cass for your tattooing expertise inputs.

To my fans--thank you for allowing the stories in my head to find a home. Without you, I would just be talking to myself all day.

THEN

PROLOGUE
Easton

"Mom… talk to me."

Only the rattle of the car engine and the tires crushing the snow answer my anxious plea. She looks bad, so bad. He turned her face into a bloody melted wax figurine this time, completely destroying the image I associate with all things good in this godforsaken world.

Why did she hide the money in the trailer? I should have never gone over to Ben's place. I could have stopped him.

The old *Dodge* jerks into another slide on a patch of ice. I think my diaphragm is broken from his sucker punch, seizing my breath as I grip the steering wheel.

This is crazy. No one in their right mind would be on the road tonight. There aren't even any snow plows out. It's not like I have a choice, though. Staying at the trailer and waiting for Leonard to finish the job wasn't an option. The prick. The fucking prick. It's quicker to say *Dad*, but that word has never given me the same satisfaction.

I don't even know where the edge of the road is, so I hope to hell the fading tire tracks in front of me don't lead me astray.

Blinking doesn't help clear my vision. The big fat flakes are coming at us like warp speed in a spaceship. It would help if my right eye wasn't swollen shut. And it really would help if that fucking bastard hadn't shot the only person in this world who matters to me.

"Mom?"

The word comes out garbled and broken, tears stinging my open eye. I'm supposed to be strong for her, the way she's always strong for me, but I need to hear her voice. I need to know I'm not alone.

There's so much blood. The kitchen towel pressed to the side of her head is no longer white. Her golden hair is saturated and plastered to her cheek.

A moan. Just a soft one. It was barely a breath through her swollen lips, but it was a sound.

She's still with me. He didn't take her from me. We still have a chance.

I don't care that he found the money. It was such a pathetic amount, anyway. Between the bills and this worthless car that rarely runs, my grocery bagging and her house cleaning jobs left little to squirrel away. It took so long to convince her to leave once and for all, and now it was all for nothing. I've been living on false hope for months.

We should have just gotten in the car the last time he was gone on his trucking route and drove until the car gave out. We could have slept in it and gotten jobs wherever it died. Anything would be better than this.

"We're not going back," I warn adamantly, but that, too, comes out sounding like the frail voice of a frightened child. "I don't care about school. I'm getting a job, and I'll take care of you, but we're not going back. We'll be fine. I promise."

She doesn't answer, but she doesn't need to. *I'm* in charge now. Things are going to be different. I'm freezing, shaking so bad my teeth are clacking together. I don't have a coat. We don't have a dime be-tween us, but I don't care. We're going to make it to the hospital. They'll help her. And Leonard Bennick can burn in hell. If he doesn't, I don't understand why I was born.

CHAPTER 1
Easton

Death by pudding—*that's* how they'll get me. It hits me with clarity as I stir yet another serving of the brown glop on my lunch tray. And here I thought it'd be from going stir-crazy from being trapped in this hospital bed. Something a little more guts and glory, like the electric chair after I jab a spork into that stupid psychologist's jugular.

Feelings.

Is she for real? Like she honestly gets paid to ask people the obvious? How do I get *that* fucking job?

'How do you feel about what happened, Easton?'

Gee, let me think…

I have freaking metal plates and screws in my leg and there's some kind of primitive-looking torture cage fastened to it. The doctors don't know if I'll have a permanent limp. I had to learn how to fucking swallow again like a damn baby. I can't talk, and hm, what else? Oh, let's see.

Mom is… dead.

Gone-forever dead. Never coming back because I didn't save her from that miserable bastard.

Everything is fucking peachy.

At least he's in jail, so they tell me.

They tell me lots of things—like how they buried Mom last month while I was in a coma. How I'm a ward of the state now since I have no available or appropriate guardians. How, if or when I do regain my voice and the ability to walk, I'll be set up with a foster family since I'm only seventeen and essentially an orphan. In short, they tell me all the new ways in which I'm fucked.

That's what I get for thinking I had it bad before the accident. Life decided to make me earn my self-pity the hard way. Staring at the glop, I blink at the liquid heat in my eyes.

Before the accident.

That's the definition of my life now—*before* the accident. There's no *after*. Not any way you look at it. No matter how many screws they put in my leg. No matter how many specialists they send in here to try to fix me physically or emotionally. Mom is gone, and I'm just a kid, a poor kid from nowhere, from nothing, with nobody, and now I'm broken.

How do I *feel*?

"I fucking hate everything!" The raspy words tear from my throat in no more than a whisper, but it's like I'm ejecting broken glass. I can't even scream to expel my demons.

IFUCKINGHATETHIS!

The tray clatters to the floor from the sweep of my arm. The minor exertion, the carnage of the pudding spattered on the floor, brings zero relief.

MJ is on duty today, which means I won't even get scolded for my outburst. She's too… patient. I'm sick of everyone feeling sorry for me. Sick of learning terminology I've never heard of before: *prolonged intubation, vocal fold paralysis.* Sick of the pitying looks when I refuse to speak. Sick of the stupid tactics to get me to communicate.

I'm not going to fucking type or write notes, saying I'm sad, pissed off, and maybe even a little terrified about what the hell will happen to me. If I don't feel like saying it out loud, I sure as hell don't feel like writing it down. What difference will it make? It's not like it'll change any-thing. Can't they at least allow me the dignity of not complaining?

I'm alive. Mom isn't. If I'm supposed to feel grateful for that, I don't understand how it's possible.

I just need to walk. If I have to sound like an eighty-year-old who deep-throated someone for the rest of my life each time I speak, fine. As soon as I can get out of this fucking bed, though, I'm gone. I'll find a job somewhere. One that doesn't require speaking. I don't have any-thing to say anyway, nor do I have the desire to speak to anyone, even if I could.

Flopping my head back against my pillow, I dig the heels of my palms into my eyes just to feel pressure somewhere other than in my chest and my leg. My cheekbones are so pronounced they feel bony under my touch.

I'm so damn weak. I should have eaten the fucking pudding.

With my luck, they'll think I had trouble swallowing again from my vocal fold paralysis and threw my tray in frustration from that. If they downgrade me on this abysmal dysphagia diet, I really will lose my shit. I was already on the scrawny side before the accident. Now, I'm as puny as a thirteen-year-old. I should have bulked up so I could have stopped Leonard.

I should have…

Should have…

Stop, Easton.

Stop it.

You promised not to do the 'should have' *game again today.*

Pinching my eyes closed, I exhale deeply, trying to ward off the ever-present crowd of regrets. I'm not sure what's worse—being a prisoner of my grief over Mom or being a prisoner in general. If I had more mobility, at least I could burn off some of the restlessness over the things twisting me up inside.

Reaching over to my nightstand, I feel for the folder of printer paper that Dr. Deetma, the psychologist, left for me to communicate with like a caveman. Swiping up a pencil, I flip the folder open and pull the drawing out that I tucked behind the unused pages. Dr. Deetma doesn't need the chance to dissect my sketches. I'd never get out of here if he saw this.

The demon, engulfed in a backdrop of hellfire, however, soothes something in my agitated soul. I feel a sense of kinship staring at it, as though it's my reflection. I don't need a psychologist to tell me the comparison probably isn't healthy.

Putting the graphite tip on a blank page, I wait for inspiration—*healthy* inspiration. Less violent inspiration. Good thing I have a fuck load of time because nothing comes to mind.

The vise grip around my heart that squeezes at night when it's silent as a tomb here at Hampton Hills Rehabilitation Center gives a tug on the dead organ in my chest when a vision comes to mind. The happy memory calls to me, begging for me to give it life. I shouldn't. I really shouldn't because I'll end up a sobbing mute mess that will get me put on some prescription I don't need, but my fingers move.

They trace out the outline of almond-shaped eyes, long lashes, and sparkling irises. My thumb rubs in the shading of cheekbones, moving with fervor now as some of the gnawing rage melts away. My gaze gets lost in the illusion coming to shape before my eyes.

It's not her. I know it's not her, but it's the only way I can see her now. I don't even have any photos of her here. Who knows what will happen to my meager possessions in our trailer back in Wayside? It was in Leonard's name. I might be a kid who doesn't know shit about the world, but I'll bet because it was his, he had to sell it for lawyer fees. I doubt there was little concern over what to do with the crap inside.

Scratching the lines of Mom's curly blonde hair, I'm determined to resist the pain threatening to choke my heart. It feels traitorous to cling to a happy memory when I should be mourning her, but God, I can't help it. I need something positive for just ten minutes, even if it is just a trick of the mind, a vision that's forever lost in time. Her smile takes form under my ministrations—the recall of her laughing last summer at me and my buddy Ben when we were whipping *POP-ITS* at each other in the backyard on the Fourth of July. He kept screaming like a girl each time I connected one of the little paper TNT bombs in his vicinity. Mom and I nearly pissed ourselves at his shrieking.

We stole a few of his dad's beers later and camped out in the woods behind his house. I can still remember the feel of his hair against my arm when I wrestled him into a headlock while teasing him over his fear of the cracking pop noises from earlier.

I knew he was curious. I think I'd always known. Our tit-for-tat dares and talking shit over the previous school year when he moved to town had escalated to the point I knew it was only a matter of time until one of us caved in and took the leap. All our joking and feigned brotherly love pecks to the other's head or cheek for months weren't the mockery we played them off to be. At least not to me. I was just waiting for him to find his nerve.

I can still feel the way his trembling hand cupped over my fly as we lay in our tent. That was the start of it. The real start—the beginning of no more lying, no more pretending to be people we weren't.

I wonder what he's doing now. Unlike me, he's always had the chance to go to college. Is it wrong that I feel bad, though, for not being at his sexual-discovery disposal for the rest of senior year? He's too damn shy about it to try with anyone else at Wayside High.

High school. Another memory.

I never expected to go to college, but I at least thought I'd finish high school. I'll be even further behind the curve than I thought whenever I get the hell out of here. As long as they don't dump me off in Wayside when they evict me, I'll make the most of it. There's nothing for me there.

"You like him a lot, don't you?"

Studying Mom's mouth, I can almost imagine it moving as she vocalized that ridiculous assumption. Yet, I think she knew even then that Ben and I didn't spend time together because of some teenage infatuation.

"He's all right," I'd told her. I'd boldly elaborated then—because I suspected her curiosity—the way I always did, "Cute butt, even if he does scream like a girl."

Maybe it's the honesty I miss the most. Because right now, I'd love someone I could be completely honest with the way Mom and I always were with each other. Being honest with yourself doesn't feel as good as it does with someone you can trust.

A clatter near the door to my room has my hand flinching. My discarded tray slides across the floor amid the soft exhale of a man's voice cursing, "Oh shit."

Following khaki slacks up to a belted waist and a neatly tucked in green polo shirt, my eyes take in the way its snug fit spreads over its owner's chest. The way it clings to a set of broad shoulders. How the sleeves hug his biceps. I didn't know ridiculous clothes could fit someone so well, but it might have something to do with the head attached to the most enticing body I've encountered in my seventeen years.

A faint shadow of stubble frames his jaw and his... smile. Fuck. Maybe it's because I was just reminiscing over my romps in the woods with Ben, but a tingle trickles down to my dormant cock like his smile is sending a radio signal to it.

Ben's lips made me curious about kissing, simply because I knew he was into guys and would let me. This guy's mouth, though? It's an education because I'm suddenly imagining how well everything else would go with kissing it, letting me know anything I've done before was just child's play.

Side-stepping over my pudding like it's an afterthought, the fuck-me smile, the sparkling jade-green eyes, thick brown hair, and the sexy, youthful face that can't be too much older than me approaches. One hand extended, the other holding a takeaway cup from *The Shake Shack*. The mouth moves in a way that shouldn't be so hypnotic.

"Hi. I'm Aaron. Aaron Manicki."

Somehow, my palm ends up connecting with his like I'm a robot that has no control over my body. It defies every rebellious behavior I've exhibited during my stay at Hampton *'Hell Hole'* Hills where I've been shipped to in the armpit of northern Maine. I don't consort with the enemy. My brain seems to be ignoring the fact Hampton's logo is embroidered on that well-fitting polo shirt. His warm grip makes my heart flip.

What the hell is that all about?

"Oh, my God," he whispers, his face going slack.

Can he feel it too?

Every muscle in my body goes rigid. Instinct has me wanting to check if my dick has gone hard beneath the hospital bed sheets and I've been caught, but I remember my folder is open on my lap. He can't see anything, even if my teenage hormones decided to make their first reappearance since before the accident right now.

Except, he sees *something*. *Mom.* My drawing of Mom.

"Jesus. That's absolutely incredible," he whispers.

Those ashen eyes flick to mine like I'm a world wonder. It's the first time someone here has looked at me like they're trying to figure me out, but in a way that doesn't make me want to punch them in the throat. It's a look that makes me think his statement means *I'm* incredible. That I'm not some unfortunate kid who lost his mom because his dad is a piece of garbage. That it's completely irrelevant for once that I had a traumatic brain injury, smashed my lower leg to smithereens, and am just a number waiting to be ejected out of here and into the system.

A sliver of guilt threads its way through my marrow over how good that makes me feel. I'm not supposed to feel good. I'm supposed to be miserable. Mom can't feel good, so I shouldn't either.

Except, the longer I stare into those eyes that seem mesmerized by me and feel that strong, warm hand surrounding mine, the more I don't want to let go or look away.

"Um, sorry," he stammers, releasing my hand and shaking his head like he was lost. It's a heady idea, the ability to make someone feel lost over me. "I tried to draw when I was in high school art class, but I was terrible at it. Not a talented bone in my body."

By all that's holy, I think I'm smiling. Who am I?

"I'll be your new speech pathologist," he adds.

Fuck.

Speech. There goes my smile and him thinking I'm incredible.

But then he smiles again, like the prospect of talking to me is the reason he was put on this earth. It's such a goddamn sunshine-y sight that it should make me sick, not send a ping of static down my limbs.

"I'm looking forward to getting to know you and, if you don't mind…I'd love to see more of those drawings sometime."

It's probably cordiality, trained professionalism, and more fake pleasantries because he's a staff member here. Maybe I hit my head harder than I thought because it doesn't register as a ploy. It just sounds like exactly what I want to hear.

Ben and I must have been really bad at our camping explorations because not a single blow job from him left me as breathless as I feel right now at the idea of Aaron Manicki wanting to get to know me. Hampton Hills must have had him locked up in the fuck-me-running-closet and just unleashed their biggest weapon because if he keeps smiling at me like that, I think I might try to say anything he wants me to for him.

CHAPTER 2

Aaron

Dr. Norton's pipe tobacco fumes hit me like a dense fog as I walk into his office. I don't have the heart to tell him that the window he has cracked open behind his desk does little to conceal his habit.

"Aaron! Planning on lunch at your desk today?" he asks, nodding at the carryout bag in my hand. The lines in his forehead multiply as he squints over the top of his bifocals. "Don't suppose you could encourage the rest of the staff to adopt that work ethic?"

"I just wanted to kill two birds with one stone." Trying to limit how much contaminated air I inhale, I approach, setting my reports down on his desk. "Here are my summaries from my morning cases. Thought I'd drop them off before my next session."

Before I can pivot and make my escape from the ashtray office, he asks, "The Bennick boy? How's that going? He talking yet?"

It shouldn't bother me that his question seems like an afterthought, the way he redirects his gaze back to the mess of paperwork on his desk. He's in charge. I'm just at Hampton Hills for my fellowship, but maybe I'm in danger of doing the one thing you're not supposed to do—getting attached to a patient.

I'm not. I just can't believe Easton Bennick has been here for almost two months and in that time, no one had gotten him to complete his swallow therapy or speak. Granted, he was intubated for three weeks, which is part of his current problem, but I didn't fathom anyone in the medical profession would ever consider washing their hands of a patient, especially one so young. Then again, I never fathomed a patient would refuse to do their swallow and speech therapy.

"Um, not exactly…"

"Mm. That's a shame. We don't get many patients that young. Shame to think of the difficulties he'll have ahead of him, but we've done what we could." He sighs. "Well, I warned you. Edwards and Wagner had a heck of a time just getting through swallow therapy with him, so don't beat yourself up. Just file your close-out report when you have time, and I'll put it in his record, so they can consider it when they make placement for him." Glancing up, he hands me a new file. "Here's one that you should be able to make some headway on. Sixty-two-year-old stroke patient."

Is he…suggesting I'm done with Easton? It can't be that simple.

"I…didn't mean to give you the impression all was lost," I assure him, taking the file. "I made some progress yesterday."

Squinting, he nudges his glasses higher up his nose. No. Not the pipe again.

"I thought you said he still hasn't spoken yet."

"Well, no…not verbally, at least. I…taught him how to sign *yes* and *no*."

"Sign language?" He blinks at me.

"Y-yeah. Um, my older brother is hearing impaired."

"Yes…I remember you mentioning that in your interview," he says thoughtfully. "But…he's not a candidate for signing. You should know as well as I do that ASL is difficult to learn past childhood. I just don't know if you're doing him any favors. We don't want to encourage him *not* to use his voice."

Heat creeps up the back of my neck. I know that well enough, but where the hell did Edwards and Wagner get with him? The kid's been through major physical and emotional trauma. I studied selective mutism in school, but hadn't seen it until now. At least, that's my assumption. There's something about the shadows in Easton's eyes, a wall of pain like I've never witnessed. He has things to say. I cannot in my soul believe that someone who looks like they have so much to say cannot at least attempt to speak. The session notes I received from my predecessors said there were vocal sounds. Not many, and they were followed by outbursts or Easton shutting down, but there were vocal sounds. He *chose* not to speak. I don't care if it's well past the date he should have done his vocal exercises. I'm not giving up.

"I'm not," I say with polite determination. "I think it's a trust issue with him. And…I have a plan. I'd like some more time with him."

Taking a puff off his pipe, Dr. Norton considers my request. I'm going to smell like an ashtray by the time I get out of here if I don't pass out first. The milkshakes in my hand are starting to drip sweat onto my slacks. At least, they'll be a thinner consistency by the time I get to Easton's room.

I nearly jumped for joy after realizing he'd snuck a drink of my shake when I took a break from our last session to use his bathroom. The dribble on his shirt stood out like a stop sign, giving me the idea for my *in*. If he can swallow that well, he can try to speak. He just needs the right motivation. I can't fathom that a kid whose eyes light up when I talk about his drawings is the same one the other therapists say throws things and shoots death glares at the mere mention of any suggestions.

Dr. Norton lets out a tired breath, making me wonder if I'll look that exhausted at his age after a lifetime in this career. "I admire your determination, Aaron. I really do, but if you haven't noticed, we're kind of like a bus station here. Overrun with cases and very little staff to get through them all. This is a state-run facility. We just do the best that we can. You'll get that shiny quality time to change lives that all new therapists want when you sign on with your first private hospital. I remember wanting to change the world myself, even though it was about a hundred years ago."

"I understand. I do, but I can still handle all my cases and keep taking more. I won't get behind."

I *don't* understand. I hate it. I hate seeing how the system works, but there's not much I can do about it—besides insisting on not giving up and working myself to exhaustion since everyone else here has burnout. I refuse to give up on someone relearning how to communicate after a lifetime of seeing what my brother George has gone through being deaf.

Dr. Norton must see the determination in my eyes. "All right," he relents, smirking. "He's slotted to be a resident here a little while longer due to his physical injuries, anyway, before they find placement for him, so consider Mr. Easton fortunate to have a motivated fellow like you in his corner."

"Thank you." I exhale. Eyes burning, I make my escape while I can and beat feet toward the south wing where the long-term care patients reside.

Sitting upright in his bed, the look on Easton's face as he gazes at his window, drumming his fingers on the mattress, would kill birds. Great. Maybe I've just been lucky so far. Tapping on the open door, I make my way inside in as unpresumptuous a manner as I can.

"Hey, I'm so sorry I'm late. Boss wouldn't stop talking."

I set the shake I got him down on his wheeled table with no fanfare, and then make my focus appear to be on getting situated in the chair by his nightstand. One thing my brother always hated growing up was looking like a spectacle because of his disability. I'll never understand why people stare at people they think are different than them.

"I think we'll have an early spring," I say casually, glancing out the window with a smile, hoping to look in commune with the gazing he was doing upon my arrival. When I finally bite the bullet and make my first eye contact of the day, I find him looking confused.

His gaze moves from me to the milkshake in my hand, and then to the one I left on his table. Right. Not as casual as I thought.

A college degree doesn't mean I'm any more mature or suave than a teenager, I suppose. Mom says I'm twenty-five, going on fifty, but she's always had a generous amount of faith in her children.

Maybe that's why I'm so eager to have a breakthrough with him: we're only eight years apart. Every other patient I've seen at Hampton Hills has been old enough to be one of my parents. I need to learn to connect with younger patients if I want to impress wherever I end up when I finish my fellowship.

"Oh," I laugh in self-deprecation. "*Nutella* milkshake. Kind of an addiction of mine. I didn't want to be rude and pig out in front of you. Got to eat on the run here. They keep us pretty busy."

Taking a sip of my drink, I toss his file down on the nightstand and lean back in my chair. I need him to be comfortable enough to work with me, not make him feel like I'm here to analyze him.

From the corner of my eye, I catch him glancing hesitantly toward the door. His hand moves, bringing the straw to his mouth, eyes slipping closed. Although it looks like he has to make some effort to swallow, his face shows he's pleased with the results.

"It's kind of an acquired taste," I digress. "I'm not big on sweets, but Nutella's my weakness." Making a show of working a kink out of my neck, I ask, "Want a different flavor next time? They've got everything you can think of."

My lungs freeze at the sight of his hand coming up, his index and middle fingers together. I hold my breath, watching him bring them down to his thumb.

No.

He just signed the word '*no*' to me. Easton Bennick just spoke to me. He remembered.

I showed him the signs casually last session and used them a few times while I talked. After a lifetime of signing to my brother, it's second nature to me, one that I sometimes have to try to shut off in public if I've been around him recently.

Blushing, he averts his gaze down and shifts in his bed with a grimace but then nods to his drink and lifts it in the affirmative before taking another sip. I have to bite my cheek to keep from grinning with joy. I don't care what Dr. Norton said. Easton just communicated. Baby steps.

Smirking, I hoist my cup up and tap it against his. "Cool," I sign back as I say the word aloud. "*Nutella* Addicts Anonymous."

I'm pretty sure the amused little smile he flashes me has a bigger one behind it, but I'll take what I can get. A smile is only one step away from a laugh, after all. And one day, I'll hear Easton Bennick laugh.

CHAPTER 3
Easton

'If you promise you'll try doing a few of the vocal exercises, I'll see if we can sit outside sometime.'

Staring out the window of my room, I don't even care that the landscape is covered in white the way it was the day of the accident. I want to cash in on the offer Aaron made the other day if it gets me out of this building for even a few minutes.

I don't want to know how fickle it makes me that I've been practicing my swallow therapy and vocal exercises since he introduced his pretty face. Motivated by sex appeal and fresh air—I'm going to get far in life.

Why am I anxious? It's not like I need to impress him. It's not going to earn me any life points or make my future more promising. Not like it's going to get me laid, either.

Ugh. Get a grip, Easton. This is so dumb.

"Any fucking time now, Manicki," I rasp, glancing at the clock on the wall.

Wow. My hoarse words are awe-inspiring. Not even my drawings will earn me a smile this time when he shows up and hears that.

"Sorry," a soft laugh comes from the doorway, making me go rigid in bed. "I'm here."

Shit. He heard me.

I mean, that's the reason he's here. And it's the reason I practiced after hours like a brown-noser, but… I wasn't sure if I was going to go through with it. Looking at anything but him as he walks into the room proves difficult. My peripheral drinks up any sight of him it can, like he's a shiny new penny. Milkshakes, again? I didn't think he was serious.

They quickly become an afterthought, though. *Why do I want to stare at his face, and… Wait a minute. What the hell is wrong with his face?*

Grimacing, he sets a cup down on my bedside table and then fingers a reddened spot above his right cheekbone. "I have a patient with dementia who took a swipe at me. I'd have been here sooner, but it's protocol that we have to document stuff like that when it happens and get medically cleared to stay on duty."

When I just blink at him, unsure of what to say or, rather, *if* I want to say anything, he must take that as a regression to my oath of silence. Moving to the window, he leans against the radiator, making the view there now a thousand times better. "So… that was really cool," he adds.

Cool? I'm sure it's sarcasm, but I can't find anything funny about being hit in the face. Maybe it's because I have way more experience receiving the act than he does, but then he clarifies, "Even if it was just to cuss me out."

Oh…

Right.

I take it back—getting hit in the face might be better than confirmation he actually did hear my broken-ass voice. Great. Now he's staring at me… just like all the others.

Why did he have to ruin what he brought to the table? Good looks and Easton-praise.

I can hear my mental sigh as loud as a school bell. Tit for tat. I know that's what this is. If I want him to stay, I'll need to say something. Lord knows if he gives up on me, anyone else they send will probably be as awful as everyone else here I've had to deal with.

Taking extreme interest in a ripple in my bedsheets, I throw him a nod. "You going to live?"

It would be a miracle if he heard that. My voice has one volume now—*secret*. How freaking embarrassing. You wait for puberty to make you sound like a badass and then life ruins it. My face is on fire; even though I doubt he can see it fully the way I'm staring down at my mattress. I never blush. It's this freaking place—it makes you feel weak in every way.

A soft chuff flits past his lips. "Yeah. I'm fine. Just enough of a mark that I'm sure my mother will give me an inquisition is all. That'll be more painful than the damage, trust me."

I'm not sure if it's his casual reaction to me speaking again or if it's that telling admission about his relationship with his mother, but I find myself glancing up. He honestly looks more self-conscious than I feel at the moment. The weight on my chest is suddenly lighter.

How the innocent wear their emotions on their sleeves.

A lifetime of tussles with Leonard taught me not to make a big deal out of a black eye. If I made them a big deal or told anyone the truth as to how I got them, people would think they were a big deal, and that's the last thing I wanted for Mom. Besides, he rarely got the better of me, saving his wrath for Mom whenever I was gone—the snake.

"I just feel bad for Mister… um, the patient," he catches himself and nudges the tile floor with the toe of his shoe. "Maybe she won't notice," he murmurs more to himself, fingering his cheek again.

Three things occur to me as I stare at the puddle of goo he is. We're not patients to Aaron—we're people. Two—he doesn't want his mom to worry about him, which shouldn't be as adorable as it is to me right now. And, three—even though my voice is a distant memory of what it was or ever could be, and I'm younger than him, maybe I can impart some life wisdom that will keep his pretty face intact.

I gesture to preface that I'm going to attempt more words, so he'll listen up. "Never stand within… reach of someone you… you can't trust." He looks equal parts thrilled by hearing my wreck of a voice *and* advice. It pulls on something needy inside me I didn't know existed, so I continue with more nonsense just to keep his attention. "And maybe just tell your mom… you were helping an old lady pick something up… off the floor, and she elbowed you."

I hate how it sounds like I'm winded. It doesn't help that his expression is so damn grateful and pleased, further stealing my breath.

"Very noble of me," he concedes with a smirk. "And sounds like it'll keep me from hearing how dangerous my job can be. I might have to schedule a few more appointments for your services."

I'm glad he picked up what I was laying down, but my air supply doesn't improve, watching him move from the radiator to the easy chair next to my bed. Either my advice about not getting within arm's reach of someone went in one ear and out the other, or he trusts me. I'm not sure why that means as much as it does.

I don't trust anybody.

I don't.

His lips wrap around his straw, innocently. His mouth ticks up at one corner, smiling while he takes a drink. Eyeballing my dripping cup, I can't believe he actually followed through on the milkshake thing.

Anybody kind of sounds like one few too many people all of a sudden.

Ah, fuck.

What has he done to me?

CHAPTER 4
Easton

The crisp April air floods into my lungs and soothes the heat in my face over my last blunder. God, I hate this. My voice is wrecked. I never knew how much pride I took in the sound of it until it was destroyed. Why can't Aaron just talk?

I think I could listen to just about anything he'd say. He's one of those people who radiates positivity, but in a calm, non-suffocating manner, not an overzealous, director-of-fun manner. He brought me outside, and I'm pretty sure he had to fight for the right to do so. This freaking place—heaven forbid, a patient actually doesn't hate life for half an hour. Granted, I'm in a wheelchair for now, but it's still fresh air. None of the other staff ever contemplated that a seventeen-year-old who's been in either a hospital or this hellhole for two and a half months might like to smell something other than bedpans and latex gloves.

Glancing over, Aaron's patient eyes greet mine from where he's sitting in one of the wrought-iron patio chairs at the little table. His mouth ticks up at the corner, but he says nothing, and that says more than any words can. From what he's told me about his life, he hasn't gone through anything like I have, but he doesn't try to pretend he understands nor steamroll me with insincere sympathy.

"Sorry," I croak, clenching my fingers into a fist at the sound that comes out.

Maybe if I only try to talk to obnoxious or ugly people, it'll be easier to speak once I get out of here. Why does he have to look so good?

Listen to me. A guy brings me milkshakes and babbles on about silly stories from his childhood and college, and I like… care about his feelings. Mom would snicker at my personal growth.

He has a brother who's deaf. Maybe that's why he's the first person I've met since the accident who looks at me like I'm normal. Maybe he's just used to people with limitations.

"You've got nothing to be sorry for," he chuffs. "This isn't easy—physically or emotionally. None of it. But I'm so impressed by you…"

That has my gaze flicking to his for some reason. How many times have I heard that in my life?

Jesus, he blushes. Someone is going to gobble this man up and eat his candy center. If only I could walk, and talk, and be legal, and…*not* in here. I'd be a defender of the candy center. I mean, someone should. He's too… good to be gobbled by the wrong person.

His soft, self-deprecating puff of air is an adorable sound as he shakes his head, trying to find the right words. "Easton…look at all you've gone through, and all you still have to go through—"

Yeah, no shit. Where is he going with this?

"And you have no one to help you go through it. Of course, it's going to be difficult as hell and aggravating and painful, but look at you." He gestures to me with a smile that I must be imagining is so dreamy because I'm an idiot with teenage hormones looking at the perfect shape of his mouth. "You're doing it," he declares with this disbelieving little laugh. "You learned to roll that chair when it's something you've never had to do before. You made a decision to be out here working with me today. You made a decision to try to work your vocal cords when I know it's the last thing you want to be doing. You're tough, and you don't have to be. You choose to be tough, and it's…"

The silence dangles like a prize I want to win. *'It's what?'* I want to ask, but he chews his lower lip and then sucks in a breath.

"*That's* what's so impressive."

Was I hoping for the word sexy? What the fuck is wrong with me?

Still, the word *impressive* has me fidgeting in this stupid wheelchair under his smile. Who in the hell has ever thought I was impressive? I don't even think Mom did. She loved me, sure, but let's be real here—*impressive*?

Leaning forward, he clasps his hands between his legs like a coach having a heart-to-heart with a team member. "I don't care how long it takes or how many breaks you need; I just want to know that when you're a famous artist someday, you'll feel confident giving interviews and telling your critics to fuck off. Knowing you're out there knocking the socks off the world and not hiding because you don't sound like you used to will make this random, boring guy in some medical office who used to annoy the heck out of you really freaking proud to say he knew you once."

Did he actually just drop an F-bomb? Perfect, buttoned-up Aaron? Wow!

Snorting, I shake my head. Famous artist. Okay, he's laying it on thick now, yet I'm still preening. He shows up to our sessions early just so he can ask to see what I drew since the last time. I wouldn't give a damn if he infringed on our session by perusing my sketches, but it's thoughtful. It gives me more time with him. And… it's kind of cool that he's so into my stuff.

"Quit feeling sorry for yourself," I finally let out, ignoring my soft volume. "It's not my fault you're boring."

Snickering, he grins and leans back in his chair. "True. That was unfair of me."

I feel the urge to hang onto the lighthearted mood before it fades. I don't want him to have to pull nails to get me to talk. When I know I have to talk, I don't want to. It's not him, it's this place and how I got here. That's not Aaron's fault. He's just doing his job and is damn better at it than anyone else here.

A famous artist. Ha!

Something competitive in me, however, gets a mental picture of what that would look like. I'll probably have to sell blow jobs in the back of an alley to even buy art supplies when I get out of here, but I'd be my own boss. At least, I'm pretty good at blow jobs.

Thank God he can't hear my thoughts, or he might think I'm serious and sign me up for more therapy.

"So…" I clear my throat, staring at a hawk soaring over the tree line behind the facility, inspired by the fact that will be me one day—getting far the fuck away from here to a life that's my own, even though I have no clue what kind of life that will be. "Explain to me…" I have to pause to swallow, my throat feeling like a jumbled mess. "How in the hell you ended up…in the gynecology department on your first day doing your shadow hours?"

"Oh, my gosh," he moans into his hands. "I don't know why I even told you that."

His ears are red, eyes sparkling, and his embarrassed expression is so full of joy, I just can't with him. The man even makes taking a good ribbing look sexy. He's got the body of a tight end and told me he puts puzzles together with his mom. Puzzles! *With. His mom.*

"That hospital's signs were all screwed up!" he defends. "They'd just remodeled and apparently, they forgot to remove some of the old signs."

Something occurs to me at that moment, seeing the way his eyes crinkle at the corners. I don't care what I'm going to be when I leave here. It doesn't feel like a countdown to an escape any longer. I think I have a goal. The talented son of a bitch actually got his wish and motivated me, after all.

Artist, back-alley-blow-job-giver—whatever I end up doing, I think I want to have a voice again so I can find someone like him to laugh with. It's certainly a heck of a lot better than feeling dead inside.

CHAPTER 5
Easton

It's embarrassing how fast I hobble to my appointments with Aaron, but they're healthier than sitting in my room, contemplating violent deaths that Leonard could meet. If someone had told me four months ago that a handsome speech pathologist would swoop in and make all my undiscovered dreams come true like some sugary tween romance movie, I'd have laughed them out of the state. I never imagined I'd have a purpose beyond surviving and being pissed off.

When I'm not exorcising my mental demons, staring at the walls in my room, or trying not to gawk at Aaron Manicki's ridiculously perfect face and body… and hands and ass, I draw. I'm starting to give up denying that it's just to pass the time, especially as my stomach flutters when I hear the sound of Aaron's laughter coming out of his office.

I live for that laugh now. It's been the soundtrack of my dreams for the past month and a half since his motivational speech on the patio, longer, if I'm being honest. I didn't know a specific sound was capable of making me so happy.

Sucking in a breath, I squash down the stupid butterflies in my stomach and adjust my sketchpad to keep it away from my sweaty armpit. I'm going to have some balls and show him the sketch I did of him. One of them, anyway. He doesn't need to know I have an entire book full like a certified stalker.

I don't doubt he'll like the portrait I'm going to unveil. He's loved everything else I've shown him so far, but this is the best thing I've ever drawn. Granted, it's of the best model I've ever had. I don't just want him to like it, though. I want to really impress him.

That invite-only summer program he's been talking about could be huge for me. If I win the grant they offer at the end of the summer, I could actually go to a freaking legit art school. You don't have to be a high school graduate. They take seniors if their submission comes with a referral from a patron of the gallery that's hosting it, which apparently, his mother is.

He assured me that putting in a good word with her to recommend me was no problem, but no one's ever done anything like that for me, let alone a stranger. I want to thank him somehow. I know he probably doesn't want any thanks or would prefer I do so with an hour's worth of spoken words, but I want him to know his faith in me is well worth it. Judging by the quaint, happy stories of his life and childhood, we come from such different worlds. That's why I want to earn it so badly. I can't stand the thought of being some pity case to him because I'm his patient, even though I doubt he thinks so. He treats me like I'm just a young guy like him, laughing over the stories of my high school shenanigans, which makes sense since we're not too far apart in age.

Okay, eight years is almost a decade, but he's still young. He's addicted to Nutella shakes and still lives at his parents' house. I can easily see him being some congenial, preppy kid at school—the kind you *don't* want to smother with their letterman jacket. The kind who's friendly to everyone and doesn't judge.

We had a kid like that at my school—Devon Willmington. Ben and I used to joke that he'd probably become the mayor because no one had anything bad to say about him. Aaron's so good he'd probably be kind to assholes, so I want him to know he's not making a mistake by sticking his neck out for me. I want to be that famous artist he dreamed of, so I can walk back into his office someday to gift him some top-selling portrait rich people are vying for.

And maybe… maybe I kind of want to earn *him* too.

I read Ben right. There's no way I could have read Aaron wrong.

He's into guys. I just… know.

Yeah, you 'know' with your dick, a cynical voice in my head teases. I tell the voice to shut the fuck up because this has very little to do with my dick. I'd be perfectly happy just to lie next to him and listen to that laughter.

Okay, my dick certainly wouldn't complain if it was involved in the scenario either, but whatever. I get a vibe from him. And what will it hurt if one little sketch in particular gets him to direct that vibe my way? I'll be out of here soon—a free man. I won't be his patient anymore. And one day soon, I'll be eighteen. Eighteen and legally available.

What's he laughing about? An ugly sensation clouds my head as I nudge the half-closed door to his office. It feels a lot like jealousy over not being the reason for his amused state. Scoffing, I shake my head at myself. Man, I have it so bad.

"Did you get into the laughing gas?" I rasp out, rounding the doorway, still mystified how little I care about the hoarse sound of my voice as long as it means I get to make Aaron smile from hearing it.

It's instantly and painfully obvious that this smile is not because of me. My throat closes up, taking in the man holding him in an embrace, kissing his neck, and gripping his ass. Dr. Reider—a visiting plastic surgeon. Dr. Norton swung by my room with him when he gave him a tour three weeks ago.

"Stop it," Reider purrs teasingly, tugging him closer as Aaron chuckles, pushing at Reider's chest like he intended to break free. "You're going to get me fired."

I want to shout that he's not funny. That Aaron's clearly trying to be professional and not make out at the workplace, but I can't. I can't shout yet. I don't know if I'll ever be able to again. I've only been speaking the past month and a half, barely above a damn whisper. It's only further evidenced by their obliviousness to me. They didn't freaking hear me when I walked into the room. I thought the way Leonard used to call me names like '*sissy*' and '*queer*' made me feel like nothing, but this might be worse. I've never felt more invisible than watching another man touch what I want, and I can't even yell at him to stop.

Clearing my throat, I shift on my crutches, bumping the door on purpose to make more sound. Reider looks up, brows pinching together like he's annoyed.

Seriously? What kind of doctor does that?

"Easton!" Aaron exclaims, spinning around. His cheeks are in full bloom as he smooths the front of his shirt and puts some distance between him and the ass-grabber. "Sorry. I didn't see you there. This is…Dr. Reider."

Reider adjusts his tie, leaning against Aaron's desk like he has no shame about being caught, and throws me a nod. "Are you Aaron's prodigy?" he asks, smirking.

Prodigy? What's that supposed to mean? And how can Aaron let some guy he's only known for three weeks grope him in his office?

The guy looked like he was trying to swallow him, body and soul, like a demon. I don't like his dark eyes or his arrogant-looking face and perfectly trimmed goatee. He looks like a used car salesman with a fancy watch who gets too much sun.

"We have an appointment…don't we?" I try for indifference but hear the saltiness in my stupid fucking whisper voice.

I hate how it makes me sound like a scared child. Like less than this clearly slightly older-than-Aaron ass-grabber. This is a state-run facility. Why is he wearing fancy-ass shoes like that here for his stupid charity visit to plastic surgery us low-class citizens?

"Y-yeah. *Yes.* Yes, we did. Um, *do.* Sorry. Dr. Reider was just…just dropped by to visit me." Aaron's smile kills something inside of me. It's the same as always, but also different. It's… polite. A little too polite.

"Um…did you want to go out into the courtyard?" he asks, anxiously glancing from me to Reider. "It's a little chillier today, but the fresh air might be nice."

It's a small consolation prize to see that he's clearly ashamed of his sex office at the moment, or maybe he came to his senses and wants to get away from the ass-grabber. I never want to step foot in here again, and getting Aaron as far away from this major mistake sounds like a solid plan.

"Yeah." I back up, swiveling around toward the doorway to encourage him to flee with me.

"I've got to go," he tells Reider, voice hushed.

Reider straightens up finally, getting the fucking hint, but then his lids droop as he stares at Aaron's mouth. His freaking mouth. Hello! I'm standing right here! His hand comes up, brushing a thumb under Aaron's chin. I might vomit. Leaning in, he dusts a kiss on Aaron's cheek.

"I should go look up flights," he says. "Call me later."

Aaron smiles and nods sheepishly. Reider pauses near me like he thinks a crippled kid should move out of the way for his Highness. I lean back about a centimeter and flash him a bright smile that says my IQ is probably what he expects it should be from someone from a trailer park. I hope he fucking trips on my crutches.

I've never felt so feral; keeping my eyes trained on his back to make sure he disappears down the hallway. My blood is pumping overtime. Aaron is into guys—just as I suspected. Part of me wants to celebrate that fact, but another part of me has just seen the equivalent of the evil witch making out with Prince Charming, leaving the princess crying in her tower. There is no way he could truly be into that guy.

"I'm sorry," he says softly, running his hand through his hair. "I've never…done anything like that at work."

I want to be that hand. I want to slap him for being so stupid, but I also still want to be that hand. "It's…new," he adds, sounding helpless and abashed. "He just…showed up."

The awkward reminder of our roles earlier—that of patient and therapist—dies away as I take in the discomfort in his expression. He owes me no explanation, and yet, I'm receiving one. That has to count for something. His show of remorse is a feather in my cap. Somewhere in there, I matter to him. I matter to him, *and* he's into guys. It's enough to take the edge off my embarrassing cloud of jealousy. I've never crushed on anyone before—this is freaking awful. I'm not going to blow it by letting him in on my infatuation, by acting like a bratty teenager.

Swallowing back the bitter panic as it ebbs, I shrug and flash him a smile. "We're young. But, yeah, get laid on your own time. You owe me five," I snark, nodding toward the clock.

Chuckling, he pats me on the shoulder. "I'll give you ten."

He leaves his hand resting there as I crutch through the doorway. Every inch of my skin goes taut under that touch. I can feel each of his fingers, searing my flesh through my shirt, making me wonder if we'd set the room on fire if we were skin to skin.

Can Reider do that to him?

No way.

He said he needed to go buy plane tickets, which means he's finally leaving soon. You don't leave someone you're serious about. He's just a passing fling.

I said it myself. Aaron's young like me. Young, with an active sex drive. I can't hold that against him.

Just as long as the fucking ass-grabber fucks back off to wherever he came from.

Then Aaron will be all mine again. Aaron, who's into guys. Aaron, who's going out of his way to recommend me for an art program. Aaron, who laughs at all my jokes and looks at me like I'm something. I've never been something to anyone other than Mom. I can't possibly feel this stupid over a guy and not have there be some potential for reciprocation.

Glancing over, one look at the smile he gives me tells me I was wrong before, clouded by a haze of worry. That's *my* smile—the one he gives just to me. It's back. Ass-grabber didn't kill it.

Everything will be fine.

His family lives in Hampton. He's not going anywhere. And that art program is in town. I'll be busted free from here soon, and then we'll just be two guys who live in the same zip code. Two available guys who happened to meet at a rehab facility. We'll laugh about it someday. I'm sure.

God, I have it so bad. The damnedest thing is that I don't mind a bit.

NOW

CHAPTER 6

Aaron

Eight years later

"Are you sure you don't want any furniture? We have some stuff left over that renters leave behind."

"No, I'm good," I mumble back, feeling drained just from lifting my hands to sign to my brother in case he can't see my lips, since I'm still staring at my new residence rather than him.

I should take him up on the offer of furniture, but my pride can't handle accepting it after what he's already doing for me. This cottage isn't glamorous by any means, but it's a lakeside property. He could get a decent rental rate out of it. Certainly more than the agreement that I just pay utilities.

Mustering a smile, I break the awkward silence between us. I hate how he keeps looking at me like I'm… damaged.

I feel damaged. Damaged beyond repair. I'm sure I do look it. Nothing like adding '*dramatic*' to my image of pathetic and broke. Moving back home was supposed to be a saving grace both financially and emotionally, but it certainly doesn't feel like it yet.

"Thanks again for this. I really appreciate it," I say, signing along emphatically, hoping George knows just how much it means to me that he's helping me get out from under Mom and Dad's roof.

The last few weeks have been a fatal blow to my self-esteem. I don't know how much more I can take. In a way, I knew coming home meant that Mom and Dad would see past all my reassuring phone conversations from the past year and a half. The ones where I told them I was managing everything fine.

When I got the call that Hampton Hills accepted my application to take Dr. Norton's old job, I really thought it meant there was finally a light at the end of the tunnel. I'm grateful to my parents for letting me bunk in my old room, but I can't take another minute of seeing their worried looks, their disappointment.

How the mighty have fallen.

Why did I think crawling back to Maine on fumes would be better than staying in Seattle? God, I'm so stupid.

I left Hampton happier than a pageant winner, but the return has proven to be far less glamorous. The caseload and disorganization at Hampton Hills make me regret any time I judged my predecessor harshly. I've only been back there for two weeks. I know things will improve once I wade through the mess, but I'm not the same motivated me I used to be in my professional career. I've lost something, and when you lose enough of yourself, everything seems daunting. I hate myself for it. If only everyone else didn't look at me like they know it, too.

Mom and Dad would never claim to be disappointed in me, but I can see it in their eyes—those looks that shout they know I've changed and will never be the same. The bitch of it is, I know they're right. And I can't do anything about it.

George nods at me soberly and steps closer like he knows it's bad form to leave his nearly homeless zombie of a brother alone in the woods, but is trying to figure out how to make his exit. I flash him a flicker of a smile, sparing him further discomfort. A silent message to tell him it's all right. That I'll be fine. I know I'm not fine, but I can't stand for him or anyone to see me like this a minute longer. I just want to be alone and miserable in peace.

Raising his hand, he slowly claps it down on my shoulder momentarily and nods. I lean into the brief touch instinctively, possibly something in my body or soul, yearning for any kind of physical touch. What I'd give for a hug right now, not a mom hug that will make me feel like a teenager who didn't make the football team. But George and I have never been huggers—not with each other. He doesn't like to be touched, at least by anyone other than his wife. He and Rachel are cuddlier than any couple can be. It still baffles me to see him like that with someone after being so serious when we were kids.

I miss him. I didn't realize how much until I came home. Our texts to each other became so infrequent after I moved to Seattle eight years ago, and I know I'm to blame. I was so… caught up in my own little world that I can see now that, in some regards, I lost my brother. Maybe I'm imagining things and had already lost him a long time ago. We were close when we were kids—until we hit our teens. He's three years older than me, so I suppose it isn't cool for any guy to have his little brother in high school with him.

Watching him walk to his truck, his profile has me wistful. Thirty-three and thirty-five. We're no longer kids. We can never get that window of time back when we used to shoot *NERF* guns at each other in the backyard. This is as close as we'll ever be. Politely obliging each other simply because we're family. He has his own family now, after all. It feels immature and selfish after remaining oblivious for so long about the growing distance between us to wish that I could make him laugh and smile the way he does with his daughter and Rachel.

I'm being stupid again. This is what people do; they grow up and live their lives. It's not George's fault if mine didn't work out the way I had hoped. He shouldn't have to rewind because I'm stuck.

Making my way up to the little porch that wraps around two sides of the cottage, I smile thoughtfully at the new planks, a stark contrast to some of the weathered ones. George is a hard worker. Did he replace those for me or simply because he wanted to keep one of his rental properties maintained and takes pride in doing a good job?

The sound of my phone chirping has me sighing, knowing it's probably Mom calling to see if I got settled in. She really needs to stop feeling like she has to hold my hand. I haven't even had time to hang up my clothes in the closet or unpack the box of dishes I brought with me from Seattle.

Except, it's not Mom. It's a Seattle number, making my heart skip a beat.

Seattle seems so far away now, regardless of the fact it's on the other side of the country. It might as well be another planet. All the friends I made out there were Jason's friends, save for a few co-workers at the hospital where I worked. These days the only reason I'd get a call from a Seattle number is because of bad news. It's the only news I seem to get.

"Hello?"

"Aaron?" Jason's mother's voice comes over the line.

"Grace? I didn't recognize the number. How…how are you?"

"I got a new one," she says dismissively, as though I could forget how much she hates me. Jason always assured me she didn't, but Jason's not around to interject those comforting reassurances any longer. At the very least, I'm convinced my existence is somehow an annoyance to her. I can do nothing right by this woman, no matter how hard I try, and it sets my stomach to churning. She's never reached out to me just to chat, so I doubt that's changed since I left.

"Oh. Okay, so the other one isn't active any—"

"A creditor keeps calling me to collect on one of your credit card debts," she cuts me off sharply. "I've given him your number, but I'd appreciate it if you'd get your affairs in order and not give out mine or Jason's information in the future. I thought you'd taken care of all of that already?"

"I…a credit card?" I only have my *Visa*, but it's a debit card linked to my meager checking account. I had to close my *Mastercard* and put it on a payment plan, but I'm not scheduled to make another payment until next month.

"Yes, that's what I said. He was quite rude, to be honest. He called when I was in the middle of a luncheon, and I wouldn't be surprised if the people next to me overheard. How embarrassing!"

"Grace, I'm so sorry. I had one, but I closed it. I don't have any others and never have."

"Well, apparently you did, and I think it's highly inappropriate that you listed Jason's office as the mailing address," she scoffs, but for once, her agitation doesn't have me flustered. I'm too boggled by what I'm hearing. Jason's office? How would they have Jason's surgical office listed as the mailing address? My first instinct is that someone in his practice opened one falsely or that my information was stolen. The wave of nausea creeping up my throat tells me that instinct is the fool-hardy love a husband feels to protect the name of his spouse. Too much has happened for me to have faith in that need to protect his name any longer.

Jason must have opened it. I know it. I don't want to know it, but I know it's the only conclusion.

"Grace, I didn't—"

"I don't want to hear it. I've been through enough. My son provided you with a good home. With an exquisite life. I don't know what you're doing to throw yours away, but I will not let you tarnish his name. Take care of this. Immediately."

I'm not sure how long I stare at the silent phone or what I think doing so will accomplish. Damaged is no longer an accurate description of what I am. I'm just breathing. Nothing more. I don't know how I'm still breathing when everything in me feels like it's given up. I have nothing left. Neither physically nor emotionally. A step beyond drained.

Shuffling across the hardwood floor of the small living room, I bump into the few boxes that George and I hauled inside. The house is so empty the scraping of my feet echoes off the walls. Somehow, my body musters the strength to flop the spare mattress away from the wall that Mom and Dad gave me. It lands with a resounding thump, shaking the floor, where I collapse onto it in a heap of hot tears.

How is this my life? How can any of it have happened?

How much does he owe? I've already sold and paid everything I possibly could. I'm driving a rusty, fifteen-year-old truck that was a rent-to-own sale from a dodgy dealer in Seattle, for crying out loud. There is no more meat left for vultures to pick from my bones.

For better or worse.

For rich or poor.

No one emphasized just how bad *worse and poor* could be.

CHAPTER 7
Easton

"What the fuck do we need that for?" I ask, taking the picture frame Wolf thrusts at me.

"It's cool."

Snorting, I roll my eyes. The image shows us smirking and posing with our arms crossed over our chests. Punks. We were such wannabe punks.

It was taken the summer we met, so I was still scrawny as hell having just busted free from Hampton Hills. It definitely needs to be burned.

Thrusting it back at him, I make sure I have his attention in case he needs to read my lips. "You're fucking delusional."

Nostrils flaring, he heaves a sigh, making me chuckle. I take pride in being the more difficult friend, but he certainly pulls his weight carrying part of that title. "It shows where we came from, that we've been together for years. It helps prove we're a trusted establishment and shows part of our story. People like stories. Something they can connect with."

Now, he really is delusional. Our *story*? How much did he smoke today? I know he doesn't like his story as much as I don't like mine.

Still… I feel a twinge in my chest over his sentimental, if not ridiculous, logic. We have been together for what feels like forever. Eight years feels like a lifetime ago.

My hair was still short in the photo, but starting to grow out from the stupid haircuts they gave me at Hampton Hell. Wolf is grinning like he just felt up a girl for the first time and standing in front of the old motorcycle his mom's ex-boyfriend, Jasper, helped him fix up.

He was so proud of that thing. Shit, we rode it everywhere. It was love at first rumble for me, feeling it between my legs and the wind on my face. I thought I'd be scared to drive after the accident with Mom. Thought I'd be terrified of wiping out and shattering my leg, even though it had healed decently by then. Neither deterred me once we hit the open road, and Wolf let loose. Maybe it was the thrill of knowing turmoil could be the end result, could *still* be the end result each time I hop on my own bike now. It was a big fuck you to all the ugly fears I had when I was holed up in that shithole, all the fears I had each time I knew Leonard was coming home.

I shared all my firsts when taking my new life into my own hands with Wolf. So, yeah, in a way, I'm sentimental too. Still, I don't see why the hell anyone at this stupid festival we're planning to set up a booth at for our tattoo shop needs to see this shit.

"No way, man," I grumble.

Rustling through a box of old design work photo albums, Clark Wolverton is oblivious to my continued skepticism. Either that, or he's just ignoring me. My tone is too low and gravelly even for his fancy hearing aids sometimes, but he's good at '*playing deaf*' when he doesn't agree with me.

Tapping him on the head with the framed picture, I get his attention. Enunciating as much as my stupid throat will let me, I make my annoyance known. "We don't even have any freaking tattoos in this picture!"

His expression sours. Tilting his head, his long, wild black hair lilts over one eye as it narrows at me. Great. Here come the hands. That means he's not willing to negotiate.

Just put it in the fucking box, he signs.

Rolling my eyes, I sigh and pitch the frame carelessly into the box he's filling to take to our booth tomorrow. *Fine. But it's stupid,* I sign back.

I get the middle finger. Because I'm a bit of a sadist who likes to push his buttons, I return the proper ASL sign for *fuck you.*

I never miss a chance to call him out when he gets lazy with the speakage. He's the one who taught me ASL, after all.

Shoving at my chest, he snickers. I shove back, but we give up our playful wrestling within thirty seconds. He's too eager to return to packing this damn brag box for our festival appearance. Freaking Wolf. Total softy.

Sighing, I step out of the closet and back into our office. He doesn't need my help. He can totally handle being an idiot all by his lonesome.

Dropping into my chair, I kick my booted feet up on my desk and tug at a snarled string hanging from the rip in the knee of my jeans. It's humid as shit today. I can feel it in my leg. Maybe I'll get lucky and it'll rain tomorrow for this festival. Anything to get out of the four-hour shift Wolf made me swear to work would be fine by me. I don't feel like sweating my ass off under a tent while listening to people probe their partners over what tiny butterfly would look good and where they should put it on their bodies. Or the inked people who ask a million questions about designs and costs, want you to sketch something custom for them, and then come up with some story about how they need to think about it or save up to pay for it down the road. People who really want a tattoo come to us. Plain and simple. We don't need to make fools of ourselves at the last hurrah of the fall festivals to drum up more business. We're doing perfectly fine. Our business account and the safe that's chock-full of emergency money in the bottom drawer of the file cabinet say so.

Wolf wants to become a chain, though. I don't doubt that he'd shit himself if we were offered some reality TV show either. Anything to embarrass us. I know he inks for the love of it like I do, but he's more ambitious than me; like he always has something to prove. I have nothing to prove to anyone and am perfectly content living my best life as it is.

Except my mood seems to be teetering now. Freaking Wolf. His talk of the past dug up more than just memories of fixing up that motorcycle Jasper helped us with. It hasn't escaped me that Nancy's been gone for a year next week.

If someone had told me years ago that I'd get attached to a foster parent, I'd have told them to keep dreaming. I can't deny it, though— she was one of the coolest people I've ever met. Okay, maybe not totally cool. Her obsession with *Beanie Babies* was not healthy, but she was always behind me a hundred and ten percent, and she always kept her word. Those are rare qualities in a person.

When I told her I had no intention of picking back up at some new high school after I got out of Hampton, she got me a tutor for my GED. When I asked to borrow one of her cars so I could get a job, she obliged and circled every want ad she thought I'd be interested in. In the end, I wound up finding work cleaning Jasper's shop, which was like not having a real boss at all because I already knew him as Nancy's neighbor. It was perfect. Wolf attended his tattoo school program during the day while I went to some art classes at the local college that Nancy had recommended. At night, we'd hang out in Jasper's motorcycle repair shop where I slowly picked up ASL from him. We'd work and learn about bikes from Jasper until we found jobs interning under the old owner of our tattoo shop.

Nancy cheered me on even though I wasn't going for an art degree or to become a mechanic. She never pushed and never set goals for me. I think she knew from the get-go that I wasn't the kind of kid who vied to fulfill goals set by other people. Maybe it worked, simply because she knew I was no longer a kid, even though, technically, at seventeen, I still was.

How lucky was I that Jasper was her neighbor? If he wasn't, I may have never met Wolf that first summer when I saw him over there working on that bike. The only way things could have been better was if Nancy and Jasper had gotten together. We would have been this eccentric little found family. It wasn't her fault that she wasn't into men.

'Promise you won't spend time crying over me,' she demanded at one of her chemo treatments. *'I'll beat this. I'm a tough old broad.'*

Not tough enough, apparently.

She kept all her promises, except that one. I can't begrudge her for dying. When I think about what she did, sometimes it makes it difficult to keep my promise. The zany broad, leaving me all that money. I know she'd be stoked that I was able to buy this place with Wolf because of it, but still—I never imagined she'd leave me something.

Laughing, I can still recall her cringing whenever she'd come in and watch me ink someone back when we were just renting the place. Tough my ass. How can you go through chemo and be afraid of tattoos? I'll never understand her. I guess I don't really have to. She didn't try to understand me. She just let me be who I was. That's more than I can say for most people who came before her in my life.

Listen to me. Freaking Wolf dragging me down memory lane.

I'd better either get off or get drunk before I have to deal with this shit show tomorrow. It's the only hope I have of surviving it.

Digging out my phone, I creep through the social media profile of a guy who's been eye-fucking me the last few times I've been at Pulse. I put him on my mental list of options. It's not my fault he has to wait in line, but I scroll, considering moving his number up the list of hopefuls who've hit on me at the club.

Blond. Full lips. An eagerness to please in his eyes. Totally a bottom. Yeah. He'll do.

A snort tears my eyes from my screen.

"Really?" Wolf asks in his mottled tone. "Dude, it's only five o'clock, and we have shit to do tomorrow."

"*And* we're young and healthy," I digress, getting up and grabbing my keys.

His eyes grow wary, and he shakes his head. "No, man. Come on."

"We'll grab dinner first."

Wolf's weakness is the home cooking he never received from his mother when he was a kid. I can see him wavering, deliberating, but then his mouth sets in a firm line.

"No. Melissa wants to spend time together tonight."

"Fine. Bring her along." I shrug, heading to the door that leads to the studio.

"Not that kind of time," he protests. "*Alone* time. She wants a romantic evening at home."

His phone dings just as he says it. Judging by the sappy grin on his face when I turn back around, I know who it is.

Ugh. Him and Melissa. Two years I've put up with them, attached at the freaking hip. I've suffered through every conversation about possible themes for their potential wedding, the names of their future children, and countless arguments over the dumbest shit known to man. They can detach themselves from paradise for one evening to help me get laid.

"Come on. You owe me for this festival. Tell her you'll blow her mind later."

"It doesn't work like that," he grumps, typing out a message.

"What? Is your dick on a schedule?"

"No, but apparently yours is."

Okay. That was fair. One point to Wolf.

My patience is at its limit, though, so I snatch his phone. One of the benefits of being a few inches taller than him.

Rushing out of the office while he grapples with the back of my shirt, I type out a message, informing Melissa that we're taking her out to dinner and then meeting a potential client at Pulse later. She's a sucker for promoting her man—she'll bite.

"Ha!" I laugh when she responds, confirming. "You're welcome," I inform Wolf, tossing his phone back to him. "I just saved you from a boring evening of foot rubs and scented oils."

Reading his text, he heaves out a long-suffering sigh. "Fine, but I'm not drinking."

Rolling my eyes at him, I throw a salute at Shannon to let her know we're out for the evening. It's her turn to close, so she doesn't act surprised.

"I'm not," Wolf repeats, close on my heels.

He's a total lightweight and yet lacks the ability to say *no*. I'm not going to be the only one who's miserable tomorrow. That's what he gets for disrupting our routine with this festival nonsense.

What's the point of being self-employed and beholden to no one if you schedule foot rubs and fuckery? We seriously need to have a business meeting one of these days.

CHAPTER 8
Aaron

Staring up at the sign above the doorway of the two-story brick building across the street, the mid-morning sun breaks through the clouds, warming my face. I've never been to a tattoo parlor before. I didn't even consider whether such places were open this early, but there seem to be people inside through the shop window. Do people actually get tattoos right after breakfast? A man steps out of the liquor store behind me, carrying a case of beer. Stranger things have happened than getting a tattoo before noon, I guess.

Adjusting the strap of my messenger bag on my shoulder, I let out a long breath and eye the door. S&H Ink. This is it—the name that was on the business card I snagged off that table at the festival last weekend when I was helping George haul totes of Rachel's homemade jewelry to their van from her craft booth.

That's when I saw him—Easton Bennick. Well, not him, his photo, sitting on display at that tattoo booth's table. Talk about a blast from the past.

He was smiling. Smiling and *not* at Hampton Hills. It warmed my heart knowing it means he might have had a good life after he left the facility.

There was another kid in the photo. Apparently, he made a friend when he left. Another tattoo artist—at least, that's what the woman at the stall said when I asked her about the picture.

I never would have imagined tattooing to be his profession of choice. It's certainly one medium of art, and he was, without a doubt, talented beyond reason. I'm so glad he did something with his gift.

I still don't know what I'm doing here, but for the life of me, I can't bring my feet to move from this sidewalk. That picture has been emblazoned in my brain all week. Easton Bennick. Unbelievable. It seems like a lifetime ago.

Being at Hampton Hills again has brought back memories of that fresh-faced fellowship kid I was, the one who thought he was going to leave a positive impact on the world, even if in small measures. It was life before Jason. Before I moved to Seattle. Before my entire world changed, and I somehow lost my grasp on everything I once held dear. It was back when everything was so much simpler; caring about patients and coming home to a quiet, humble life.

I miss *that* Aaron Manicki. I hadn't realized how much until I saw that photo of Easton. Some logical part of my brain asks me how I think being *here* is going to get that version of me back.

Swallowing at the thickness in my throat, I shake out the anxious sensation in my hands. I *shouldn't* be here. I know that. I'm still such a mess, clearly. I'm standing outside the business of one of my former patients, for crying out loud. I should be at home listening to self-help podcasts or possibly finding a second job to dig myself out of debt, not spying on Easton Bennick.

Except I crossed the line before I even got here. Didn't I?

I... couldn't help myself.

Maybe it was the appeal of thinking about something else other than my own problems because I gave little conscious thought to protocol while looking through Dr. Norton's old files. I told myself that *I'm* in charge now—his files are under *my* management. Both are true, but I knew well and good that only curiosity sent me rifling through them, not a substantiated medical obligation.

What I discovered turned curiosity into a full-blown obsession. Easton never came back.

He left Hampton Hills about a month after I did. That's basically where his paper trail ended. There were a few notes about follow-up inquiries, but he failed to respond to any of them. He never returned for any check-ups or any of the continued therapy that was available to him.

Innocently perusing his file was nothing untoward, but now I wish I hadn't read it. I wish I could find an ethical reason to justify this need I have to know why he cut all ties with his program. It's been the only occupant of my thoughts the entire week.

There were resources available to him at Hampton even after he was discharged, but without taking advantage of them, he might have thrown away precious chances at restoring his voice. Why hadn't he come back? How had he fared after he left?

He was a teenager from a broken home who'd suffered trauma and had a vocal disability. I was a college graduate from a stable home life and look how lost I feel. I learned the hard way that life is not a bed of roses, but Easton had already been dealt a rough hand before coming to Hampton Hills. I *have to* know that things got better for him. It's no excuse for being here, but it's all I've got.

I just… *need* to witness something *good*, one thing from my past that turned out right. If I stop to think about how selfish that makes me sound, I might not go through with this.

With that, my feet move me across the street, although I'm about as confident as a kid on ice skates for the first time over this foolhardy snooping mission. The second I'm inside the shop, it's apparent I'm woefully out of place.

The large open room nearly spans the entire floor of the building, sectioned off throughout by low partitions that surround workstations. A woman with blue hair, a nose ring, and fully tatted sleeves is working on a female client's stomach just beyond the desk. In the stall across from her, a large man with a scary build is inking a man's exposed backside—*fully* inking it. My word. There are at least three more artists at work deeper in the room, each marking bare flesh under fluorescent lighting. The thrum of rock music is drifting over the room from somewhere, melding with the ambiance of tin signs and framed tattoo model photos on the walls. It's as though this is where night comes to meet the day, and yet everyone here seems to be acting as though that's perfectly normal.

The space is a vast contrast to mine and Jason's home. He'd turn his nose up at this in a heartbeat, but I tell myself he's not here to guide my decisions anymore. As much as that instills a sense of guilt in me, it also feels liberating.

Continuing my perusal, I have to admit that what seemed rough and bold at first has a classy professionalism about it. Black tile flooring, polished to a shine. Pristine white paint on the drywall. Everything looks clean and tidy, and the workstations are impeccable. I've been in hospitals and clinics that couldn't hold a candle to this level of hygiene. It's not at all what I expected.

Hell, how did I know what to expect?

"Are you here for an appointment?" a woman calls out.

Right. There's a reception desk. I had no clue people made appointments. Clearly, my knowledge of tattooing is from inaccurate films that only portray drunk people making spontaneous mistakes in the middle of the night.

Straightening my dress shirt collar over my sweater, I smile at the familiar face.

"Hi. No. Um… I stopped by your booth last weekend at the festival…"

"Oh, yeah! You're that old friend of Easton's, right? I totally forgot your name to mention to him."

I said I was an old friend? We were friendly, certainly, but that's a far stretch from patient and therapist. This is getting worse by the second. I need serious help.

"Aaron," I supply, grateful she didn't ask me my name that day.

Would it have mattered? Maybe he won't even remember me. If he does, he'll probably wonder what on earth I'm doing here. I can't say I'd blame him.

"I…just moved back to town and thought I'd drop by to catch up with him. Is he working today?"

Slapping the cap back on the end of a marker, she chuckles. "Not this early. He's still upstairs." Leaning on her forearms, she gives me a curious once-over and then shakes her head, grinning. "All right, you look harmless. I can't believe I'm getting to meet someone other than Wolf, who knew Easton as a kid. Go through that door. There's another one at the top of the stairs," she informs me, pointing to a black steel door at the far end of the parlor.

Nodding dumbly, I thank her and make my way down the aisle between the tattoo stalls. The buzz of the tattoo guns hums in my ears as the black door gets closer.

Where is she sending me? Is it a VIP room? Something more illicit? What have I gotten myself into?

Depressing the door lever, I push through to an empty stairwell. When the door clicks closed, it's as quiet as a tomb. Only the sound of my breathing and a pool of sunlight from a window over the landing above are my companions.

I could turn around and leave, go back to the cottage, and look at job ads. I could fry up some eggs to fill my stomach that's always so twisted up I never feel hungry anymore. I'm sick of eggs, but they're a cheap, nutritious meal. I could go visit Mom and Dad, but I'm tired of pretending I have my shit together in front of them, and I need to save my gas to get to work. I already logged a few unnecessary miles coming here.

Staring up the darkened stairwell at the pool of light at the top, ascending feels like it would be a pivotal life choice. I pinch my eyes closed, shaking my head at that fortune cookie-sounding logic; but in a way, it's true.

I have no friends. The ones I had in Seattle were just colleagues or friends of Jason. I spent eight years there, and there's no one I was really close to. It took losing Jason for me to realize that. Everyone I knew, everyone *we* knew, were the kind of people who weren't really friends, but rather just acquaintances, and definitely *not* the kind of people who still check on you a year and a half after your life implodes.

I need… roots. *New* roots. A starting point to be my sounding board for my future, no matter how bleak things seem right now. Something that makes me feel like I'm making wise decisions and being a good human being—the way I felt years ago. If finding inspiration in the past gets me there, I think I need to take that chance. I can't stand feeling like a ship adrift at sea much longer. Something's got to give.

CHAPTER 9
Easton

Steam rolls out of the shower as I step out and towel off my hair. It's like it's chasing after me and knows I'm not yet healed from the effects of last night. I swear my eyelids are scraping my eyeballs. I can only imagine how Wolf must feel right now, no doubt still passed out on my couch. That's what he gets for being a serial boyfriend.

Blow-up number fifty-seven with Melissa. And who gets to do damage control? Me and my liver. Maybe someday he'll learn his lesson and stop dreaming of white picket fences. I don't have the heart to tell him that his quest to be married with two point five kids likely stems from his issues with his mom. He's a big boy. He needs to figure that shit out on his own.

The towel fibers caress my skin as I wrap the fabric around my waist and my stomach lets out a growl. My alcohol is starting to beg for food. Great. It's always fun trying to peel Wolf off the couch after one of his relationship drinking binges. I got him drunk enough that he shut up about it and had a good time, though, so he should at least take me out for breakfast. Fair is fair. I'll give him exactly ten minutes to rejoin the living.

Pulling open the bathroom door, I bask in the way the temperature change in my bedroom makes my skin go taut. Tromping across the carpet, I step out into the kitchen and living area, prepared to make a beeline toward the counter for some pot-banging practice. That should wake Sleeping Beauty, except… he's not on the couch. He's talking to someone by my front door. Who the fuck is…

That looks like…

No.

The sight before me is like colliding with a brick wall.

Aaron Manicki.

Fucking. Aaron Manicki. In my living room.

An eight years older, eight times more handsome, Aaron Manicki.

My heart gallops like a herd of elephants, drinking him in; the same solid build, that chestnut hair combed less severely, and those stupid, jade-green eyes that drove my teenage heart crazy. Damn it to hell. He's still drop-dead gorgeous.

I fucking hate him for it.

What... the hell... is he doing here?

The flicker of his gaze and his parted lips as he and Wolf notice me let me know he's not the only one sizing up an old acquaintance. My stomach squirms, watching his shocked expression as he takes in my ink-covered body.

Why do I feel self-conscious? I never give a damn what a guy thinks of me. Let him get his fill. I've got nothing to be ashamed of, so I stand seemingly unaffected as those eyes rake over me from head to toe.

Yeah. That's right, Manicki. I'm not the boy you left behind.

His expression and that dorky-ass sweater with a dress shirt underneath couldn't say more plainly that I don't run in his circles. Inhaling, I straighten up, out of spite or maybe self-preservation. I'm bigger than when he last saw me, but it doesn't feel like enough.

Why did I give this man so much power over my psyche? Why am I still?

"Easton," he says with a puff of breath. It's like he can't believe it's me. "It's good to see you."

Why am I trembling? What in the hell is going on? It's just Aaron Fucking Manicki. He is not tremble-worthy.

Shit. I'm just standing here like a mute in front of the man who single-handedly taught me to speak again.

I don't know what the hell to say to him, and I sure as shit have no desire to subject myself to his reaction over my voice, even if I could find words. Mute... That suddenly seems like a stellar idea.

I tilt my chin, the universal sign for *what's up.* Seems appropriate since he came here unannounced, and I'm standing here in nothing but a towel like we're old bros.

"I'm back at Hampton Hills and saw that you... never finished your program, so I... I thought I'd check in on you."

Wow. How cute. I'm suddenly seventeen again and need him to document my well-being.

Did he think I ceased to evolve after he left? That I couldn't possibly take care of myself without guidance from him or Hampton?

The nerve of this guy. How did I miss his arrogance all those years ago? He's good at burying it under layers of polite good intentions.

Holding my towel with my left hand, I smirk and sign with my right, ignoring the helpless memories the communication method stirs inside me now that it's for someone other than Wolf. With Wolf, it's our own secret language. For Aaron, it's just… torture.

Hampton has you making house calls now?

He blinks, watching my hand even after I drop it. The crestfallen look in his expression twists something in my chest. I shouldn't feel like I've failed him, but I refuse to give him the satisfaction—or maybe even the disappointment—of hearing me. I shouldn't care what he'd think of my gravelly baritone, but it's like one of those notes kids pin on your back to mock you.

He starts to raise his hand to sign back but drops it. Yeah. I'm not deaf, asshole. That says right there how well he remembers me. I can't believe I ever pined for this guy.

"No. I just, uh, moved back last month to take Dr. Norton's old job at Hampton and got to wondering how you were doing."

A month. It took him a month to remember me? With a tight-lipped smile, I extend my palms to indicate my flat, gloating over how it shows off more of my ink for his widened eyes.

I'm doing all right, I sign, downplaying my status. I've never been so grateful that my flat is as messy as it is right now. The satisfaction of allowing him to think I'm some tatted, speech-impaired ruffian is sheer gold. I didn't know disappointing someone could be so rewarding.

Wolf steps forward hesitantly, as though my signing is a traffic-control signal that will crash a plane if he gets too close. I nearly forgot he was still here, hovering in the background, watching this awkward show.

The concerned look on his face tamps down my agitation. He knows me well enough to know when I'm annoyed, unlike the self-centered speech pathologist pretending he gives a damn. He also knows I have no love lost for Hampton Hills or anyone associated with it.

"Hey, man. I'm gonna take off," he says. With his back to Aaron, he signs for my eyes only. *You cool here?*

Over Wolf's shoulder, I can see we've captured Aaron's attention, the odd man out, desperate for knowledge. A wicked idea curls around my brain. This is going to be awkward, but fuck it. I don't have any other tricks up my sleeve at the moment.

Wrapping my hand around the back of Wolf's neck, I tug him to me and crash my mouth onto his. Yup. Totally awkward. He grunts as I slant and make purposeful smacking noises with my lips, creating a naughty sensory effect. It's all I can do not to bust up laughing at his *what-the-fuck* expression as he grips my shoulder to keep his balance. Perfect. I hope it makes him look like he's embracing me.

Pulling back, the smile I flash him is genuine over my quick thinking. I run my hand down his arm, like a lover who just delivered a parting kiss. When I take a peek at Aaron, who's studying my floor, I can tell by the color in his prissy cheeks and the way he's shifting his stance that he caught the whole thing.

"O-kay," Wolf says, clearing his throat and wiping his mouth. He's discombobulated, but God bless him. His gaze shifts to Aaron and then back like he gets that I'm up to something. "I'll, uh, I'll see you later, then?"

I sink my teeth into my lower lip like he's a tasty morsel that I can't wait until *'later'* to have and nod. The eye roll he flashes me says he's going to kill me for this, but I don't care. When he turns, I swat his ass, making him jolt. Aaron flinches. The look on his face is priceless, cheeks and ears bright red.

Wolf lets out a nervous laugh, sparing me a glance, then musters a smile for Aaron. "Nice to meet you."

"Y-yeah. You too," Aaron replies, hands stuffed into his khakis like if he closes in on himself it will protect him from the ambiance of vulgarity I've set into motion.

"Bye... lover," Wolf says at the door, practically glaring at me.

I'm going to have to work a lot of overtime or go to more festivals. Fuck.

When the door clicks shut, it's just me and Aaron Manicki, alone in a room together for the first time in eight years. It feels like all the air has been sucked out of the building, but then I notice his mouth is still open, floundering in surprise.

Right. That was one thing we never established during our sessions.

Yeah, I want to tell him. *You're not the only one who kisses men. Didn't stick around long enough to find that out. Did you*?

I'm doing an admirable job of maintaining a sated air, a ruse of a man who experienced an evening of debauchery. Still high on the satisfaction over his discomfort, I casually tousle my damp hair with one hand and sign with the other.

You need me to sign papers or something? Proof of life for your report?

"What?" His face crumples in confusion. "N-no. I...There's no report. This was more of a social call. I came because... because I wanted to make sure you were okay...just for my own peace of mind."

Aw, how sweet. I focus on the selfish part of his statement—for *his* peace of mind. The memories of foolish teenage fantasies and pitiful feelings of abandonment and betrayal churn inside me. I sign carelessly, narrowing my eyes at the window like something in the view is holding my interest.

Cool. I've got to get ready for work. Thanks for stopping by. Just show yourself out. Okay?

With a tight smile, I throw a nod toward the door and then stride back to my bedroom. Every step away from him makes my lungs ache. Which is fucking absurd. Deep down, I know I have no right to be pissed off at him. I didn't have to believe all his bullshit. And I'm the one who chose to play mute just now.

Fuck! Why did he come here? It's been eight years—why do I still want his approval?

Stopping at my nightstand, I let out a breath and try to wipe the tension from my face with my hands. Where is my satisfaction? Would

I feel better if I'd taken a different approach and bragged about my successes? The thought of hearing him praise me for them like a puppy that just took its first shit outside makes my skin crawl. My hang-ups over him are like a damn sickness.

The floor creaks behind me, making my heart skip a beat. The loose board by my bedroom doorway—he followed me.

Trembling, incapable of speech—as if I haven't already lost all my senses—my cock twitches at the thought of Aaron in my bedroom. I hate how it means he still owns a part of me, something broken and needy deep inside. Except, my fantasies aren't the same as they were eight years ago. The one flashing through my head right now involves me grabbing two fistfuls of his sweater and tossing him on the bed, rumpling his buttoned-up exterior. Crashing my lips hard onto his mouth, eating his soul with my tongue. Plowing my fingers through his perfect hair. Ripping off buttons, leaving little bite marks on his flawless skin. Hearing him moan, watching him writhe beneath me, begging me to fuck him as I tease him until he loses his mind. Turning him into the wild animal I've let him think I've become.

But I don't do any of that.

The most resourceful thing I've taught myself is to not give in to impulse. I hook my thumb under my towel and let it drop to the floor. The sound of his gasp sends a tremor through me, rushing blood to my groin and causing a burst of victory to explode in my chest.

Sweeping my hair back, I turn toward him as though I didn't know I had an intruder and meet his gaze, or rather I attempt to. His eyes travel up the length of me, starting at my heavy cock, not erect but no longer flaccid under his perusal. Hand to his stomach, he gapes when he meets my eyes.

"I...I..."

Like what you see? I smirk and stride toward my dresser.

"Sorry. Shit! I'm so sorry," he mutters, turning away. "I just... wanted to ask you if we could talk sometime."

Retrieving a pair of jeans, I consider a pair of underwear for a second, but decide forgoing them will portray a better image, one of a wild man who goes commando. Slipping my legs into my pants, I leisurely pull them on, bending over so my ass is on full display. I've never felt so exposed in front of a man before, nor felt like my body could be a weapon.

Turning around, I'm pleased to find his eyes meeting mine. He looked. He might not like the ink on my front, but there's not a drop on my back—it's all untouched male physique. A wicked part of me hopes I outshine that husband of his he ran off with and maybe even tempt him from his precious vows. It'd serve him right for carelessly instilling visions of grandeur in kids who have nothing.

What do you want to talk about?

"I…well, it's a little surreal to see you again," he laughs breathlessly. "I mean, it's great to see you out on your own. You…you have a nice place here."

Thanks. What I really mean, though, is fuck you; I don't need your approval.

"I saw in your file you got placement about a month after I left."

My ire crawls up my spine, hearing how he has access to details of my life like a spy while I know shit about him and what he's done over the last eight years. If he expects a response to that, he can hold his breath and die waiting. He doesn't deserve to hear about Nancy— someone who kept her promises.

"So, you work downstairs?"

My decision to appear sub-standard wavers under his curious, file-snooping gaze. Pride is such a bitch.

Yeah. Me and my friend own it.

More shock.

Fuck you. Fuck you. Fuck you, Aaron! Why is it so difficult to believe I could own a business?

"Oh," he chuckles. "Wow. That's great, Easton. That's…amazing."

How is it amazing? I worked my ass off.

"Do you…how is your speech doing?"

And there it is. The crux of the visit. He came to hear his prodigy.

It's beautiful, I sign, uncaring that my sarcasm is written all over my face as I cart a T-shirt and socks over to my bed.

"Do you…strictly rely on signing now?"

This freaking guy. *Rely* is not a word in my vocabulary these days and never will be again.

I talk when I need to, and let it rest when I don't need to.

"Oh."

The disappointment in that single syllable shouldn't make me feel like I've let him down. Keep it together, Easton. This is so fucking stupid. What do you care? He's just a stranger, a stranger who never meant a damn thing.

"There's been some new strengthening techniques they've tried since we last met," he adds with an annoying optimism. "I…if you need help or want to try working through anything, I'm here."

My lungs are itching for a blast of fresh air on my bike, my skin for a cold swim in the bay. The water makes my bones ache, always giving me a pleasant reminder of what I've endured to get to where I am. Sitting on the bed, I take a pause from stuffing my feet into my socks.

Not necessary.

His expression falls. I know I'm being difficult, but can't he take a hint? When did he get so pushy?

"It's just that…we used to talk…a lot."

No shit. It took him eight years to remember that? Cry me a fucking river.

Focusing on donning my boots, I don't miss him stepping forward. I couldn't miss a move of even one of his muscles, apparently.

"Um, I brought you something." He flips open that dorky messenger bag he's toting, retrieving a little device no bigger than an electric shaver. I tense, recognizing instantly what it is.

No. He did not. Really?

Holding up an electrolarynx, I hate the pontificating smile on his face. "I don't know if you have one of these, but we get samples of the newest upgrades. I wasn't sure if you'd even need it, but if you're still struggling with vocal function, it might be a useful tool to have when you're around people who can't sign."

Nostrils flaring, I wish I could melt the device with my eyes, wish I could melt him into a pile of ashes. Did he hit his fucking head? Was he in a coma for the last eight years? How can he stand there and talk to me like I'm still a teenager who just got discharged from Hampton?

No, thanks. I'm good.

"No, really, we got more in than we can use," he assures me, stepping closer, holding out the damn electrolarynx. "We won't even miss it. Here."

Pressing my palm against his closed hand to refuse, I tremble at the contact of skin on skin. I didn't need a reminder of how many times I yearned to know what that touch would feel like. I was stupid then and I'm just as stupid now.

All I can muster is a shake of my head, standing here like that frustrated kid I was, the one with a tsunami of pent-up emotions. He sees me as a patient, or even worse, an inadequate child, a project that needs fixing. This guy was never my friend, never worth crushing on.

Lines of disappointment mar his forehead. I grind my teeth at the desire they give me to be compliant.

"Easton, it's really no big deal," he says in that soft, understanding tone that suckered me years ago. "Lots of people use them. It's just something nice to have in case you ever have a bad day."

Cupping my hand, he tries to turn it like he's going to place the damned thing in my palm. *Bad days?* What the fuck does he know about bad days? I remember every story about his privileged life, but apparently, he remembers fuck all about mine.

Snatching the electrolarynx, I whip it across the room, sending it ricocheting off the wall. He jumps back, watching the body of the device split open and fall to the floor. The way he gapes at me like he can't fathom the reason for my outburst is just another wedge in the proverbial distance between us. I've never felt so petulant in my life, and it only increases my shame and anger twofold.

The new model looks a little faulty, I sign with as much indifference in my expression as I can. *I think it's time for you to go.*

"Easton, I…I'm sorry. I didn't mean to upset you. I just… wanted to help."

It takes everything in me not to use my voice, not to scream at him. Gripping a handful of his shirt, I tell him with my other hand what I think of his offering of help as I drag him out of my room and toward the door.

Are you fucking deaf? Maybe you're the one who needs therapy. I asked you to fucking leave.

I release my grip on him unceremoniously, and he staggers to a stop in the hallway. Breathless, sweater rumpled, face flushed—he looks like he just saw the boogeyman. He still has that youthful innocence about him and that annoying do-good spirit, as though all the world is shiny. His face says I've just taken a big old dump on it.

Well, I'm not a fucking fairy godmother. I *am* the fucking boogeyman, and he stepped into this pile of shit willingly. I didn't ask for him to come calling. I remember what happened to me and I got over it. He needs to get over whatever the fuck brought him back to memory lane.

His hand trembles as he brings it up to smooth out his collar. The morning light glints off his wedding band, assaulting me with images of him being devoured by Jason Reider on his desk all those years ago. Three weeks later, he'd up and run off to Seattle to move in with the guy. One of the nurses told me they got married about two minutes later. He never said a word about it, and I didn't get so much as a fare-thee-well.

I know he didn't need to, but damn. I guess his whole art program recommendation for me hadn't been as high on his priority list as he'd made it sound. The time I stewed over that is too humiliating to acknowledge.

Right now. I could fucking care less. I did fine without his charity. I was young and dumb then. The fact I let him get under my skin today makes me a dumb adult. I'm actually glad he stopped by. It's good that I got this closure. Apparently, I needed it.

But I'm done. So fucking done.

Slamming the door shut, I know I'll feel better in a few minutes. Aaron Manicki…or Aaron Reider—whoever the fuck he is—won't even be a memory anymore.

CHAPTER 10

Aaron

Killing the engine outside the cottage, my truck rattles, adding to the vibrating sensation that's been coursing through me the entire ride home from Easton's. I'm lucky this thing made it across the country from Seattle with what few possessions I didn't have to sell. Right now, though, I kind of wish it hadn't.

God, that was stupid. What was I thinking?

I violated his privacy, not to mention a medical ethical code about contacting former patients outside of work. Granted, I had no clue he lived upstairs when I walked into H&S Ink. I assumed it was a second level to the tattoo parlor or the office, but I still willingly went to his place of work.

Staring out at the stream beyond the yard, I feel numb, as though I've been tased. Easton. Easton Bennick in the flesh. The thick sensation in my throat hints that was a poor choice of words.

Yeah. He was definitely in the flesh. He's certainly not the shy kid I remember him to be. Not shy about anything. Nor a kid.

Somehow, I make it out of the truck and into the cottage without even comprehending my movements. I'm aware of the sound of the door opening and clicking shut, the scrape of my feet on the hardwood floor, and the clatter of my keys when I drop them on the sideboard by the entryway, but I'm not present. I'm still in that room.

He hates me.

That much was apparent. Is that hate particular to me or is he still mad at the world over what happened to him?

I stare dumbly at the floor, reliving every second of those ten foolish minutes. A veil of invisible heat swaths my face.

That guy in his apartment…the one he…kissed.

That wasn't kissing, Aaron. That was…

Another wave of heat assaults me as the phrase 'face fucking' comes to mind. I find my hands reaching for a glass from the kitchen cabinet and filling it with water, throat parched.

Well, he didn't seem to hate *him*.

I can't think of any reason Easton would hate me. Our interactions were always pleasant. He was probably my favorite patient when I was at Hampton years ago. The most entertaining for sure. We started out a bit rocky, but by the time I left, it felt like we were as close as friends or like he was a little brother.

My mind must really be fried from all the stress in my life because the image of him in all his naked glory reappears in vivid, inked color. Lean but well-defined arms and chest. Strong, chiseled legs. A dark thatch of…

Christ.

Definitely not like a little brother.

It has to be all that ink, not letting me free my mind of the picture. It's everywhere. His body is a canvas of art.

I've never been a fan of tattoos. Instinct has me wondering why he'd do something so dramatic to his body, but it wasn't… repulsive. It was beautiful in a rugged way, and I wonder if it's his own art.

I thought I was drawn there to appease the sentiment that crept up on me from being back at Hampton and seeing his picture at the festival, but I know now that's a lie. The enigma of his life story after Hampton was a liberating distraction from my misery. I don't think I cried once this week, nor did I have a panic attack. No wonder I dove headfirst into his file like it was a cold case.

"Jesus, Aaron," I mutter, shucking my clothes on the way to the bathroom like they're from a crime scene. "That was freaking brilliant. Can you get your shit together now?"

With a deep breath, I step into the tub under the showerhead, determined to forget my momentary lapse of sanity today. Steam builds, the heat soothing my tense muscles. The ever-present cage of loneliness reminds me it's still there with its suffocating claws. The sympathy I now have for complete strangers who've lost someone is unfathomable. There, too, is the taste of bitterness, for everything that follows loss. Learning to re-live a life as one after being a couple for so long. Facing unpleasant discoveries that strip away everything good you thought you knew about the person you loved.

Sometimes, I hope the scalding water will wash it all away. There's not enough water in the world to do that, though. So, I turn off the faucet and face my new existence for another evening.

In the security of my comfortable old sleep pants, I topple onto my mattress. A bed frame is not a necessity, I remind myself. It's not. They're pretty useless, actually, if you think about it. A floor is just as solid as a bedframe, and this way I don't have to clean dust bunnies out from underneath the bed.

Exhaustion doesn't win when I close my eyes. If the panic attacks start again, I might cry. They've been fewer and far between since moving home, but the anxiety is still there under the surface like a coral reef, slowly building. I wait for the anxious thoughts to creep in, but it's not my usual worries that come to mind.

It's skin. Tattooed skin. A strange feeling over the memory of Easton unabashedly kissing another man mere feet away from me. Intelligent, daring eyes that turn into a glare. The electrolarynx crashing against the wall.

He was just a memory, and then he was real, vividly real right before my eyes. Now that he's real, I can't shut him out of my mind.

Why doesn't he speak anymore? What happened to him when I left?

Questions brought me to him, but now I have so many more. At least thirty minutes pass as I stare at my ceiling, unseeing. It's long enough for me to realize that I can't un-think the current of thoughts about Easton any more than I can unsee the living, breathing canvas that he's become.

I know I don't know much about tattoos, but the times I've heard people talk about them, they sounded like they either got one to beautify their body or memorialize someone or some struggle. I can't recall a single image on Easton's body other than what looked like waves expanding across his chest and biceps, from his ribcage and up the front of his neck. Embarrassingly, all I can seem to remember with much clarity is the way he bent over, baring his backside. Pinching my eyes closed, I rattle the picture from my mind.

Focus, Aaron. You've seen men naked before. Maybe not in a while, but you've seen them.

Remembering his completely covered front from neck to thigh, I can't imagine the hours he must have sat in a chair being needled. *Pain.* All I can think about what that much ink represents is pain. And the thought of him being in pain doesn't sit well with me.

Well, that did absolutely nothing for my resolve to erase today from my brain. I've never wanted to help someone more than I do right now.

Listen to me. I can't even help myself. And I very obviously pissed him off. Even if I knew how to help him, I doubt he'd let me. He basically shoved me out of his apartment like I was an intruder.

I was. God, I was.

The look on his face…

'Are you fucking deaf? Maybe you're the one who needs therapy. I asked you to fucking leave.'

Groaning into my hands, I whisper in my shame. "Shit."

I have to make this up to him. Somehow, without getting a restraining order thrown at me. My throat makes a miserable noise realizing I've engaged in restraining order-worthy behaviors. Thank goodness, Mom and Dad don't know what I was up to today.

Things are going great. That's what I told them earlier this week when I went to dinner.

I just… stalked a former patient, invaded his personal space, and stirred up his past trauma. Yeah. Everything's terrific.

CHAPTER 11
Easton

Tattooing isn't for the weak. The urge to roll and crack my shoulders is strong, but I'm almost finished adding the color to this piece I did for Hank, one of my regulars, so I press on. He travels a lot, and I don't want him out there in the world with naked art on his arm.

See, Wolf? Who says I don't help advertise?

"Man, that's sick. I love it," Hank gloats when I finish and grab the wrap to seal him up. "No one does color like you, Easton. Don't ever get so booked up you can't fit me in."

Snorting, I stretch the aftercare film over his ink, lining it up to cover the area. "Always a spot for you, Hank. You know that."

He praises me a few more times before shaking my hand and heading out of the stall to go settle up with Shannon at the desk. That part always supplies me with validation. Granted, I don't think my art is anything to be praised since it came naturally, but the fact I learned to apply it to flesh professionally is something I take pride in. I'm happy when my customers are happy, but tonight Hank's flattery doesn't do for me what it usually does. I'm itching to get out of here. So help me, if I get a walk-in, I'm going to feign an illness.

Glancing over the half-wall to Wolf's stall, I wait for him to feel my stare. Arching a brow, I glance at my wrist, where a watch would be, with a satisfied smirk. A little friendly competition is healthy amongst friends. His mouth forms a thin line, and he shakes his head dismissively.

Sore loser. Not my fault he's a slow poke.

Snickering, I start cleaning up my station until I feel a pull from that unspoken, silent bond we've shared for years. Catching his gaze, I watch his eyes flick to the front of the shop and then back to me. That's a warning signal if ever I saw one.

Son of a bitch. Did we seriously get a walk-in?

Spinning my stool around, I regret my curiosity. I read Wolf's signal wrong. I expected it to be someone drunk or possibly a difficult regular, but it's worse. So much worse.

Aaron stops a few feet away from my stall. I've never seen him in blue jeans and would have preferred to keep it that way. The snug, faded denim fits him exquisitely in all the right places. The blue *Henley* under his jacket compliments his stupidly pretty eyes.

Ugh. I should jam this tat gun into my cerebral cortex. What the fuck is wrong with me?

Throwing me a sheepish wave, he smiles. "Hey."

There's that trembling sensation again, bubbling under my surface. My lungs feel thick, almost like I'm holding my breath underwater. What was the point in learning how to speak again if I can't seem to think of anything to say to him each time I see him?

I went the whole damn week convincing myself I'd struck him from that pathetic mental record in my mind only to have him reappear like a bad penny. A still terribly sexy bad penny that has no business being voted as *'sexy'* by yours truly.

Turning back around, I busy myself cleaning up my work tray from Hank's job. I went with signing last time Aaron appeared in my life, so if I look indisposed, he'll know why I don't answer. That, and I'm pretty sure I told him in so many words to fuck the hell off, so he shouldn't even expect me to respond.

"Easton…I owe you an apology."

Fuck.

Fuck. Fuck. Fuck.

"I'm so sorry I just barged in on you like that. I didn't know you lived upstairs. The girl at the desk just told me to go on up. I thought it was the office or something. Not that it makes it okay," he lets out in a rush.

That explains part of it. Shannon is so getting demoted.

"And I'm sorry it probably seems like I'm barging in on your life again right now too, but I feel terrible about last weekend. *Really* terrible. Your…" he trails off. "How you're doing is none of my business. I didn't mean to stir up any unpleasant memories or come off as pompous, like you need anything from me or Hampton. I… I'm just so sorry. I hope you can forgive me."

Jesus. Is he finally done talking?

It's like there's an invisible cord tethered between the two of us. I can sense every shift of his body and feel every ounce of tension between us. What do I even sign after that ass-kissing?

He's sorry? Not as sorry as I am.

It still explains nothing as to why he came knocking at my door. And it explains even less why my mantra of *'forget Aaron Manicki'* all week was as weak as a puff of smoke. As much as I thought I adored him years ago is how much I can't stand him now. Or… can't stand that my body hasn't yet realized that I can't stand him.

I spent so long hating Leonard that it turned me into a cynical prick—until Wolf and Nancy finally knocked some sense into me in their own subtle ways. Hate and I do not mix well together It makes me reckless and ugly—it makes me like Leonard Bennick. I may never be or do anything noteworthy in my life, but I refuse to be like Leonard.

So, I angle my stool around and let my nitrile-gloved hands dance the lie I presented to him. *No problem. Forgiven.*

"Thank you."

His sigh is audible. The fact my forgiveness brought him relief sends a tremor through me, a heady sensation over his approval. And then the bastard's face lights up.

Damn it.

That face. That smile.

I've had a week to relive that moment in my apartment. A week to realize there was something broken and different about him. Less confidence. An anxiousness he never had before. Right now, though, the smile on his face is bright and beautiful, highlighting every gorgeous feature of his handsome face. It's the smile I fell hard and fast for all those years ago—that sweet, innocent, genuine Aaron smile.

I swallow. Hard.

He needs to fuck right off again, pronto.

But he doesn't. He speaks again because Aaron of the present is a cruel pain in the ass that has zero compassion for my internal dilemma.

"Um, would it be all right if we could hang out sometime?" he hedges. His hands come up quickly, cautiously. "And *not* talk about anything to do with Hampton. I just moved back and I'm a little short on friends. Even if I wasn't though," he adds in a rush, like he realized his admission wasn't exactly a compliment, "I'd be really happy to be one of yours."

He wants to be *friends?*

I'd bark out a laugh if it wouldn't break my code of silence. I'm so fucking mad right now, there's probably steam coming out of my ears. What the hell were we before, I want to ask, instantly regretting the question flitting through my head.

Nothing. You were nothing to each other, you idiot. Remember?

Shifting anxiously, he fidgets with the collar of his jacket. His wedding ring only adds fuel to the fire. *'Short on friends'.* What the fuck is that supposed to mean? Married people aren't short on friends. They're freaking married—they don't need friends. They stay home at night, cuddling like Wolf and Melissa, or go everywhere together. Does his husband know he's here slumming it in a tattoo shop at nine o'clock at night with a former patient? I smell trouble in paradise, which rouses not a drop of pity in me.

Glancing over, I catch a look from Wolf. Brows hiked, he eyes me curiously, silently asking if there's a problem. It's the answer I need right now.

Smiling, I turn back to Aaron-wants-to-be-my-friend-Manicki. I've got just the hangout for a lonely married man.

Grabbing a pen from my workstation, I scribble down the address to Pulse on the back of one of my business cards. Handing it over, I soak in his dumbstruck expression.

We're heading out for drinks after we close up. I can meet you there in about an hour.

"Oh. Uh…okay. Great." His surprise as he checks the time on his phone tells me that will probably keep him up past his bedtime.

Good. I hope hubby shows up to drag him home. Until then, I'll enjoy every minute of seeing the new Aaron survive the snake pit he just walked into with his offer of friendship.

I can't be friends with this guy. I thought we were friends years ago and look where it got me—eight years of ignoring that I was still obsessed with my first real crush. I'm not making that mistake again.

No way.

I'm a fucking mature adult now. There's only one clear solution—I need to fuck him out of my system.

CHAPTER 12

Aaron

I once grabbed a navy-blue sock and a black sock while getting ready for an early shift at Mercy Hospital in Seattle, where I worked. I didn't notice until halfway through my workday, but it was all I could focus on after that. I never realized how much of a contrast there is between navy blue and black before that.

Right now, I feel like I'm wearing that mismatched pair of socks again, even though it's so dark in this club that no one would notice if I were. *Pulse* is an accurate name for the place. The loud bass of the dance mix music has been reverberating in my eardrums since the second I walked inside. Not the ideal place for talking, but then again, Easton and I won't need to use our voices, I remind myself.

If he ever shows up…

Scanning the crowded club from my barstool again, I check to see if I missed his arrival. The patrons are predominantly male. I've been offered two drinks already in the hour I've been here, and the redhead at the bar either thinks I'm someone he recognizes or is trying to send a not-so-subtle hint that he's interested. There are straight couples here, quite a few on the dance floor, but it's apparent the club is queer-friendly and I'm on the radar.

"Ready for another? You've got one coming if you want it," the bartender says, motioning his head toward the redhead at the end of the bar.

Fantastic. The perfect, quiet, getting-reacquainted evening I was hoping for with Easton. Minus Easton. Did he dupe me and send me here on my own as payback for bombarding him yet again?

"Uh, no. I'm good. Thanks. I'll have a *Sprite*, please, but let me pay for it. Okay?"

Pulling out my wallet, my face heats, knowing I'm being watched. I haven't been single in a club for ages. I don't even remember how to turn someone down or know what could happen if it doesn't go well. The last thing I want, if Easton actually does show up, is to be half-buzzed while stuck chatting with another man. That wouldn't look like a sincere flag of friendship.

Glancing down the bar, I give the man an apologetic smile and wave of thanks, and then point to my wedding ring. He smirks and gives a shrug, but then looks out at the crowd like he's already searching for his next mark. I've never been so grateful to be easily forgotten.

A flash of light by the entrance catches my eye. Each time the door has opened, it lets in a flood of the exterior light. This time, a gaggle of people is illuminated by it, two of them familiar. One is the woman who works the desk at S&H and the other is Easton's… well, I'm not sure what he is. He's the long-haired man who was in Easton's apartment that morning, the man whom Easton devoured with his mouth, mere feet away from me. His arm is around a slender woman with long, sleek black hair, though. Her arm is wrapped around the back of his waist, her hand hugging his hip. I don't even have time to contemplate if Easton knows when he walks in right behind them, laughing at something another tattoo artist said that I recognize from his shop. I guess that answers the question of whether he's aware of where his business partner's interests are focused at the moment.

His party approaches, angling through the crowd. I stand from my stool with every intention of flagging him down, but he looks over, saving me the trouble, and flashes me a smile and a wink. The stupor I'd started sinking into over the thought of being blown off evaporates with that wink and something like joy flutters in my chest. It resembles something like a sense of belonging.

How bizarre. We're veritable strangers, yet I know him better than anyone else I've seen since moving back, short of my family.

A bubble of anticipation creeps up my throat knowing I might get to fill in some of the blanks between what I knew of Easton years ago and now, as long as I don't mess this up and mention Hampton. Except, I'm left with a sinking feeling when he and his friends walk right past me without slowing or as much as a word or another glance.

Odd. Not exactly what I'd call an invitation.

I watch, suspended in an awkward limbo, as they proceed to a cordoned-off section at the front of the club where a bouncer attends a roped gate that leads to a series of oversized booths. He gives Easton and his friend both a high five and releases the rope to allow them entrance.

Still… not a look from my stalwart former patient. Great. What do I do?

I wait, assuming he might return to the bar to get drinks for himself and his friend, but then I spot a waitress approaching the booth they sat in.

He saw me, right? He didn't wink at someone else and miss me, did he?

Shit. *Am* I being duped? Was this another *'I asked you to fucking leave'* gesture but just played differently?

My dignity tells me to leave and accept my humility, but I've nearly run out of dignity in the last year and a half. I also promised myself all week that I was going to find the courage to face him again to make up for setting him off with that stupid electrolarynx.

The flash of a memory assaults me as I remember the sweet kid I spent so much time with years ago. I can still remember the storm in his eyes one cold spring day when he was frustrated with his progress and still burning with rage over his accident and the death of his mother. I don't even recall what I said to him to get through to him that day, but I'll never forget the way his hostility slowly melted away. It came to a point, and then it was like the flip of a switch—a carefree shrug, a wry grin, and then some crack at my expense and he let me in. I had to earn it. How could I have forgotten that?

You had to earn everything with Easton. I took for granted that he let me earn his audience while he wouldn't let anyone else at Hampton.

Striding over to the roped barrier, I don't calculate any dialogue. I just move with purpose. I want to earn his respect again. Hell, maybe I just want to respect myself. Maybe for once in a long time, I just don't want to think about everything I say or do.

Memories of arguments with Jason taunt me in a quiet hush, along with all the doubts I carried over the last few years of our relationship. Doubts that turned into poisonous seeds that took root in my soul and infected every bit of confidence I had in each aspect of my life until I became a sad being who only existed to make a marriage work. And then I became a sad being who reaped the weight of all those regrets when his husband died, strangled with equal parts guilt over my unhappiness and grief over the good times.

Shaking off the thoughts, I focus on the bouncer. I do not want to be mental right now. I don't know whether I'm doing this for me or Easton, or because I really do need a friend. Maybe I'm doing it because it scares the shit out of me since it means I've taken a step toward really living for the first time in forever.

"Hey, I'm supposed to meet my friend," I yell at the bouncer and point toward Easton.

Said *friend* glances over, laughing at something someone said. What I'd give to know what that sounds like. The bouncer looks over at Easton for approval. Easton raises his hand with a let-him-pass motion, loosening the tight knot in the pit of my stomach.

As I pass through, every jittery apprehension I had returns, my false confidence abandoning me when I need it most. This was my idea. I asked to hang out sometime. Why didn't I register that meant making small talk with someone who clearly has nothing in common with me?

He slides deeper into the half-arch booth as I approach. The welcoming gesture brings me a modicum of ease, knowing it means my presence is being accepted.

"Hey!" the woman from the shop desk calls from across the table. "I'm Shannon, by the way!"

"Hi. I'm Aaron."

The muscular tattoo artist they came in with has an arm slung over the back of the booth behind her, making me wonder if they're a couple. He reaches out his inked-up hand to shake mine.

"Fro," he states, making me give his buzzed sandy haircut a second glance, at which he grins before settling back.

Instinct has me looking at the last of Easton's party, but they're indisposed. The guy that Easton lip-locked is currently doing the same to the woman with the long black hair, both oblivious to everyone around them.

Sitting back in the booth, I decide introductions aren't important right now. The back of my shoulders touches something solid that doesn't feel like the booth padding. I find Easton smiling at me, his arm resting on top of the seating behind me.

That's Wolf and Melissa. They don't come up for air often.

Laughing at his joke, I hate the anxious way it sounds. I feel so awkward. It doesn't help that the question on my lips is if he joins them, so I bite the inside of my cheek and glance out at the dance floor.

A brush of skin against my hand snaps my attention back to the table. I find Easton palming my glass and bringing the straw to his lips. I didn't even think to offer to get him a drink. Fail number one on my part… or fail number three, I guess.

Coming up, he narrows his eyes at the clear bubbly liquid and then scrunches his face up at me with a shit-eating grin. Sprite. Right. I'm such a party animal.

"I…already had one while I was…while you were still at work."

One? Wow. He grins, sighing animatedly.

I don't mind that his humor is at my expense as long as he's showing me this lighter side of him. It feels like I've been let into a locked city.

"Thanks for letting me join you guys. You all work at S&H I take it?"

God, that was a stupid question. He knows I've seen them all there. I'm nailing the small talk already.

Nodding, he leans back in the booth, no doubt as enthralled by my segue as I am. His face lights up, however, when the waitress approaches with a tray loaded with drinks. Drinks and a whole lot of shots.

"Easton? Who's your friend?" Melissa calls from across the table as the waitress unloads her tray.

"Hi, I'm Aaron," I repeat like a parrot. At least I have that phrase down.

"Melissa," she chirps, flashing me a dainty wave. "And this is my boyfriend, Wolf."

Wolf hoists his beer bottle up in a salute, but I don't miss the guilty look on his face. I sneak a glance at Easton to see if I can decipher anything between the two of them and find him smirking at his business partner. Wolf's eyes narrow, his frown looking unimpressed and an evident raucous under the table tells me he just kicked my booth companion.

I try not to gawk at Easton's profile, but can't help myself. He takes notice and shrugs, staring out at the crowd of people dancing.

I'm not his type, he signs casually.

That does little to draw my baffled attention away. Sliding a shot in front of me, he withdraws his arm from behind me and smirks as he lifts one up for himself.

There's a devilishness in his eyes as he looks at me. *He's shit at getting you to leave too, apparently,* he confesses.

I don't know whether to laugh or drown in my utter foolishness, remembering that kiss from last weekend. He kissed his straight friend just to get me to leave? That… rash and, I suppose, hilarious if I were outside looking in. As he gestures for me to pick up the shot of liquid, I stare blankly but oblige his wishes just to prevent myself from looking like a statue.

As the alcohol burns its way down my throat and I gasp, I still can't shake the importance of his confession. Does he even realize what he just told me? Easton hated me before I even walked into his apartment.

Why?

Shuddering, I feel the liquid balloon in a ball of warmth in my belly. No sooner do I recover and another shot is slid into my reach.

"Oh, no. I'm fine. Thanks," I tell him. "I had…"

One. I remember. Loosen up. The night is young.

'Young?' I'm usually in bed by now. I was never one to fall for peer pressure when I turned the legal drinking age, but I casually palm the shot glass just to claim it as I watch him down another.

"Do you come here often? I don't remember this place being here."

It opened about five years ago. I did work on the guy who owns it.

"S&H. Does that stand for something?"

The corner of his mouth ticks up, his fingers drum in a frenetic motion on the table as his head bobs to the beat of the music. I can't seem to look away from the angles of his face. The shadows under his cheekbones, the smooth-looking texture of his skin, the cords in his neck, the dark curtain of lashes lining his intelligent eyes. He's exactly the same, but completely different. He was always real, but is somehow even more so now. I never contemplated my patients' looks. I saw only cases, only symptoms or struggles that I needed to remedy. Maybe because he's no longer a patient, I'm seeing him with different eyes. Easton Bennick is beautiful. Strikingly so.

Yeah. Speak no evil—hear no evil, he replies, gesturing toward Wolf on the last of the idiom.

Looking across the table, there's barely any space between Melissa and Wolf. They're practically nose to nose as she whispers something to him. Except, no one would be able to hear a whisper in this place with the volume of the music. His gaze is focused on her mouth.

He's lip reading.

His profile affords a clear view of his left ear. In the hollow of it, I spot a tiny device.

Hear no evil.

He's deaf. Easton looks pleased with himself when I glance back at him, obviously seeing the understanding in my face.

I don't know whether it's from my years of working with the non-verbal or if it's because I know Easton isn't the kind of person to just blurt out facts. It makes sense now, however, how his friendship with Wolf may have come to pass. It also explains why Easton's signing far exceeds the few ASL words and phrases I taught him.

I'm both glad he found a friend he felt comfortable around and sad that it means he might have isolated himself on purpose from people who were more verbal. Frowning, I bring the shot to my lips, determined not to get caught looking analytical. I promised both him and myself that I'd leave Hampton out of this hangout.

Gasping for breath after the fire in my throat subsides, I let out an embarrassing groan. How does he look so fit if he drinks this stuff on the regular?

Got any hair on your chest yet? he asks, grinning.

I'm too young to be a prude and too old to be competitive. I can at least not be boring, though. "A few after that, I think."

Sighing, I lean back against the upholstery, letting the effects of the liquid ooze its way into my veins. The sedating sensation is a welcome one, uncoiling tight nerves that have been tense for so long that I didn't think they'd ever give me a reprieve. Alcohol was only ever a social affair for Jason and me, with the occasional glass of wine at dinner. I never contemplated it after he died. It seemed like it would be a dangerous way to handle grief, and I was a big enough mess without it. If I knew I could have some self-control, I might indulge now and then, given how I feel at the moment. The movement of the dancing patrons in front of us almost seems hypnotic as I stare in a blissful haze, free of worry for the first time in a long time.

I'm jostled when a body presses against my side, only to find it's Easton. He's shifted closer to me. A surprising spark of static filters through me at the contact and the proximity until I catch him nodding toward the dance floor.

Oh, brother. He's trying to get out of the booth and I'm sitting here like a lug. I scramble to move and let him out. It's still strange to see him eye level with me. He was either in a wheelchair or hunched on his crutches back when I knew him before. We're the same height now.

Just as I move to reclaim my seat, his hand hooks under my upper arm.

Come on, he gestures and angles his head toward the dance floor.

"What? Oh…no. No, I'm not much of a dancer."

Maybe in the kitchen to something less fast-paced… back before life pulled the rug out from under me, I don't add. His mischievous smile returns, however, accompanied by another tug on my arm.

You can go back to Hampton and put all my new moves in my file.

Grudgingly, I concede, taking his outstretched hand. I blame guilt over his mention of Hampton for part of it. The other part is possibly because of the smile he gives me and those eyes… I never noticed how they can draw you in. Mostly, I just tell myself that I want to keep him smiling to make up for any of the grief I caused him.

Bumping past a few patrons, he releases my hand once we're deep in the mix of the crowd. It is sensory overload upon the realization that I am fully out of my element. Some remix of Måneskin's *Beggin'* is thumping all around us. Easton's promise of new moves doesn't disappoint. He bursts into fluid movements as frenetic as the light in his eyes that both mesmerize and intimidate me. I tell myself that my one drink and the two shots I downed are making my hips sway in a comparable manner, but likely resemble a junior high student at their first dance. Whatever he sees, he approves of or is thoroughly amused because his smile brightens. One of his moves brings him in closer, but he doesn't retreat. His chest is nearly flush with mine. He's so close I can feel the heat of his body and the brush of his thighs as he shifts and those deep sea-blue eyes of his lock onto my gaze like I'm the only thing in his focus. It's freaking intense and… and *something*. Something else that I can't name.

I feel centered suddenly. It's as though he cast a line, caught me, and reeled me in with one look, like he knew I was floundering. I'm no longer bobbing out of time. The music is flowing through me, through both of us like we're one.

It's probably him. He's clearly the better dancer and more in his element than I am—one of those guys who can make any dance partner look good. I'm just along for the magical ride, getting a hit of his glory. If that isn't alcohol talking, I don't know what is.

The spell thickens when he spins and slips behind me. For a second, I think the line has been severed, that I'm back to free-falling on my own, but I feel hands on my hips. A chest pressed to my back. I should have no idea that it's Easton, but I do, without a doubt, even without looking back. I can feel it in his presence as though my body knows his.

There are so many sensations I thought I'd never feel again in my life. Joy has predominantly been the one I've mourned saying goodbye to forever. Laughter, another. Arousal, however, I think I parted ways with far longer ago than I care to admit. If I admit it, it makes me the bad husband I've avoided acknowledging that I was. You're supposed to love and want your husband through thick and thin—through droughts and floods. I didn't even care that our spark had died. I loved him any-way. At least, that's what I told myself, but is it love when you no longer crave your husband romantically?

Throat thick, mouth dry, pulse skittering erratically, I am reintroduced to that forgotten phenomenon. It hits me with the force of a frigid burst of winter wind, blasting you when you first leave the warmth of your home. I've drunk more than one drink and two shots in my life with-out getting light-headed. The way my knees threaten to buckle when Easton's stubble brushes against the side of my neck and I feel his hot breath ghost my skin has nothing to do with alcohol consumption. I can't breathe, but it's not the suffocating kind of shortness of breath. It's the top of a roller coaster kind of gasping, the knowledge that something exhilarating comes next.

And *that*... is when I do stop breathing.

It's a panic attack like none of the others. This isn't what I came here for. I'm not supposed to be... turned on. I... I'm grieving. Or should be.

If I'm being honest, all I've been doing is feeling sorry for myself and trying to understand all the riddles left behind by Jason's death. That bit of truth only makes it worse. I should be feeling more sorrow over losing him rather than concern over what bills he racked up will find their way to me next. I did grieve at first, but then it turned into an unsolvable mystery that left me practically homeless. And what am I doing? Getting aroused by a guy who I told I wanted to be friends with.

I'm about to turn around and make polite apologies and excuses to Easton when I feel his arms close around the front of my waist. That should not feel so good that it quells my panic. I said *friends*. I never had any intention of thinking of him as anything other than a friend. I'm not only letting Jason down but Easton, too. Why did I think I was figur-ing anything out? I'm still as big a mess as I was last week.

Gripping his hand, I start to pull away but freeze at the feel of a soft lip at the shell of my ear. It drags slowly upward, teasing. My God, he's...is he coming on to me?

I'm freaking frozen like a pheromone-induced baby gay who just got a whiff of his first all men's rave. When I feel Easton's cheek brush against mine, his lips mere inches away from my own, the panic returns in full force. He... wants to kiss me. It would be the first time I kissed someone other than my husband in eight years. Damn me to hell for being excited about it.

"I...I need some air," I blurt, pulling away.

I don't even look back, barreling through the crowd with the urgency of needing to get out of a mosquito-riddled jungle. The glow of an *EXIT* sign above a side door near the bar is a beacon to my starved lungs. The thumping music and throng of the club are muffled background noises to the pounding of my heartbeat in my head as I push through the door and out into the alley.

Staggering, I feel the coarse texture of the brick wall and gulp in the cool night air. I am such a fool, a fucked up, emotional fool. What will that poor kid ever think of me now, watching me race out of there? The friend proposition is surely blown out the window. Kid—what a joke. He's not a kid. He's a man who has a better handle on himself than I ever did. He can tell people to fuck off when they piss him off. Every time Jason's mother calls, I shrink like a caterpillar.

He probably didn't even want to kiss me. He was just dancing, dirty dancing like everyone else here was, like everyone does to this kind of music.

He hates you, remember?

Sagging against the wall, I lean my head back and pinch my eyes closed. A sour laugh bubbles from my throat. I guess I had one sliver of dignity left, but I've successfully stomped on that tonight. This was me, all me. Maybe getting horny is some latent phase of grief that hits a year and a half after the loss of someone. People told me I might find someone else. I used to get mad about it. I have no desire to find love ever again. I'm not so ignorant to understand that there is a possibility I could kiss someone again someday. It could happen. Maybe ten years from now, when I'm not a dumpster fire, but not like *this*. Not like an inferno that creeps up on me the first time I go out to a crowded public place with a guy who, for all intents and purposes, I barely know.

"Holy shit, Aaron," I curse under my breath, pressing the heels of my palms to my eyes.

The door hinges creak, flooding the alley with the end of the sex-riddled song that broke my brain moments ago. Out walks that beautiful face, no longer behind me, no longer unavoidable.

My pep talk and momentary freak out prove as weak as I am because even though my guilt and sense of diligence tell me to book it to my car, I look directly at his mouth. The mouth I still want to kiss.

CHAPTER 13
Easton

Well, that was easier than I thought. Someone was about to melt into a puddle in my arms before his conscience hit him. And looky what we have here… still lingering outside. I've played cat and mouse before. Can't say it's my favorite game. Or rather, I'm usually the mouse, but whatever works. I don't do infidelity—one, because I'm single. And two, coupled-up guys aren't my thing. They come with problems, and other people's problems can stay their own problems. Sauntering over to Aaron, I remind myself of that now. It takes two to tango. This is a search-and-destroy mission that can only be initiated by two willing parties. I'm destroying Aaron Manicki from my system tonight, and he made it clear he was more than willing with that labored breathing he was doing on the dance floor and the sex haze that came over his eyes.

Everything all right? I ask.

"Yeah," he lets out on a breathy laugh. "Sorry, I haven't been out to a crowded place like this in a long time. I just…needed some air."

Mouse—one. Cat up to bat.

Sidling up to him, slowly for effect, I eye his jugular, pulsing as he watches my movements and wets his lips. I shouldn't be enjoying this so much. I know I dreamt of it a hundred times over, but it's different now. It's not a fantasy—it's a means to an end. It's just therapy. An antidote to cure the incurable disease I've lived with for eight years.

Planting my feet on either side of his, my pulse kicks at the way his throat undulates when he swallows. His gaze flits all over my face and up and down my body. Fuck it. Sex is sex, even if it's an anger bang. Why shouldn't I enjoy an antidote if it's going to set me free?

Cupping the side of his face, my breath practically stutters to a halt. That's the smitten, less-experienced teen in me talking, though, so I remind him he doesn't exist anymore. Aaron and I are equals now. Man versus man. Horny man versus horny man. Cat *et* mouse.

He didn't want to kiss seventeen-year-old me. He wanted the guy in the club. The one who worked him over on the dance floor like a *Fruit Roll-ups* until he melded against my body like a layer of cake icing. I'll give him exactly what he wants. Just once. I'll just give it to him so good he wants it more than once and then I'll walk the fuck away like he did eight years ago.

Mouth agape, he seems to be floundering for words. Likely more juggling of that pretty conscience he thinks he has. People who think they have consciences are so fucking predictable it's a joke. Not me. I don't do on-the-fence off-the-fence. If I want something, I kick the fucking fence down and go after it without apologies Life is too short to care about consequences and morals.

Leaning my forehead against his, I tell myself the gentle, patient gesture is because he's still clinging to that sweet persona of his, the one that fooled me years ago. I bet he moans his head off in bed when all the lights are out.

I brush my nose against his, delighting way too much in the way he shudders under the touch of my hand and grips the sleeve of my shirt, whispering my name like it's a plea, "Easton, I…"

I want him so badly I'm freaking vibrating, and yet some part of me is scared shitless, like I'm coming on to a teacher who will report me and shoot me down. Not now, though. Not now. That was then.

Brushing my lips over his, I move them upward once. Just a nudge, a tease to make him wait one second longer. He pants like he's out of air. It's exactly where I want him. And I damn well better get on with it before I'm out of air from the suspense, too.

Placing my other hand on the wall, I lean into him, chest to chest, and cover his mouth. I'm out of foreplay the second his silky lips meet mine. Angling his jaw, I swipe the tip of my tongue across the seam of his mouth, a silent message to open. He does on a little whimper, and there's no stopping me from seeking more of the first taste I got. I'm finally kissing Aaron Manicki and he's sweeter than I ever imagined he would be.

With each stifled moan and whimper he makes, clawing at my arm, I become more carnal. His mouth is a damn drug and has no business delivering such pleasure when it belongs to someone so boring. We're lucky the wall is holding him up because the entire front of my body is slumped into his by a magnetic force that can't be broken. Hell. I could fuck him right here and I'm pretty sure he'd let me.

He keens high and loud, squirming against me. It nearly does my head in and rushes all the blood to my cock until I realize he's pushing against my shoulder. Tearing his mouth away from mine, he turns his head to the side, eyes pinched shut tight.

"Wait," he pants. "Wait."

Oh, brother. The mouse is back.

Who is he fooling? I can feel his dick pressed up against my groin. Come to think of it…

The filthy grind of my hips into his makes another moan spill from his lips. I lean in and nip one of them playfully, putting the ball back in his court.

When he opens them, his eyes are so fogged over by lust, I know it's just a matter of moments before he gives up the bashful act. Except, their color seems to deepen… and then glisten.

"I can't… I…"

A twinge of something foreign stabs my chest, seeing him on the verge of tears. I don't do guilt. Guilt can go fuck itself. Aaron is responsible for at least half of his hard on. This is for my mental health, damn it. I need this man out of my system.

Brushing his nose with mine again, I decide that now is as good a time as any to play dirty. So, I glide my thumb under his lower lip as I whisper, "You don't have to tell your husband."

The shock on his face does stupid things to my heart. His expression flickers between awe and then immense sadness, crumpling before my eyes. Is my hoarse voice that much of a disappointment to him? He's the one who fucking wanted to hear it, or so I thought. Maybe that was just sociopathic insanity I built up in my head.

A tear spills down his cheek and his jaw hangs open, silent. I wait, hanging on the moment for his verdict over my voice.

"I don't…have a husband anymore."

It shouldn't relieve me I'm not corrupting a married man. I'm here to destroy, remember? But I believed him once before. Granted, it was over an art program that could have changed my life, but the point is he's a liar. Once a liar, always a liar.

I could have told him Reider was bad news. Maybe Prince Charming ran off and left him, and *Mr. Innocent* never got over it.

Smirking, I reach for his hand and bring it up between us. Tapping my finger over his dreaded ring, I cock a brow at him, accusingly.

"He… he died. He's dead."

Dead… as in… dead?

What…

My grip goes slack. The reason behind Aaron's current pliancy reveals itself in the way his hand falls lifelessly from mine like he's got nothing left in him. I'm not sure how long I stare at him, my jaw agape as his eyes pinch shut again and more tears spill onto his cheeks. At some point, I have the decency to drag my body off his, but then I'm at a loss. I just stand there, paralyzed by the sound of his sniffles, watching him bury his face in his hands. I remember what a love lost feels like, and it is not a comfortable sight.

Sucking in a breath, he finally drops his hands and blinks at me. It's as though he's seeing me for the first time, or possibly not even seeing me at all, his pupils like pinpoints.

Glancing up and down the alley like he's lost, he murmurs, "Shit. I'm sorry. I…I need to leave. I need to go."

He turns, and just like that, he's gone, hustling down the alley toward the parking lot while I stand in what oddly feels like a giant quagmire of guilt. Search and destroy wasn't supposed to destroy me along with it.

CHAPTER 14
Easton

What's six-foot-two, a fucking idiot, and carrying two milkshakes as he walks into a place he swore he'd never set foot in again? A jackass who apparently has a conscience after all.

"Still not my fault he fucking cried," I mutter under my breath, getting off the elevator on the second floor, trying not to shudder at the familiar surroundings.

Hampton Freaking Hills. Kill me now. When did I become as big of a sap as Wolf?

Dead. Dr. Reider's dead.

Fuck me. Did not see that one coming.

One minute, you're about to anger bang your teen crush into a wall, and the next, he's crying on you over having his heart broken. So... I bought freaking milkshakes. What the hell else was I supposed to do? I don't know where he lives, and a card or roses seemed like they would be an inappropriate way to apologize for rutting a widowed man into the back alley wall of Pulse.

I'll admit I was a bit of a dick, but that was before I knew Reider was dead. I thought he was having a marital crisis. Not that I'm into home-wrecking, but he's a big boy. He can make his own decisions. What was I supposed to think?

Jesus.

The internet said it was a car accident. A year and a half ago. Had to be a freaking car wreck. Fate has a cruel sense of humor. It knows just how to sucker me.

This explains why he moved back to Maine. I've had the weekend to mull over how this development played into him looking me up. The best I can figure is that he's lost. It explains the change in him, the heightened fragility that I mistook as innocence when I put him on a pedestal so long ago.

I'm not quite at the point of admitting I was wrong, though. I bought Nutella milkshakes for crying out loud. That's enough. Baby steps.

Stopping at the reception desk, *not* as a patient, is surreal. I know I've been a free man for years, but it's invigorating to be reminded of it.

"Delivery for Manicki," I inform the woman behind the counter.

Frowning, she glances over at a roster on her workspace. "Um, we don't have anyone by that name here. Are you sure you've got the right floor?"

That old feeling of inadequacy creeps over me, typical of Hampton. "Reider," I mumble.

"Who?" she asks, leaning forward the way people do when they can't hear me.

"Aaron Reider," I repeat with more volume.

"Oh! Okay. Yes, Director Reider is making his rounds right now. If you'd like to leave that here with me, I can get it to him."

Shit. Now what do I do?

"Easton?" a familiar voice calls from the opposite hallway door, and there he is.

In the same style of green polo shirt with Hampton's logo embroidered on it that he wore when I was here, it's like being sucked back down memory lane. For eight years, I've told myself everything has changed, and yet, for a split second, it seems as though nothing has. Except, that's not true. I'll never be able to look at him now without remembering that I know what it's like to kiss him.

Bad reminder.

Fucking hell. How am I supposed to console someone I wanted to wipe from my memory and now want to eat alive?

"Hi. What...what are you doing here?"

Right. My presence isn't exactly in line with my you-and-Hampton-can-go-fuck-yourselves behavior.

Hoisting up the bag from The Shake Shack, I flash him an impish grin. The way his expression softens is truly sad, as though he's just been given the gift of a lifetime. Is that how I looked when I was here and had just lost Mom?

"Um, how about we go to my office? I was just headed there to file these," he says, gesturing to some papers in his hand.

There's a new coat of paint on the walls and new light fixtures in the hallway as we walk in stride, but you can't hide the past. The smells are the same. The sounds are the same. The air is the same suffocating air. I try not to let my skin crawl, reminding myself it doesn't matter. Yet maybe... in a way, it did. I had to end up somewhere after the accident. Who knows if there were worse places than Hampton?

Following Aaron inside an office, I vividly remember that it belonged to Dr. Norton, the eccentric old man who oversaw this level when I was a resident here. Hints of tobacco smoke linger in the air from ages past and oddly fill me with a sense of being home.

Stopping in front of his desk, Aaron gives me a bewildered once over. Yeah. I can't believe I'm here either, I want to tell him. He makes a breathless laugh and smiles.

"This is a nice surprise." Glancing at the bag when I set it on his desk and remove the contents, his expression turns fond. "Are those Nutella? I can't believe you remembered. I haven't had one of those in years."

It's like I don't know what to do with myself since I'm not a kid on crutches with a scheduled appointment. Locking onto a leather couch at the side of the room, I tote my milkshake over to it and take a seat. Maybe this will be easier if I'm not close enough to be in his orbit, close enough to grab him and put my mouth on his.

I need to say something. I used to have to contain my excitement over getting to talk to him, but now that my speech is more improved than he ever heard it, it's like I don't have the backbone to use it. It might have something to do with the only thing I've said to him verbally was a taunt about his dead husband before I knew said husband was dead.

Did you make it home okay? I sign.

Leaning against his desk, he drops his chin, cheeks going pink. "Um, yeah. I'm so sorry about flaking out like that…about…not being myself."

I'm sorry about your husband. That doesn't seem very sincere since the thick air between us says he remembers the feel of my tongue in his mouth, so I add, *I thought maybe you were divorced.*

"Um, no." Craning his neck back, he looks up at the ceiling and blows out a breath. "I can't say I didn't think about it sometimes. We didn't exactly know each other very well when we got married, so it took some work after the honeymoon phase was over." Fidgeting, he stuffs a hand in the pocket of his khakis and flashes me a chagrined look. "Not what you asked, I know," he digresses with a nervous laugh. "But I'm just explaining because…because I guess that's part of what's made losing him so difficult. Not that it's probably any easier losing someone you had a perfect relationship with." Pushing off the desk, he goes to the window and stares out at the dreary landscape, everything going dormant and caught between the end of summer and fall.

"I got completely swept up and lost in Jason when he came along. I'd never met anyone like him. He had this incredible resume and was so confident and worldly and…convincing." Glancing back at me, he lets out another of those pained laughs. "I honestly don't know how anyone would have said *no* when he asked me to pick up and move out to Seattle with him. He made it sound like the world would be at our fingertips and our life would be full of sunshine and rainbows. And it was…for a while."

His silence infects the room with something dark that has me wanting to go to him. I'm here to cut ties amicably, not get pulled further into the fog that is Aaron.

"That's what I get for believing in true love," he mutters with feigned humor and lets out a sigh, turning back around to face me. "I… lost sight of who I was and what I wanted to do with my life. I won't pretend I came back here solely by choice. I honestly couldn't see many other options, but…I'm here now. So far, I've made a mess of nearly everything. For starters," he hesitates, fingering his collar and eyeing a spot on the floor. "Thinking I should look up one of my former patients."

I used to be the one who was embarrassed all the time during our sessions. Sure, I teased him to keep the playing field even, but this is a different shade of humility in him now. It wars with the chip I've carried on my shoulder. His life choices destroyed the invincible image I had of him, making part of me want to scold him for pissing on my fantasy. I can see now that he was just a pop icon on a poster, and yet, the icon sought little old me. It still doesn't make any sense.

Why did you?

"I…had to know if you were okay. If you were okay, I thought maybe it meant I'd done one thing right."

Shit. If he starts crying again, I don't know what I'm going to do. The urge to get up and hug him is way stronger than it should be. I don't fucking hug.

"Honestly, though," he admits with a forlorn smile, "wondering what happened to you after you left here was better than thinking about everything I usually think about these days."

And there it is. He was just looking for a distraction from his pain.

It's not exactly a compliment, but it's forgivable. Understandable. I feel it in my damaged bones. What the hell is life but a distraction, anyway? Maybe that's all he ever was to me and why it hit so hard when he disappeared. I was forced to face everything after that.

I nod because there's nothing to say.

The phone on his desk blares, slicing through the poignant silence between us. Frazzled, he turns and answers it.

"Oh? All right. No. No, just wait. I'll be there in a minute. Okay."

That's my cue to leave. Peace offering delivered. Guilt successfully shucked off. I stand, giving him a knowing look when he turns back to face me.

"I'm sorry. I have to go."

The remorse in his voice shouldn't please me. He's just lonely. It's not like he wants my company in particular. It's not like I want his company. I don't.

Take it easy on them, I tell him, gesturing to the phone.

"Always," he laughs. "If Dr. Norton taught me anything, it was to not rule with an iron fist." Grimacing at the room, he adds airily, "Or…smoke a pipe indoors."

I didn't need to see that he still possesses his easy humor. *Leave, Easton*, a wise voice in my head tells me.

Giving him a salute with my melting shake, I head toward the door. I didn't even want to come here. Why is there an invisible pull making me want to stay?

"Easton," he calls just as my hand touches the knob. "If you ever want to chat or…get together. Maybe not at a club or with alcohol involved—I think I've made it obvious that I'm in no condition to handle either of those situations," he chides himself with that annoyingly adorable goodness in his expression as he scribbles a number on a *Post-it Note*. "God knows why you'd want to. I must look completely deranged after how I burst into your life again, but…it really is good to see you."

Reaching out, I fully expect the slip of paper to snap me like a mousetrap. He is the freaking mouse, after all. He just didn't know it, apparently, or I'm a bad fucking cat who can't tell a cry for help from a come-on. Whatever. I can throw it in my drawer with the rest of the numbers I've collected.

"Thanks," he adds, lifting his cup. "For the shake."

I need to burn that damn place to the ground so no one can ever buy him one again if he acts like this over a freaking malt. Protect him from more Jason Reiders.

Whoa…

What?

Get back to work, slacker.

With that parting sarcasm, I hightail it out of my former prison faster than I've ever moved. This is the last place I want to be if I've apparently lost my fucking mind.

CHAPTER 15

Aaron

This isn't going well at all. After a week of lighthearted texts back and forth with Easton, I was under the impression we'd reached some kind of budding camaraderie. I shouldn't have ruined it with a lunch invitation, but I was still desperate to make up for acting like such a fool the last few times I'd seen him.

> **You should get one of these for your office.**

That was the message it started with, accompanied by a picture of a milkshake machine, letting me know who the sender was. It's been so long since I've had any kind of silly exchange with someone that the text made my smile nearly break my face. I think I was also astounded that he'd actually reached out. It felt like a victory, not the way it is when I break through with a patient, but because it's Easton and he has no obligation to speak to me.

I had to take the morning off to get my oil changed. While I don't have much leave accrued, meeting Easton for lunch was far more appealing than going to work for half a day. The hundred and twenty-seven dollars I have left to my name until payday would probably be wiser spent on one of the many bills I have to pay, but I can't remember the last time I enjoyed myself or did something for someone else. I was a bit taken aback by Easton's offer to pick me up since I was the one who wanted to treat him, but my bank account made me accept.

I can still feel the rumble of his motorcycle between my legs. Being pressed up behind him on the back of his bike as we whirred through downtown was not how I imagined our first reunion after his visit to my office. I certainly never pictured pulling up to Hampton Boarding House on a motorcycle, either.

It's still the nicest restaurant in town. Jason and I even ate here on a few of our dates when he was a visiting surgeon at Hampton Hills. If I only get one chance to spoil Easton, I figured this would be the place to do it.

Watching him drum his fingers on the white linen tablecloth anxiously as his eyes canvas the dining area makes my heart sink. He looks so out of place in a button-down with his neck tats peeking out above the collar and his wavy hair slicked back.

Tapping at the menu, he indicated his selections to the waiter with nods or shakes of his head. He has yet to speak to me again since that night at Pulse. I don't think I imagined it, which has my speech pathologist brain churning about why he's reverted to signing. No matter what I say, I feel self-conscious, wary of sounding like this is an investigation rather than a cordial meeting of acquaintances.

"I figured you do most of your work at night, so I hope lunch was the best time to catch you."

I work all day, but I can come and go as I please.

"How did you get into tattooing?"

I realize as soon as I've asked that the response could be a long one. I've spent enough time with my brother to know when someone isn't happy to sign, which baffles me even more as I watch Easton answer me. He isn't comfortable speaking to me in any format, unless it's short texts about nothing. How did I get this so wrong?

My friend Wolf went to school for it and showed me the ropes. I got a job cleaning at the studio under the old owner. I showed him my artwork, and he finally let me start doing simple designs until he trusted me to not fuck up anything more elaborate. Skin is a permanent canvas, so I don't blame him.

The way his gaze tracks the other diners watching the movement of his hands has me tensing. George was always self-conscious about being watched in public, too. I hate that I'm the cause of Easton feeling like he's a spectacle, even though I don't think it's his signing that's drawing us attention. It's just... *him.* His ink is mostly covered, but it's still apparent he possesses a lot of it. Yet, even without it, I can't imagine people not gawking at him the way I can't seem to stop doing. It's those dark-rimmed, deep jade eyes of his, those long lashes. He gets more stunning the longer I look at him.

Clearing my throat, I try to bring his attention back to me to ease his wariness. "You've known Wolf a long time?"

He stares at me for a moment and then nods. Why does everything out of my mouth sound like an inquisition? I'd shut up if he asked me anything, except I'm afraid then I'd be the one with clipped answers. My life hasn't exactly been interesting since I left Hampton.

He was friends with the guy who lived next door to my foster home.

The tightness in his jaw and the way he looks out the window as he answers tell me I'm getting too close to home. I promised not to dive into the past and that's right where I took him. Wonderful. Can't we just go back to silly texts? Why is this so hard? It feels like there's a black mark on my record bigger than showing up at his door unannounced or bailing out of a noisy club, but for the life of me, I can't figure out what it is.

"The desserts are really good here," I throw out, still unable to shut my pie hole. "Or they used to be when I came here with... Um, my parents used to bring me and my brother here on New Year's Eve each year. They let us pig out. It was the best part of the Christmas season. They shoot fireworks off out back and we'd watch them from the patio."

Luckily, our lunch arrives. Easton picks up his fork and looks at it strangely.

"Sir, do you need another dinner fork?" the waiter asks.

Frowning, he shakes his head, motioning with his three-pronged fork. The waiter's veiled expression is obvious, at least to me, as he glances at the steak Easton ordered.

"It's no trouble to bring you another. Steak is much better enjoyed without a salad fork," the man informs him and bustles off.

Blinking at his utensil, Easton's face goes crimson when he glances up at me. I never considered he might have never set foot in a place like this before. It was supposed to be my way of showing him how much his offer of friendship meant to me, not to humiliate him.

"I'm sure that one works just fine," I assure him.

Mouth in a thin line, he picks up his steak knife and starts sawing through his meat with more force than necessary. Maybe he's just really hungry.

Or maybe, like everything else, I've fucked up again. When he pops the first bite into his mouth and lets out a loud exhale around it, I watch in silence as he sets down his utensils and unbuttons his cuffs. Rolling up his sleeves, he reveals his inked forearms, a vivid contrast to his white dress shirt. Leaning forward more casually than before, he hunkers over his plate, giving a dismissive nod to the waiter when he delivers the *proper* fork.

Yeah. I definitely fucked up.

CHAPTER 16
Easton

I rescheduled Molly Vasquez's inner thigh tattoo for this shit? No wonder Wolf acts like he has to make all the important business decisions.

Salad forks. Dinner forks. Linen napkins that don't soak up shit. Oh, how the other half live.

Turning over my bike's engine, the only saving grace of this lunch date is that I get to cart Aaron *Precious* Manicki-Reider away from this fancy-ass place Steve McQueen style. I hope they ban him after this for me rattling their windows.

What the fuck happened to him? We used to shoot the shit like it was effortless. He seemed like his old self when we were texting this week. Now, he's trying to show off with this place and acting all awkward, but not the endearing kind of awkward that used to make me melt each time he said something corny. Freaking Jason Reider is to blame, no doubt. He ruined a man who had potential.

Thinking ill of the dead, even if the dead was a dickhead before he died, is the final way to top off my soured mood. I'm no saint, but I don't need more inspiration to conjure cynical thoughts.

I let loose on the road out of town, back toward Aaron's little cottage. That part makes no sense to me. So, I was being a little nosy by insisting I could pick him up since he was springing for lunch, but I'm glad my nose let me in on new Aaron details. If he's all fine dining, why does he live in a dinky little cottage? At least it's by the water. The lucky shit. I'd be out there every day, jumping in bare-ass naked. I bet he doesn't indulge in that activity.

When we pull into the gravel drive outside his place, he goes tense behind me as I take in the change of scenery from earlier when I picked him up. The truck that was sitting out front—a rusty old one that also doesn't jive with the fine-dining type—is currently on the back of a flatbed trailer. The logo on the door of the semi hauling it reads, *Sullivan Recovery Specialists.* I somehow doubt this type of recovery has anything to do with substance addiction.

"Oh, God. No," Aaron gasps behind me, scrambling off my bike. "Shit. This cannot be happening."

Whatever is going on is urgent enough that I don't get a backward glance. I stay put, watching like a voyeur. Aaron races up to one of two men in navy-blue coveralls who is tightening tow straps down on his truck. I don't catch all of what's said, but there's something about being defaulted on a payment and repossession of his listed collateral. I'm guessing this jalopy is his listed collateral.

A man walks out of the cottage, looking flustered and… a lot like Aaron. Judging by the evident cochlear implant surgery scars around his ear and the fact Aaron starts signing rapidly to him, I've just laid eyes on his infamous brother, George, the one I heard so many childhood stories about years ago. He throws his hands up, gripping his head while Aaron elaborates animatedly about money problems and something to do with Jason… Jason and Jason's debts. How the plot of marital bliss thickens. When they disappear into the cottage, a blanket of dread covers me as I wait for them to re-emerge.

Are they arguing? Would his brother hurt him?

I'm off my bike and striding up the few steps to the porch without further thought. I can hear Aaron explaining how he consolidated debt into loans and has been doing everything he can to pay them on time.

"This is so embarrassing. My other tenants know my brother is living here. What if any of them saw this?" George's voice warns.
Looking past them, there's little to land my gaze on. The living room is devoid of furnishings save for a camping chair next to a few stacks of books. There's a TV sitting on the floor at the far end of the room, but it's not even plugged in. Through the doorway on the other side of the room, I catch a view of a mattress… on the floor, no bedframe. He told me at lunch that he moved into this cottage over a month ago.

I let my boots scrape against the hardwood floor as I cross the threshold, alerting Aaron to my presence. I get a pitying look as though he's sorry for neglecting me, which is baffling as hell, given that his current circumstances seem more pressing. The sound of truck doors slamming outside, however, draws his attention back to the yard.

Moving so he and George can pass, I make my way slowly down the stairs, regretting the view. The workers pile into their semi and start to haul the truck away. Aaron's shoulders slump up ahead of me. He drops his face into his hands as though shielding himself from reality will protect him from further misery. His brother stands by, looking helpless and uncomfortable. I can relate. I don't know why I'm still lingering. This isn't something I need to or should see.

I don't know what the hell is going on, but it doesn't involve me.

Making my way back to my bike, I straddle it with every intention of making a quiet escape. However, damn fool that I am, I take one last look and catch Aaron holding up a hand, beckoning me to wait.

He follows George to a van with *Manicki Property Management* on the side of it. *Other tenants*, George had said in the cottage. He's not just his brother, he's his landlord. The pieces start falling into place more than I care to learn. After Aaron bids George goodbye, he makes his way back over to me. I should have left when I had the chance.

His mouth moves, but nothing comes out. Eyes glassy with tears, his chest is heaving like he's out of breath. It's now that I register that the dark circles under his eyes aren't likely from age. He's only thirty-three. His khaki slacks look worn in the light of day and there's a button missing from his cuff, a wayward thread sticking out at the hem.

Running a hand through his thick brown hair, he grips a handful of it as he flounders, baring his teeth in anguish. "They…they took my truck," he blurts, stating the obvious. "I…have bills…from Jason. I don't know why. I always took care of the bills, but they just kept showing up after he died. Credit cards I didn't know about, memberships, tabs from clubs. He had properties and bad investments I wasn't even aware of, money he borrowed privately and never paid back. Just when I think I've found everything, something else falls in my lap. I don't know why he…" he trails off, staring out at the water or possibly nothing.

You didn't have to take me to lunch, I tell him, a distraction from the uncomfortable confession. That was supposed to be my purpose, right? A distraction.

Sucking in a breath, he shakes his head. "No. I did. I had to make up for making you uncomfortable." Swiping at his eyes, he swallows like he's trying to regain some of his composure and cocks his head with a smile. "And…you brought me a milkshake. I'm sorry the restaurant was…too much. I just wanted to do something nice for you." Glancing at the place where his truck was parked, he grimaces. "And…I'm sorry you had to see that. I wasn't always such a mess."

How are you going to get to work?

"Oh, I'll…go look for another one. It'll be fine," he lets out airily.

He gives me an optimistic smile that doesn't hide the fear in his eyes. His expression tells me everything I need to know. He doesn't have a damn clue, and I probably just ate the man's last dime… with the wrong fucking fork.

The pedestal I put him on topples. All my anger, bitterness, and the fog of unrealistic expectations that clouded my judgment fizzle into oblivion. He's just a man. Just a man trying to survive in the same shit show called *life* that I am.

Maybe he always was. I was just too young and naïve and angry to see it.

Shit.

CHAPTER 17
Aaron

I think I'll just live here… in this tub. I can drain the water each time it gets cold and run more. The shape of the old pedestal basin fits my exhausted body, creating a swaddling sensation that is the most comforting thing I've felt since my childhood bed. I don't feel so empty with the water all around me. I serve a purpose here, filling this space.

I've been staring at the white ceramic wall tiles for over two hours. Their brightness under the morning light that's seeping through the window makes the room feel sanitized, my soul clean, less heavy.

Shit. The water's getting cold again.

Closing my eyes, common sense reminds me I should call my mother, concoct some type of story about how my truck is in the shop, and ask if I can borrow her car so I can get to work tomorrow. I can't live in a bathtub. At least, not this one. George owns it, not me.

Pulling the drain plug, the gurgle of the water is a depressing sound, sucking down my temporary moment of ignorance of the reality awaiting me. I should be more preoccupied with my situation than the audience I had two days ago when Easton dropped me off, but avoidance is an addiction.

I can't believe he had to see that. I didn't think things could get any worse. Laughing as I step out and grab my towel, I know that's a lie. Of course, they can get worse. That's the one-way direction my life has had. I just didn't think I could *feel* worse than I already have been.

Easton grew up rough and with little from my recollection of his file and our discussions at Hampton. I doubt he'd judge me. He certainly didn't when he was here Friday afternoon. If anything, he seemed to be concerned and spared me my non-existent dignity. Still, though… I don't like the thought of being *less* in his eyes, for some reason.

Tromping back into the bedroom, I rustle through the oversized box that serves as my dresser for anything I couldn't fit in the tiny closet. It's been getting chilly at night with Autumn coming in hard and fast. Winter cannot come and go fast enough. I've lowered the heat as much as I can tolerate to save on costs, but I'm growing tired of shivering all the time. I can't afford to get sick, even if I do have medical coverage through work. Thirty-three years old, and I dread the thought of a co-pay visit. How sad is that?

Donning a pair of old sweatpants, sweatshirt, and socks, I haul the blanket off my mattress and wrap it around me like a cloak for extra warmth. At least, George hasn't said a peep to our parents about my pitiful existence here, if he's noticed. I told him I was waiting to buy furniture if I found a different place. I'm not sure he'll continue to believe that after Friday when the repo men called his management number on the sign by the main road for his cottages.

Shuffling to the kitchen, I put a pot on to boil and rummage through my selection of *Ramen* noodles in the cabinet. Getting food in my stomach might make the pain of lying to my mother more tolerable when I call to grovel for the use of her car.

The sound of vehicle doors slamming shut outside makes me jump. Do repo men work on Sundays? I have nothing left that's eligible to be repossessed, no other loans that had collateral listed. God, I hope it isn't George coming to give me an inquisition or… kick me out.

He wouldn't, would he? I know he was embarrassed by the activity the other day, but the cottages are spread at least half a mile apart, so I doubt any of his other tenants saw.

Hustling to the front door, I spy a black van in my driveway with red lettering emblazoned on the side of it. S&H Tattoo. Easton?

There's a shiny red pickup truck parked next to it with furniture in the back of it. That woman from the shop, Shannon, and that guy, Fro, head toward the back, lowering the tailgate.

Opening the door, I step out onto the porch, blinking through the last of the dew burning off under the mid-morning sun. I find yet another vehicle in the party—a silver SUV that looks like its backend is loaded to the gills with boxes. There's a small army of tatted men and women on my lawn. In the middle of them, pointing like he's directing them, is Easton.

"Morning!" Shannon calls, throwing me a wave and a smile as she and Fro slide a bed frame out of the back of the truck.

I wave back, dumbly. I'm too distracted by the sight of Easton and Wolf hauling a couch out of the back of the van. They turn and start heading my way, toward my front steps.

"What…what is this?" I babble, moving out of the way so I don't get run over when it becomes clear they have no intention of stopping.

I know Wolf is deaf, which explains why he doesn't look at or answer me, but Easton isn't. Granted, he's focused on not dropping the heavy piece of furniture, but I know he had to have heard me.

"Easton, what are you doing?"

He answers, but it's by way of nodding his head toward the door I left agape. Scrambling past Wolf before there's no room left for me to pass, I step back inside and hold it back even though I'd prefer they stop and tell me what the heck is going on. Where did this couch come from, and why did Easton bring it here? It looks... new.

Oh my God. It *is*. There are still tags on it.

Grunting, Wolf staggers momentarily as they guide it through the doorway. Easton makes a breathy snickering sound at his friend's expense, which gets him a glare, but then Wolf's face cracks into a smirk. They set it down near my camping chair in the middle of the living room with a thump and dual breaths of relief.

"Easton...what is..."

I don't get to finish. The end of a metal bedframe scrapes the side of my arm.

"Coming through! Sorry about that," Fro calls as he and Shannon guide the piece through the doorway past me. "Where's this going?" he asks Easton.

My stalwart former patient points in the direction of my bedroom. I blink after them in a daze. Glancing out the doorway, two other men from the shop are unloading a box frame from the van. What is happening? I need answers.

I meet Easton's gaze, finally snaring his attention. His mouth ticks up at one corner.

Good morning. You're not busy, are you? he says with his hands.

Busy? What does busy have anything to do with it?

"No." I shake my head mechanically.

Good. I took a chance that you'd be home.

He starts heading back outside, but I snag his arm. "Wait. Easton... what... What is all of this?"

Furniture, he signs with humor in his eyes, as though I'm being obtuse.

"Yeah. I can see that, but...but why? Where did it come from? What...what are you doing bringing it here?"

The place looked a little empty.

He grabs my arm, tugging me out of the way when the two men bring the box frame through the doorway. The magnitude of the gesture I'm witnessing is beyond touching, but I also see dollar signs. Dollar signs I can't afford, nor will I be able to anytime soon.

"Easton, thank you. This is really kind of you, but I can't..." Shifting, I turn my back to the others even though they've ventured deeper into the cottage. Murmuring in my shame, I confess, "I can't afford this. It would take me a long time to pay you back. So, please don't take offense. I'm touched by your intention, but...I just can't accept any of this."

Don't worry about it.

God, he has no clue. Loans between friends are never good—isn't that what people say? And more than a comfortable couch to sit on, more than something other than Ramen noodles to eat, I want Easton to be my friend. I know now that it has nothing to do with me needing a distraction. He's good, funny, and as fucking amazing as he was years ago. He's a life force I want to be around.

"I *am* worried about it. You don't understand how…just how bad things are with my finances right now. I won't do that to you. I can't accept it. I know you probably went to a lot of trouble. I'll help you take it back. That's the least I can do."

"Stop." The commanding sound that comes out of his mouth hits me like a cold splash of water. It's soft and raspy, but it's… vocal. "Just stop," he repeats, gripping my arms and giving me a poignant look. "Please. I don't want anything."

"But…"

"I don't," he emphasizes, giving me a squeeze. The determined look on his face softens, erasing the lines around his eyes. Shrugging, a little smile plays on his face as he adds even softer, "You helped me once."

The words are so good to hear that tears well up in my eyes. It's a reassurance I didn't know how much I needed. You're not supposed to question good things, but it feels too much like a hallucination.

"But…you hate me," I stammer. "Kissing Wolf to get me to leave. The electrolarynx. The restaurant…you looked like you were crawling out of your skin just to get away from me."

Releasing me, he blows out a breath and cranes his head back, rolling his eyes. Shifting in place, he rubs the back of his neck and chews his lower lip.

"I hate…the past. Not you."

Something still doesn't add up. If he's doing all of this because he thinks I helped him, why did he lash out like that if he can separate me from Hampton?

"I let you down when I left, didn't I?"

Scoffing, he shakes his head. With a wry smile, he reaches out and picks at a nail sticking out of the wall. It's avoidance if I've ever seen it. It brings back a flash of his little quirks from our sessions together.

As he tugs at the nail, I recall how those artful fingers created the most breathtaking sketches on any paper he could get his hands on while he was at Hampton. He was so talented. I wanted him to go to art school so he could…

Oh, God… That school where my mother used to be a board member.

"The art institute scholarship program…I told you I'd get you in before I left, and then Jason had to report to a new facility and we took off in a hurry. I…forgot." I wish I could make my crime stop coming out of my mouth, but it's a penance I need to own. "Oh, God. Easton, I'm so sorry. You were so excited about it."

He drops his hand and looks at me, his posture relaxing. That smirk, the one I'm starting to think means the opposite of whatever he intends it to mean, plays on his face again.

I think I did okay without it.

Signing. *More* signing. He was so not okay without it. I want to crawl back into the tub and draw the shower curtain closed around me until they all leave. At least, though, I've gotten to the bottom of it.

"I'm sorry, Easton. I'm so sorry. I can't believe I did that to you."

Chuffing, he runs his fingers through his hair and takes a step toward the doorway, peering outside. "It's fine," he murmurs airily.

"It's *not*. I was too self-absorbed and lost sight of what was important to me."

His gaze flicks to mine, surprised. My face heats, remembering the kiss from last weekend at the most inopportune moment. I'm sure now that it was done just to punish me, that there's nothing about me that's important to *him*, but I meant what I said. He *was* important to me then until I got blindsided by dreams of a happily ever after. Standing here, wrapped in this blanket while he fills my house with this unexpected gift and is showing me kindness when he has no earthly reason to, I know without a doubt that he most certainly is important to me now, too.

"Thank you," I whisper, too choked up to give the words any more volume.

I wanted to know more about him. It just had to be on Easton's terms, apparently. Everything in my soul wants to make the things being carted into my cottage disappear, but I have a feeling the amount of damage that would do to this bridge between me and the mysterious man before me would be irreversible. Easton with claws. Easton, the giver. Easton, the silently compassionate soul who can't stand to take a compliment. He's not careless about who he lets in, and I've been granted a pass. I don't want it to be revoked now that I have it.

His phone rings, a welcome distraction. I try not to look curious when he brings it up to his ear, knowing it means he's going to speak again. Turning, I shrug out of my blanket and fold it up. I can't believe I stood here like a snowstorm rescue victim the entire time with it around me.

Something taps my shoulder. "Here. Talk to them, will you?" Easton holds his phone out expectantly.

"Who?"

"Cable. For your TV."

Oh, my word. This is going too far. Cable is not a necessity of life.

"Easton, I don't need cable."

Rolling his eyes, he motions with his phone again. I know I likely underestimated how lucrative owning a tattoo business can be, but this is excessive. I can't take advantage of his good deed to the extent it puts him in the same position that I am.

"That's too much. Really. Don't, please."

Nostrils flaring, his hand doesn't move a muscle, the phone still presented to me. Shit. Maybe I can appeal to his sense of pity.

"I can't afford it."

Sighing, he brings the phone back up to his ear. "This is going on my S&H account, right?" There's a pause and then he swallows and enunciates with some apparent difficulty, "*S&H account.* Okay, good. Hang on again."

With a pointed look, he hands his phone to me again. How could I have forgotten just how stubborn he can be? I'm about to exhibit the same amount when he adds softly, "Talk to them, please…so I don't have to."

It's a vein sliced open, bleeding all over my heart. As much as I feel pathetic and embarrassed, I never want to see the same look on his face.

I no sooner reluctantly take his phone before he heads out the door, and I'm left listening to the salesman elaborate on all the different cable packages available to me. He only speaks salesman, though, because no matter how many times I tell him to enroll me in whatever is cheapest, he rattles on about bonus packages without detailing the prices.

Pacing, I try to muster patience, befuddled by all the activity around me. In my bedroom, I catch Fro and Shannon setting the box mattress on the now assembled bed frame. There appears to be a brand-new comforter set still in its zippered plastic packaging on the floor next to where my mattress is temporarily leaning against the wall. How will I ever repay the kindness of these complete strangers? And what does it say about Easton that they're doing all of this at his behest without a word or complaint?

Melissa flits past me with a smile. Curtains are draped over her arm as she sizes up the old lace valance that hanging in the front room window that was here when George gave me the keys to the place. Curtains? I don't need curtains.

Another guy walks into my kitchen with a case of soda and two cases of beer under his arms. I hear music. Why is there music?

A peel of laughter floats out of the bedroom, and I catch Shannon bent over, amused at Fro's sprawled-out position on my mattress like he fell on top of it when they flipped it onto the box frame. I spot a *Bluetooth* speaker on my bedroom windowsill, explaining where the background noise is coming from. It's like a moving-in party that I wasn't told about, everyone having a good time regardless of it involving manual labor.

The salesman asks if I'm still on the line, pulling me back into the painful bargain. "Look, I don't need any of that stuff. Please, just whatever the lowest package is. Okay?"

Easton wheels past me with a brand-new dresser wrapped in plastic wrap on a dolly. The expression he shoots me says he heard my plea and isn't pleased.

The sales guy just offered me something that includes *HGTV*. I don't even own a home. Sensibility makes me draw a line at just how far I'll go to appease Easton's need to give. I turn my back on him lest I be cajoled by his persuasive face and antics.

No sooner do I get off the phone, not entirely sure of what I signed up for, than Melissa nearly runs smack into me. There's a notepad from my kitchen and a pen in her hand.

"What do you like on your pizza?"

"Pizza?"

"Yeah. Easton's ordering pizzas for lunch."

Looking through the doorway to my bedroom, I learn the definition of the word *awestruck*. The man responsible for upending my day and my residence is taking in his team's handiwork with a careful eye, as though he wants to ensure everything is perfect. He inches the un-wrapped dresser over a few inches and then stands back to check that its placement is symmetrical with the end of my new bed. I watch like I'm in some kind of dream. These aren't the actions of a guy who hates me or a tatted rogue with a rough exterior.

I wanted to know so badly how he fared after leaving Hampton, and I have my answer. He did just fine, like he said. Whatever road he traveled to get where he is now, he ended up even more endearing than I remember him being.

Melissa clears her throat, reminding me of her request. He stocked my house, and now he's feeding me and all his friends. Swallowing against the thickness in my throat, a soft laugh bubbles out as I smile at her.

"Of course he is."

CHAPTER 18

Aaron

The mystery behind Fro's moniker doesn't cease to amuse when Wolf produces a screenshot of an old photo on his phone of the man with a frizzy bush of dark hair sticking up at all ends. Glancing at the now-bald man, I try to compare amidst the cacophony of laughter from his friends at his expense.

Scoffing, he grumbles in front of his beer bottle, "You try taking care of that shit all summer. This is way more low maintenance."

"He's failing to mention the gum incident," Wolf informs me, chuckling as he tucks his phone back into his pocket.

"Oh, come the fuck on," Fro grumbles. "Not this shit again."

"There's a *no chewing gum* sign on his stall for a reason," Shannon informs me with a wink where she's perched on the new coffee table in my living room.

They're a merry crowd, to be sure. I'll admit, there was a moment where I wondered if this would turn into some type of kegger when I first saw Fro carting in a case of beer earlier, but no one's overindulged. Everyone cleaned up after themselves the second they were finished with a drink or a plate. It's casual and so natural it feels like they're my own house guests.

The sun has just set, which means it's nearly dinner time, but there was so much pizza delivered, I have no designs of being hungry again anytime soon. Somehow, it seems ungrateful to be sitting in my camping chair after all the trouble these people went to, but they completely deserve the comfort of the new couch after giving up a day of their life for me.

I still can't believe everything that came out of Wolf's van. It was like Santa Claus' magical sack of presents. I managed to bite my tongue most of the day, keeping myself busy helping Fro put together the entertainment center that appeared along with all the other unnecessary items. While I'm enjoying being surrounded by laughter and the easy merriment of these wonderful people, I haven't had a chance to speak to Easton since the pizza arrived a few hours ago.

Excusing myself, I head to the kitchen, where I saw him escape moments ago with his empty soda can. One hand resting on my counter, the other clutching the small of his back, he arches his chest, stretching. Eyes closed, the cords in his neck are strained, pulling his face taut. How much anguish has he had to live with because of his past injuries? No young life should have started out the way his did. I can't believe how much moping I've done when what stands before me is clearly a fighter, a silent warrior of this earth. My younger years were basically carefree. I doubt I'd have had the strength to endure what he must have.

"Please tell me you didn't hurt yourself hauling any of this stuff in here today."

Straightening, he turns around and leans against my kitchen counter. "No. Tattoo back. Hours spent hunched over every day."

I hadn't considered that. Still, it sounds like one more reason he shouldn't have hauled a furniture store into my house today.

Something slaps the doorframe, giving me a start.

"Yo, Bossman. We're still supposed to ride back with Wolf, right?" Shannon asks, popping her head into the kitchen.

"Uh, yeah. Thanks."

"Cool." She digs a set of keys out of her pocket and slaps them into Easton's hand. "We're going to head out then. Melissa's itching to get home."

Shaking his head, he chuffs. "Surprise, surprise. Thanks."

"My pleasure." Turning to me as she passes, she graces me with one of her perpetually cheery expressions. "Nice to see you again, Aaron. If we dinged any of the walls, I blame Fro."

"Thank you. This was…incredible of all of you. Seriously. I don't have the words."

I follow Easton back to the living room, wondering if I'll miss getting another word with him. I know he doesn't want to be thanked, but how can he just up and leave after today without so much as a few minutes of chatter? Maybe it's my need to give him something in return that has me feeling like something is missing.

I thank the rest of his friends as they pile out the door. A giddy sensation comes over me when Easton remains, bidding them farewell with me like he's staying put.

I got what I wanted. Now what? What can I say to not scare him off or ruin the magnanimous gesture he made today?

After the Wolf departs, it's just the two of us left standing in my living room. He moves to the coffee table and collects the last of the pizza boxes, carting it into my kitchen without a word. Scrambling, I snag a napkin that was left behind just for an excuse to follow. Face to face in the kitchen, I'm about to blurt out more thank yous I know will make him squirm when he speaks.

"I'm gonna go too. You good?"

Scoffing, I give the cottage a scan. "I feel like I robbed a home goods store and didn't even know it."

Snorting, he reaches into his pocket and retrieves the keys that Shannon gave him. I stare dumbly as he holds them out to me.

"Here. So you can get to work," he explains.

I stare at them, remembering that I forgot all about calling my mother to ask for the use of her car. Right. My truck is gone. Forever. Shit. But what is he talking about?

As his crew pulls away, I glance out the front window and notice the silver SUV is still sitting in my yard, along with Easton's motorcycle. *Two* vehicles, but only one person left to drive. The keychain on the keys has a *Chevy* emblem on it, matching the symbol on the front of the shiny, newer-model *Suburban* on my lawn.

"What? No. I can't."

Sighing, he rolls his eyes, grabs my hand, and drops them into my palm. He starts heading toward the door, setting off a panic in me. I only have seconds to unravel this new mystery. Which one of his friends offered up an *eighty-some*-thousand-dollar ride to a complete stranger? This is getting out of hand.

"Easton, wait. Whose is this?"

Mine, he signs, and then that playful light in his eyes flickers. *Don't worry. It's not stolen.*

God, what kind of impression of him did I convey? "I wouldn't have thought that," I babble and make my feet shuffle forward. "But seriously, I can't borrow your car. This is too much. You've already done way too much. There's no way I can—"

His palm covers my mouth. It's gentle, but so unexpected I stop speaking. Leaning in, his lips press a quick peck to my temple, and he murmurs, "It's fine. Get some sleep."

I think I've been numb most of the day, too swept up in the events that unfolded to be fully present. My brain comes back online, however, the second I feel him pull back. It's pure instinct and gratitude, and probably still more self-pity, but I latch onto him, hugging him tightly.

I know he doesn't like talking or praise, but I have to let him know how much this means to me. I hope he understands that it's not even about furniture. It's the chance he's giving me to exist in his world again.

He's stiff under my embrace as I try to hold back my tears. Will I ever stop getting teary-eyed?

I don't blame him for not knowing what to do with such a mess of a man in front of him, but then I feel his arms go around me. They're loose at first but then tighten. It feels like they glue some of my pieces back together. I let out a breath that sets free something painful from my chest. For the first time since Jason passed or perhaps even longer than that, it feels like everything is going to be alright. And it feels like it's because of the man I'm clutching in my arms.

When his arms loosen, I have the gumption to do the same. Drawing my face out of the crook of his warm neck, I find a strange look on his face. It's not the guarded mask of humor. It's something closer to awestruck.

"Goodnight," he rasps. Nodding toward the TV, he adds, "Don't order any porn."

I bark out a laugh through the congestion building in my sinuses. "Not a problem."

The words hit his back, though. Seeing his hand on my doorknob has my chest going tight. The fairy godmother only visited Cinderella once. I'm well past that many visits from the enigmatic man about to walk out my door.

"Will I see you again?"

I cringe at the foolish question, feeling his car keys in my hand. Of course, I'll see him again. I'll have to return his car to him, but that's not what I meant.

Freezing, his hand stills. It's probably only seconds, but seems much longer as I wait for a reply. He cants his head to the side without looking back.

"Do you want to see me again?"

"Yes," I answer without missing a beat. "Yeah…I'd like that."

Swallowing, he nods before pushing through the door. "Then you will."

I don't move as the rumble of his bike fires up. I don't move when his headlight flashes across the front room window, nor do I, until the purr of his engine is out of earshot down the road. Turning around to the silence of the cottage, it no longer feels like a place to wait out a stay of execution. Lights blazing in every room, television broadcasting a hockey game, all the once-empty spaces now filled with things that make it look like a home—not a single memory of the miserable hours I've spent in here comes to mind. All I see is Easton. Easton hauling in a couch and a dresser. Easton setting a stack of pizza boxes down on the coffee table. Easton cursing at the remote to get the cable set up. Easton screwing the legs into the sockets of the table, now sitting in my kitchen. He gave me more than things. I think he just gave me a clean slate.

I remember when I first met him, how disgruntled and bitter he seemed. And yet, I could tell there was genuine kindness and optimism about him, hiding inside that scared kid who'd been through hell.

It no longer seems cold in here, but I haven't touched the thermostat. The most unlikely man just filled my house with warmth. All those good qualities I saw are still in there, no matter what the years have done to either of us.

I make a vow that this is the last time I'll cry. For this month, at least.

"Thank you," I whisper, choking on the overpowering sensation of being so undeserving.

I'm not thanking him, though. I know he wouldn't want it. My decree is addressed to life for bringing us together.

"Thank you."

CHAPTER 19
Easton

If I hurry, I can make it across town before he gets home. Ripping my nitrile gloves from my last job off as I head into the office, I ignore how much that sounds like planning. I'm spontaneous. Always have been. Even spontaneous people do a little planning.

Tossing my gloves in the trash can, I call out to Wolf, where he's updating our website on his computer.

"I'm going to head out for dinner. I'll be back by seven."

"*Seven?* That's a long dinner."

Snorting, I ignore him and check my hair in the mirror on the wall. It's starting to curl again the way it does after my hair gel has worn off for the day. I'm not running upstairs for more. Rinsing my hands in the sink in our private half-bath, I wipe them over my head to tame down my flyaways. There. Good enough.

Walking back into the office, I head to my desk and open my top drawer to find my breath spray. I give my tongue a spritz and then grab my can of deodorant, misting the underside of my arms underneath my shirt, trying to remember if I forgot anything.

I sense a presence in front of me and look up to find Wolf. His face looks like it does each time one of those commercials for women's underwear pads plays on TV.

"Where are you going?"

"Dinner," I say louder. Did he not hear me?

"For three hours? It's not even four o'clock yet."

Scoffing, I level him with a look. "It's a Melissa-length dinner. You know, the kind you like to take *every fucking day.*"

Huffing, his face goes red. "I do not."

Delusional. So delusional.

Snatching up the shopping bag on my desk, I head to the door, but something holds me up. *Hey, watch it,* I sign in his line of vision when I find him gripping the bag, prying it open to look inside.

"What the fuck is this?" he asks, pulling one of the puzzle boxes out of the bag.

"A chemistry set, clearly."

Taking it from him, I stuff it back into the sack. Since when he did get all handsy?

"Are you going back to Aaron's?"

"No, I joined a puzzle club. We're ranked top in the state. I'll give a shoutout to S&H when we win the televised championship."

I'm nearly free, one foot out the door when his urgent call hits my back. "Easton!"

Ugh. If he starts asking me about web banners and ad spaces again, I'm going to spike his root beer. I handle the books. He handles the marketing. That was the deal when we opened the place, but he's always trying to pick my brain about his side of the business. So freaking needy.

What? I sign impatiently.

"I thought you hated the guy? First the furniture, and I didn't say a word, now puzzles and dinner? Dude, what's the deal?"

Laughing, I don't understand his motherly concerns. "I don't hate him."

Fuming, he glances behind me like he's checking to see if anyone in the studio can hear us. It must be something sensitive if he's bringing his hands up to sign. *You freaking kissed me just to get him out of your hair. Not fucking cool, by the way!*

I wondered if he was ever going to bring that up. I thought maybe it was so uncomfortable for him that he would never mention it, and I'd be off the hook. Frowning, I go for full sympathy, setting my bag down and walking over to him slowly. Capturing his hand in mine, the look on his face is priceless.

"I'm sorry I've neglected you." Flipping a lock of his long black hair away from his face, I hold back a laugh when he recoils. "Did you want me to take *you* to dinner?"

Hands hit my chest hard, shoving me back. "Fuck off. You're such a jackass. You know that?"

Snickering, I grab my bag and head for the door again. He's so easy. Why does he even try to mess with me? I thought we established years ago that I always win.

"I just don't want to see you get all fucked up again the way you were when you got out of that place."

That stops my feet like a car boot got strapped to them. Did he really need to go there? What the fuck? It's just dinner and a puzzle for a guy who's down on his luck.

Turning back, I refuse to look at him and his stupid bleeding-heart face. He always has my best interests at heart, even when I don't want him to. Maybe it's also just too uncomfortable to say the words out loud after all the fuss I made.

I won't. I don't hate him. I never did.

"You could have fooled me."

Craning my head back, I sigh at the ceiling. From the looks of it, his mom left him for good the last time, then Jasper. Who's had to bear the brunt of his emotional side since then? Thank you very much, you bitches.

"Do you want me to say it?" I mumble, but facing him so he can read my lips. "Cause you're only going to hear it once."

"What?" he asks, the epitome of confusion.

Oh, sweet Wolf. This is what he gets for trying to have a heart-to-heart with me.

"He's not a dick. I was wrong. Okay?"

Is he… having a stroke?

Shit. I just killed my best friend.

His body flinches on a puff of air, though. Good. He's still breathing. And *now* he's fucking smiling like the damn *Cheshire Cat.*

Messing with his hearing aid, he waggles his fingers at me. "Wait. Tell me that again."

I give him a wave with my middle finger. "Bye, *Wolfiekins.* Have a good night."

"Hey!" Aaron's face lights up as he gets out of my Suburban. I was starting to wonder if my ass was going to fall asleep sitting on this cold ass porch of his. "This is a nice surprise. At least…I hope it is," he hesitates, walking up the steps. "Is everything all right?"

Car drive okay for you?

Frowning, he watches my hands even after I lower them. Why is it so important to hear my voice? I thought we were over that. I let out enough word vomit with Wolf a little while ago. Sometimes a guy just doesn't feel like talking.

"Yeah. Yeah, it's great. I made sure to go under the speed limit."

Of course he did. Man, this guy cracks me up.

"Don't you need it, though?" he asks. "It'll be getting really cold soon. You probably don't want to be on your bike this late in the year."

Rising, I ignore the ache in my leg from the chill and lift my bags up with me. "Hungry?"

There. Words. That should make him happy enough to forget about my stupid car.

Laughing like he knows I'm avoiding the topic of my car, he nods. "Yeah, actually."

Does he know his voice sounds like sex when it comes out all soft and sweet like that? I never freaking stood a chance as a hormonal teen. He should have been barred from seeing patients between the ages of puberty and retirement.

Fuck. Focus, Easton.

Inside, I'm glad to see that none of my offerings have been removed or neglected. There's an ass indent on one of the couch cushions, so I hope it means he sat on it.

Following him to the kitchen, my mind goes to a strange place, wondering what his house with Reider looked like. Did Reider ever buy him gifts, and if so, what kind?

Aaron chatters about how sweet and wonderful my staff and Wolf were as he gets glasses out of a cabinet. I pull the food out of the carry-out bag and take plates from him when he hands them to me. It's oddly domestic and quite surreal to be in a living space with him even though I was here once before. It's just the two of us now, however, and I can't hide behind text messages like I did all week again.

"Do you have any clients tonight or are you off today?" he asks, taking the seat next to me rather than the one on the opposite side of the table.

"Later," I mumble just before stuffing my mouth full with a bite of a taco.

Our exchanges this week ranged from food to veritable nothings. He complained about an orderly who's a close talker and has bad breath, whom I dubbed Mr. Itosis, first name Hal. Each time I got a laughing emoji from him felt like a prize until my old doubts crept in, and I'd force myself to sign off for the night. I'm not seeking approval. I know I'm not. It felt natural, is all. Maybe that just makes me a bit of a dork like him, too.

It even felt natural to pop by for dinner when I realized it was Friday night and he wouldn't have to work tomorrow. It was a safe bet he wouldn't have any plans, and he *did* ask to see me again, after all.

"Oh my God, this is amazing," he exclaims, eyes slipping shut while he chews his food.

"You look like you need it." It's true. His college boy baby fat is gone. I can see it in his face.

"Thanks," he scoffs. "I won't read into what I know that means. I just haven't had much of an appetite."

"I'll fatten you up." Shoving the container of tortilla chips that came with our meals closer to him, I jest, "Quit whining and eat."

Snickering, he grabs one and shakes his head. "Were you always this charming?"

It's now that I realize what I liked about him so much. As calm and kind as he is, he was never afraid to rib me back, even if it was passively. People act like they're wary of me, even Wolf sometimes. Aaron only acted like he was wary that he'd hurt me. Grinning, I nod around a bite. "Yeah, but I've had a little more practice."

"Thanks for the warning."

I doubt he meant that to sound flirtatious. I don't think Aaron even knows how to flirt. He already seems to have written off our kiss at Pulse as a lack of judgment on his part, not giving any indication of what he thought my intentions were. I'm grateful for it. I'm not here to flirt. Fuck if I know how to make a new friend, but it's not gotten too awkward yet, so I rifle into the shopping bag as a segue.

Pulling out the puzzle box, I set it so it's standing on its side on the table. His jaw pauses mid-chew, forehead crinkling. I present my hand in front of the ridiculous image of a collage made up entirely of rubber chickens, soaking in his bafflement.

"That's…quite the puzzle."

"I got another one more to our taste." Pulling the other box out, I waggle my brows, getting a laugh out of him when he takes in the giant dick mosaic. The way his ears turn red, I'll take that as a no. I slice the chicken puzzle box open and dump the contents on the table in front of us.

"You remembered," he murmurs, making my hand freeze.

I *remember* now that he didn't mention anything about his love of puzzles in any of our texts this week. Shit. There are drawbacks to having a steel trap memory.

"Not your thing anymore?" I mumble, casually reaching for my soft drink cup.

"No. I still love them."

Smiling, he starts flipping over the pieces so the image sides are face up. Part of me wants to run out the door for being so corny, but as the seconds tick by and I catch the serene look of his profile, the urge to stay wins.

Friends. This is what friends do. Dorky friends.

So, for the next two and a half hours, I dork out with Aaron Manicki over a rubber chicken puzzle.

I get up to use the restroom at one point and return to find him washing our plates. I guess he was just humoring me about still liking puzzles.

"Did you quit on me?"

"No. I was waiting for you."

That's… sweet. Reclaiming my seat, I study the scattered pieces that remain. I'm not waiting for him in return; I'm hunting for new matches.

The water from the faucet sluices over his fingers as he scrubs a glass hurriedly. It's like he wants to get back to this ridiculous distraction

I brought. He's wearing jeans today, with a dress shirt tucked snugly into the waist underneath his black belt. An errant memory reminds me that the staff at Hampton used to have casual Fridays, so I'm guessing this was Aaron's attempt at conforming to that ritual. Although I wouldn't call a dress shirt casual, it's typical Aaron. I don't think the guy could look shabby if he tried, even if his dress shoes do look a bit worn. With his sleeves rolled up, I find myself studying the thin layer of hair on his forearms and the faint cords in his arms. Grabbing a dish towel, he dries the glass carefully. Gently. It's strange how much enjoyment it brings me, watching the most mundane tasks and movements, watching *him*.

I'm so lost that he catches my gaze when he turns around. Glancing at my watch to not appear so obvious, I see that it's six-thirty. My next appointment isn't for another hour, but there's no need to give Wolf any more reasons to gloat about me being gone so long or wear out my welcome here.

"I should get going. I have an appointment."

"Oh."

A giddy rush flutters through me at the sound of his disappointment. It was tacos and a puzzle, Aaron, not a *Porsche*.

"Well, thanks for all of this." He smiles. "This was…nice."

More flutters. It was tacos and a puzzle, Easton, not a date. Jesus, I need to leave.

Getting up, I start for the kitchen doorway but pause as Aaron cuts me off, moving past me. He walks me to his front door just like he did last time, all gentlemanly and shit. I don't think I've ever been walked to the door unless it was to tell me to get the fuck out after I turned down a sleepover from a one-night stand.

"I'll let you know if there's a missing piece at the end," he teases.

Shit. Why didn't I think of that? I should have pocketed one just to fuck with him. Then I could have texted that I was holding it for ransom.

Oh my God. Go!

"Don't start the dick without me," I warn, because I have officially been infected by his dorkiness.

"Deal," he laughs, opening the inside door.

And then… I just stand there for no goddamn reason like I don't know what to do with myself because I can't look away from him looking at me. I should grab the screen door handle and step outside, but I blame his face. It always looks like there's something paramount on his lips that I need to stick around to hear.

I'm not the only one feeling the awkwardness. I can tell by the way his lips are parted. The next thing I know, he's moving toward me. When his arms wrap around me in an innocent hug, I realize I'd been holding my breath like it was for something more. What the hell—did I actually want him to kiss me?

I'm hot-blooded. He's a guy. Of course, I wouldn't have been bent out of shape over it.

Except, this hug, just like the last one he gave me, makes me helpless in a way that doesn't make me miserable. Is there such a thing as a comforting kind of helplessness?

Awkwardly, I give him a little squeeze so I don't look like a mannequin. That soft chestnut hair of his is like feathers against my cheek. Everything about the unexpected embrace fits. I didn't know that people could fit together like this without sex involved. It's an oddly deeper connection than when I've had my dick deep inside someone. It has my entire body feeling heavy and sedated. Why do I have the urge to thank him?

Pulling back, he drops his arms, looking so content and it's got me contemplating if we just created magic. A strange little laugh bubbles past my lips before I get my shit together and nod, booking it out the door.

Maybe Wolf was right—I do feel fucked up again, but not the way I was when I left Hampton Hills. This is more like *ten shots on my birthday when I feel like the king of the world* kind of fucked up. There must have been something in those tacos.

CHAPTER 20
Easton

"Oh, my gosh. You don't want to do that. I'm sweating so much it's gross," Aaron shouts over the music when I grip the back of his neck to give him a playful shake after his return from the dancefloor with Shannon.

"Woo! Your man can move!" Shannon shouts, stopping at the table's edge to take a drink from her highball.

"Too bad moving isn't dancing," Aaron replies with a laugh, wiping his brow.

It's a nice recovery from her innocent accusation, but I still want to crawl under the table. *My man?* Is that what everyone thinks, or has Wolf been talking shit behind my back? That's not like him, but I glance over at him just to be sure. He and Melissa appear to be in one of their regular disagreements, judging by their body language, so he's currently dead to me on the intel front. They'd better not flake out. He told me he'd be the DD tonight. I'm not getting in some nasty ass cab because of boo drama.

The waitress brings another tray of shots that I have no clue who ordered. Me? Who's to say at this point?

Aaron drops his head and groans into his arms. So, I do the natural thing and nudge his elbow with a shot in my hand just to see his reaction. Rising, he shakes his head.

"No. I can't. Everything's starting to feel like it's in slow motion. I'll start talking nonsense if I have any more."

"You talk nonsense all the time already. How will that be any different?"

Elbowing me, he snickers. "I do not!"

The strand of hair hanging down on his forehead gives him an adorably disheveled appearance. I want to both ruffle it up to see what he'd look like getting out of bed and put it back into place since I know that's what he'd do if he could see himself right now. Reaching out, my hand opts for stroking it back into place.

"Am I a mess?" he asks, running a hand over his head, his eyes slow to blink.

He's perfect. So damn perfect my heart feels like it's swelling in my chest. Raking my fingers through his thick hair, I fuck it up good.

"Yeah. You're a mess."

Gasping, he gapes at me, strands sticking up all over the place. "You did not just do that!"

Reaching over, his hands grip either side of my ribcage as he cracks up, and… is he fucking trying to tickle me?

"You're not ticklish? How can anyone not be ticklish?" he slurs.

Groaning, his hands still and he drops his face into the crook of my neck, letting his weight lean into me. He lets out a sigh, and I can feel his lips move against my jugular.

"No more shots, please."

Wow. Aaron: down for the count.

Cupping the back of his head, I lean in close to his ear so he can hear me. "Yup. A total mess."

His skin has a hint of saltiness to it when my lips leave the spot where I pressed them against his cheek. He needs to be freaking tucked in, is what he needs. Was I ever this sloppy?

Reaching for my beer, I find a pair of eyes on me from across the table. Wolf's brows hike, humor playing on his lips. I want to give his shin a kick, but that'd make him think he's right.

Is he? I probably look like I'm cuddling with Aaron and just gave his cheek a peck.

I can see how that must look off to Wolf. I don't invite guys back to our booth. *Ever.* I don't wrap my arms around them and ruffle their hair. I don't give them kisses on the cheek like teens going steady. I make them earn it and wait till we get out the door.

Fuck.

This is different, though. It's Aaron. He's… We're…

Ah, double fuck.

Okay, maybe things are getting a little out of hand. It's been a month of puzzles and dinners. I keep showing up like a lost puppy and he keeps eagerly letting me in like another lost puppy who's looking for a pack.

Now we're at Pulse after I gave him this whole optimistic speech about how he should get out of the house more and enjoy life. The guy never goes anywhere, but why did I say that? I was perfectly fine hanging out in his little cottage.

I cannot believe I brought him here… *again*. On top of Shannon's verbal diarrhea and Wolf's smug-ass expression, there are at least three people here that I've fucked, which should not matter in the slightest. However, the fact it bothers me is *bothering me.*

When I was seventeen, I had an excuse for acting this idiotic. I was a kid with a crush. What do you call it when you're twenty-five and want to spend every free second with the dorkiest man you've ever met because just being in the same room makes you feel like you're walking on air? Because... I *like* how dorky he is. I fucking dig it way too much.

I've never had so much fun putting puzzles together. I don't think I ever put a puzzle together before, to be honest. Now, though, I've become a damn puzzle connoisseur. I've found myself looking for ones with more than a thousand pieces so I can prolong our time together. Seriously, I cockblocked an old lady at the store last week who was reaching for the last two-thousand-piece puzzle on the shelf at the department store. The picture was of a sewing room. She looked at me like I had a dick growing out of my forehead as I scrambled past her with my find like I'd be willing to run over a family of four on Black Friday.

Aaron's grip on my right side loosens, sliding farther around me, turning into half a hug. He groans into my neck, a sleepy sound that makes me want to take him home and curl up on his couch with him just so I can watch him sleep on me.

I know it's not my norm. It's so much farther than my norm—it's new territory, but I've been having a lot of thoughts like that lately. They're getting worse.

What happens, though, when Aaron doesn't need a shoulder to lean on anymore? What happens when he gets sick of puzzles? What happens if he decides to transfer, and up and leave to some other state again? What if I'm the only one who fell down the stupid tree and hit all the branches, and he just thinks of me as his buddy or a dead husband rebound?

Shit. No wonder Wolf is looking at me like I'm pathetic. I'm turning into him.

CHAPTER 21

Aaron

"No! Don't do it!" I cringe watching the actor on the horror flick that Easton chose make terrible life choices. "Oh, God…he did it. He opened the damn door. You're dead! You know that, right? Ugh."

Groaning, I pinch my eyes closed and shake my head, unable to watch the predictability that I know is coming, but a noise next to me draws me from my revulsion of poor cinema.

Easton. *Belly* laughing.

Is there a better sound in existence? I don't even care that it's at my expense.

Jason always looked mildly annoyed watching movies like this with me. He'd change the channel, thinking it would solve my crisis, when really being vexed by the film was more preferable than not discovering if my predictions would be proven right.

Watching Easton's body shake as he tries to contain his laughter where we're lounging on my couch like pod people, I want to hug him for the simple act of not changing the channel. I want to thank him for enjoying one more of my idiosyncrasies. And I kind of want to kiss him for a million other little reasons that have happened over the last two months since he showed up on my doorstep with tacos and a rubber chicken puzzle.

Last weekend, he took me to his secret swimming spot on the opposite side of the lake near an abandoned water pump shed. I'm only guessing it's a secret because he coyly said, *'If no one knows where to find me, I'm probably here, so don't tell anybody.'*

The water was so cold, I don't know how we didn't get hypothermia, but I'd do it again in a heartbeat to relive one particular moment.

I slipped on a rock under the surface and nearly submerged until he caught me, or so I thought. As soon as he helped me get my footing, the sneak dunked me. I came up sputtering, shoving him for payback, but it ended with us in each other's arms. The frigidness of the water died away and there was this pull between us making me warm all over. I wish I could play the memory back from the outside looking in so I could see if I moved in closer, he did, or both of us. Whatever happened, he turned abruptly and swam away like it was forgotten, nothing.

He had said he comes there to think. Did I ruin that sacred place for him by reading the moment wrong? Regardless, there are other moments I don't think I've read wrong.

It feels like something is happening between us. When he took me to Pulse two weeks ago, I thought maybe it would be a replay of the first time I was there—minus me running out into the alley in tears. This time, I was prepared. Excited even. He was sweet, and playful, and open, but then…nothing. He helped me to the door when Wolf dropped me off, but unlike at the club, there wasn't a kiss goodnight on the cheek. Was I foolish to hope for one?

It wasn't the first time he's done something like that. More and more, there are little touches. Grazes of his hand. Sweet pecks on my head when he walks by like he's sneaking them in while he's on the move. He never pauses long enough for something more.

The thing is, though…I want more. I've decided I want his mouth on mine again with no regrets or doubts this time. No guilt. I'm sure of it.

Laughter tamped down to a snicker now, he reaches into the popcorn bowl on his lap. Does he know how many times I've snuck peeks at the way his long legs are stretched out, stocking clad feet resting on the coffee table? I like how comfortable he looks sitting on this couch next to me. I like the idea of it becoming permanent.

The skin at the base of my neck tingles, and I have to steady my breathing when I realize why. It's his fingertips, tracing little circles over my Tshirt at the base of my neck.

Sometimes the way we joke around makes me forget that I'm the older man. Maybe Easton's waiting for me to give him a few more green lights, just…not in his secret thinking place. Jason was seven years older than me, and he's the one who made all the first moves. I'm so hapless that I'd have had no clue what to have said to him and probably wouldn't have ended up married if he hadn't initiated.

I've never had a friend who's drawn imaginary circles on my body like this. The way he kissed me at Pulse that first night—there was so much passion there. Granted, it kind of felt like I was being devoured, and I don't exactly remember all of it since I was so out of my damn mind, but I kept telling myself he only did it thinking I'd be a fling.

A guy who shows up regularly for movies, stay-at-home dinners, and puzzle nights isn't just looking for a fling, though. No. Something has definitely changed between us, and I know I'm not the only one feeling it.

Slowly, I ease further down into the cushions, slumping into him as I go so my head is practically resting on his shoulder. "I'm glad my cinema hostility amuses you."

Snorting, he gives my hair a playful tug. "I had no idea you had it in you to be so aggressive."

"*Aggressive?* I'm just stating the obvious. It's frustrating that every horror movie ever made has the same red flags." The killer pops out of the bushes at that exact moment, and it's all downhill for the supporting actor. "Do you see?" I shout, pointing at the television. "He's dead! *Why?* Because he went *outside. Alone!* I fucking called it. *How?* Because they're all the damn same. Ugh. What a dumbass."

His body jostles mine on another round of belly laughter. "Oh, my gosh. *You* are out of control. Excuse me! Now here this! Aaron Manicki just used swear words!" he exclaims holding his hands outward like he's making an announcement.

"You swear all the time!"

"*I do.*" He nods, his tone sage as he bops me on the nose, "*not* Aaron Manicki. If you start throwing popcorn, we're signing you up for anger management."

"Oh, brother," I sputter, swatting his hand away. "You make it sound like I have a problem. I cannot be the only person who gets aggravated by ridiculous plots."

Squeezing my shoulder, he leans closer and whispers, "I know this will be difficult for you, but if you can make something nice come out of your mouth for the next five minutes, I might believe you."

Watching his lips move, I picture something so nice it steals my breath. I'm ready. I know I am. I'm sure there are parts of me that aren't fully healed from losing Jason and from the mystery of his spending habits that I've discovered since his death, but maybe we're not meant to fully heal. Maybe scars form and we grow from them.

Closing the distance, I go for it. His soft peach fuzz tickles my upper lip. His lips are soft and still. It's a chaste thing, so different from our first. It's the way a first kiss should be—a moment so wonderful it's frozen in time. Little tingles of electricity ping through my entire body. When I pull back, his stunned face looks back at me. He…seems almost conflicted. The amused sound he makes next has me even more baffled, especially when he gets up from the couch and heads to the kitchen.

"You need another drink?" he calls.

"N-no. I'm good."

What the heck was that? Shit. Am I that bad of a kisser?

Returning with a bottle of water, he drops back down into his same spot as before, but sitting upright. Resting his elbows on his knees, he hunkers over his popcorn bowl, gaze fixed on the movie. And now…he's eating popcorn.

Did I just commit an error of epic proportions? He was caressing the back of my neck and bopping me on the nose a moment ago. Now, it's like I'm not even in the room.

I don't understand. The way he looks at me sometimes—it makes me think he's fallen as deep into this thing that's built between us as I have.

"I…hope that was okay. I guess I should have asked first," I hedge.

Turning his head for a second without looking at me, he smirks. *I am officially violated. Shame on you,* he signs teasingly before reaching for more popcorn.

Signing. Sarcasm. They're Easton Bennick defense mechanisms. I've always respected his invisible walls, but right now they feel like weapons drawn unnecessarily. Does he have nothing else to say? What is so wrong about a little honest communication?

Glancing around my cottage in a daze, I don't think his avoidance of the subject is a question of sparing my feelings. The furniture and use of his car are one thing. I get it. Some people are givers when others are down on their luck, but two months of hanging out at least four nights a week is well beyond a giving kink.

The last two weeks, I've seen him every single night and spent most of the day with him each weekend, even being invited to watch him work. He acts more domestic than Jason ever did, easily moving in tandem with me when we cook dinner in my kitchen together.

The other night, he dragged my feet into his lap and *rubbed* them. Those are things that couples do. He's quickly become my world, and I don't see how I haven't become his.

Inhaling, he arches back, stretching and checking the time of his phone. *I should get going.*

With that, he gives me a brotherly squeeze on the knee and gets up.

Wow. He's actually walking to the door to put his boots on. Unbelievable. I know I'm terrible at this sort of thing, but…that's it? How can he not have some kind of reaction?

Defense mechanisms or not, I'm suddenly salty. There's no other way to explain it–I'm being ignored. Jason did that to me all the time whenever I voiced protests about not wanting to go out to another dinner to schmooze with people. When I'd suggest going away to camp or drive down the coast for the weekend, he'd laugh like it was a silly idea and not take me seriously. I can handle not clicking with someone—I learned plenty about that—but being ignored is like being invisible. I don't want to be invisible ever again.

Getting up, I inch my way over, watching him finish the laces on his boots. Straightening up, he flashes me a polite smile. I officially hate that kind of smile on him.

When he heads toward the credenza by an old mirror that George had in the place when I moved in, I realize he's going to fetch his keys. He really was planning to leave without a word.

"What is your deal? I don't understand you sometimes," I mumble glumly, my thoughts airing themselves like dirty laundry.

When he replies by pantomiming me with an amused quirk of his brow, frustration wins over my sheepishness. Shaking my head, I throw my hands up.

"You kissed me at Pulse," I explain, but since we've never mentioned it, it feels like I need more evidence. "You're always kissing me some way. You touch me. You look at me like…"

Kicking one leg out as though it's taking patience to endure my inquisition, he hooks a thumb in the pocket of his jeans and signs with his other hand, *Like what?*

"Like…maybe you're feeling something."

Snickering, he shakes his head. *Don't get sentimental on me. I'm not the marrying type.*

And then he heads toward the kitchen where his black leather jacket is slung over one of the chairs. My heart probably has no business breaking into a million pieces. Mostly it's for him, though, not me. It feels traitorous to realize things about him now based on memories from years ago, but I'm grateful for it.

He's a runner.

If his leg hadn't been in traction when he was at Hampton Hills, he'd have no doubt been gone like the wind. It explains why he was so hostile toward me when I first contacted him. Some people shut down when they're uncomfortable. Easton shuts down by fleeing the scene. Fleeing on foot, or motorcycle, or by stealing away the sound of his voice.

"Damn it, Easton, don't do that."

Coat in hand, he turns around with a stony expression. *Do what?*

"Close up."

Scoffing, he shrugs into his coat, forcing him to finally use his words. "Are you fucking shrinking me because I turned you down? Get over yourself."

The fact that they're ugly words makes me sad for him. I don't deserve them, and I know he doesn't mean them. How many times has he isolated himself in his life to avoid facing things that are difficult for him? You can't live in a bathtub, proverbial or real.

When he waltzes toward me like he's intent on heading out the door, I see a window closing. Jumping forward, I grab ahold of his arm to stop him, but he whirls back around.

"What the fuck?" he laughs a bitter sound.

"Stop it," I demand, even though it comes out shaky over my bold move. "I *know* I'm not wrong. You want me just as much as I want you."

"What?" he laughs breathlessly, shirking my hand off. "Get the fuck off me. You're delusional."

"I'm not," I soothe, placing my palms on his shoulders as gently as I can. "Talk to me. What's the problem?"

"There's no *problem*. You want to play rough? I can play rougher than you," he says testily, swatting my hands away. "Don't test me."

My arms fall easily showing just how *not* rough I was playing. The glower on his face is all posturing, but apparently I'm the only one in the room who knows it.

I'm ashamed to admit it, but I forgot him once. I won't forget him again and that includes ignoring whatever he's running from. When he spins on his heel like he's going to storm out, I panic.

You're not supposed to keep people who want to leave from leaving, but Easton walking out that door is more than just someone fleeing an argument. It's a sentence, a nail in a coffin that tells me I'll never see him again. It's a ticker tape repeating that he'll continue to run for the rest of his life whenever someone scratches whatever old wound I just did.

Throwing my arms around him from behind, I steer him away from that opening that'll take him away from me. "Bullshit!" I scold, holding him against the credenza. "You blow hot and cold, and then tell me *I'm* delusional? I'm not buying your tough guy act anymore. I lived with lies for years, Easton. I'm not doing it anymore. I need the truth."

"What truth is that?" he scoffs, his fingers pulling at my wrist like he's trying to worm free of my grip.

He could if he wanted to. We're the same height and although I'm a little thicker, his muscles get more active use than mine ever do. His feeble attempt tells me he doesn't want to hurt me, and *that*…is all I need to know.

"You're scared," I whisper aloud, the realization softening every fiber in my body. "Just admit it."

The hardness in him evaporates like he transformed from a solid to a liquid, and he goes completely still against me. Gaze fixed on the surface of the credenza, he lets out an unconvincing laugh. "What the fuck would I be scared of?"

His heartbeat is pounding under my palm. He might as well have been a child uttering that he isn't afraid of monsters while cowering underneath a blanket with a flashlight for all the weight that held. Peering over his shoulder, I watch the rise and fall of his chest in the mirror. As self-conscious as I was a moment ago about latching onto him, now I never want to let him go.

"*Us*," I tell him softly. "*This. Me… yourself.*"

For a second, I stop breathing right along with him. It's like watching dominoes tumble, staring at the reflection of his lost gaze. I want to comfort him so badly, want to reward him for this quiet moment of facing his truth, a truth that I'm humbled to be a part of.

Bringing my mouth to his neck cautiously, I press a delicate kiss there. He trembles at the touch of my lips. His gaze flicks to mine in the mirror. There's a new kind of terror in his eyes, that of a thief who's just been caught red handed. Cheeks tinted pink, his heart still hammering under my touch, I watch him swallow, staring back at me with a look I haven't seen in eight years. Except, it registers so much differently this time.

My God...

"*This* is what you wanted, isn't it?" The disbelieving words tumble from my lips. "All those years ago?"

His face blooms, and he looks away. I can feel him stiffen in my arms again.

Shit. No. I can't let him go like this.

"Don't," I caution, reaching up to his jaw, urging him to look back at the mirror so he can see me. The shame on his beautiful face chokes me up. It's such a compliment and yet so painful to witness. I had no idea. I know there's no way it would have been possible back then to reciprocate what I'm seeing in his eyes as he lowers them again, but my heart shatters for leaving him the way I did now that I know.

"Let me see," I plead. "Please?"

His feet shift like an anxious rodeo bull in a cage. With a labored breath, he looks slowly back up. It's proud, and stubborn, and gorgeous, as if he's confessing to a crime. I've never been more honored in my life by a single look.

"I...didn't know. I'm sorry."

It's barely a whisper. "Well...now you know."

He looks like I just lanced him. How do I tell him that he doesn't have a damn thing to be embarrassed over?

I remember that day I came to his apartment above the shop. Regarding his voice, he said, '*I use it when I have to and give it a rest when I need to.*' It's sound advice. I struggled to figure out what I could do to make up for leaving without a goodbye and then dropping back into his life uninvited. Now that I know *I'm* what I could have given him to ease his pain, I welcome the end of the struggle with open arms. I don't need words to show him he can have what he wants.

Sighing, I lean my head against the back of his and take in a hit of his familiar scent. I give his waist a squeeze, hoping he receives it as an extension of what now feels like an embrace rather than a stockade to keep him from leaving. The wavy curls of the ends of his hair tickle my nose as I trail my mouth lower to reunite with his skin, pressing a kiss to the nape of his neck.

All the while, he trembles in my arms.

Don't be afraid, I want to tell him. *Don't be ashamed.*

Trailing my hand slowly down his chest, I move my lips to his ear. I'm shivering with nerves myself. He has to feel it. He's not alone in this.

"Let me give it to you," I whisper, watching his throat undulate when I place a kiss there.

His stomach flexes under my touch, and he finally looks back at me. The transformation is astounding—completely open and vulnerable.

I'm not practiced at taking charge. I was under the mistaken impression that Easton grabs what he wants from life by the horns, but I can see that's not the case where little old awkward me is concerned. Maybe for a moment that night at Pulse he did, yet I realize now that was him trying to teach me a lesson, but it wasn't the real Easton. Not the one laid bare before me.

Stepping back, I slide his jacket off and toss it to the floor. Gripping the hem of his shirt, I draw it carefully upward, thanking the stars when he raises his arms. He's still with me.

A scene of colorful designs from his neck to his navel reveals itself–a serpentine dragon threaded all across his upper body, at war with a demon of the sea that refuses to be drowned. I want to tell him he'll never drown, not with me.

I tug my own shirt over my head and let it fall, baring myself in equal measure. I stand still, letting him take a look, feeling giddy at the way his eyes travel curiously over my flesh. He turns, still gaping like I'm made of something more fascinating than other human beings.

When he catches me watching him watch me, he makes a nervous sound. Be bold, I tell myself, stepping forward and cupping his face. It's no longer difficult to manage when my lips meet his again.

One brush of our mouths isn't enough. It opens a floodgate of need. His lips part for the tip of my tongue and I taste. Gripping my arms, he moans, meeting my enthusiasm, and then I'm lost. He kisses like he's been studying a map of my mouth his entire life. How have I kept my hands off him for two months?

We take a step forward, a step back. We're two starving people who've been denied the thing they want the most. When he palms my back and his hand slides to the base of my spine, pulling me closer, my head goes light.

Coming up for air, I have to force myself to move away. Before that confused look of his can take over the rest of his face, I grab his hand and tug.

"Come to my room?" I venture not caring how out of breath I sound. "I'd like to see what you look like in that bed you bought me."

Smirking, he follows, sidling up behind me as we walk. Bumping pleasantly into me with each step with his hands on my waist, he peppers a few kisses across the back of my shoulders, letting me know exactly what I want to do next. I want to know every inch of Easton Bennick until he's imprinted on my soul.

CHAPTER 22
Easton

I'm at a loss as to what just happened. First, I was laughing at how ridiculous he was over that movie. Next, he was prying my soul from my body with that hurt look on his face. Of course, I feel something. I can't be around him and not feel or *not* be around him for that matter.

I can't believe he *knows*. Now that he figured out what a heartsick fool I was, I'm helpless to turn off whatever is showing in my eyes. It's a miracle he didn't realize it sooner, to be honest. I'd say it's mortifying, but the reward is far from anything to complain about. My knees are still shaking. He kisses like each touch of his lips mean something. Aaron Manicki knows a game I've never played, and it both excites and terrifies the hell out of me. I only know one game and kisses in the past have only meant I wanted to get off.

When he stops at the side of his bed and turns to me, I nearly swallow my own tongue. Now what?

I… I don't think I can fuck him. Is that what he wants?

God, I can't believe I just thought those words, but I mean, it's *Aaron*. It's dreamy smiling, puzzle-loving Aaron, not *I left town and now I'm back with an electrolarynx Aaron*. Things are…different. This would *mean* something. What happens when you fuck someone and it means something? I fantasized plenty about something meaningful with him, but fantasy is less discombobulating than reality.

When his palms glide down my stomach, I forget whatever the hell I was thinking. His warm breath hits my lips. There's nothing I can do to stop myself from tasting them again, so I don't even fight it. Each little puff of air of his I steal, each of mine that I hand over willingly to him, sinks me deeper into this blissful quicksand of the unknown.

His fingertips dip into the front of the waistband of my jeans, loosening my button. God, yes. I want them off even if just to feel all my skin against his. I'm glad he's not being reserved for once because I don't know what my problem is. It's like I'm afraid if I move too suddenly this will all end. I have no choice, though, when my jeans pool around my ankles.

Stepping out of them, I stare at his fingers working his sweats down over his hips. My heart wallops against my ribcage. He didn't just grab his sweats; he's taking his boxer briefs down with them.

I've seen so many dicks in my life, one more shouldn't be fascinating, but it's Aaron's. It's hard, adorned with a thatch of dark hair at the root, and bobs as it slips free of the fabric. He flashes me a self-conscious smile. Shit. I'm gawking.

Right. We're doing this.

I *want* to do this. Whatever the hell *this* is. I just... have to show him *my* hard-on now too. Why does that feel like more proof of my former infatuation? He clearly doesn't mind.

Stripping my underwear over my hips, I let them fall and kick them off like I'm ripping off a bandage. Nice finesse, Easton.

I feel like a piece of artwork up for criticism as he takes me in from head to toe. I don't even think I was this self-conscious as a virgin. If any of my former conquests were watching right now, they'd be struck speechless or laughing their asses off.

I watch the way his thigh muscles and stomach flex as he backs up onto the bed on his knees. My legs move dumbly and I join him, colliding with the force field of his body heat. His touch is so soft, guiding my elbow all courteously, but it might just be an excuse to touch me. I'm looking for my own excuses, still baffled that he's reciprocating. Gripping his sides, I give them a squeeze to show more participation. There's a thin layer of 'love' to them that I want to knead like clay. My cock brushes up against his and kicks because I haven't embarrassed myself enough tonight already.

"Well," he whispers, "what do you think?"

Think? I'm not capable of that right now.

Leaning down on his forearm by the pillow, he pats the top of his comforter. "Want to see if you got your money's worth?"

Oh... His comment earlier about the bed.

Right.

Settling down next to him, maybe someone else might feel some sort of benevolence over him since I did buy this stupid thing, but it's just the opposite for me as he leans over and starts kissing his way down my arm.

"It'll work," I croak, which sounds way too much like the slut that I usually am. "I'm not the one who has to sleep on it every night."

I'm about to reach up when he rises to his knees, but I'm at a loss when he bends further over me, placing kisses on my shoulder and back. I stay put in my awkward pose, half-leaning forward on my side. *Foreplay*—I should tell him he doesn't need to bother, but I'm so anxious that prolonging things for once doesn't sound like a bad idea.

Reaching out, I trace the side of his thigh, the soft hair there adding more realism to what's always just been a fantasy. Running my hand up his hip as his feathery kisses pepper their way down my spine, I gulp against a lump in my throat when my fingertips reach the curls of his groin. Gliding my palm down his cock, I revel at the resistance of it against my hand because of how hard he is.

I did that. That's for *me*. Un-fucking-believable.

The satisfied sound he lets out makes my blood burn hotter. I feel his hand go to my hip and nudge.

"Turn over?" he asks.

I have so many questions, but I comply, settling onto my stomach. His body heat covers me like a blanket. It's so strange, like being… found. When his lips brush against the back of my neck, I close my eyes at the shiver the chaste contact sends through me. How can so little evoke so many sensations?

Moving lower, he traces the lines of my back with his nose and lips, stopping occasionally to place more kisses. His palm runs down the outside of my hip, a slow, delicate caress that doesn't end when he reaches the middle of my thigh. He returns with a brief detour of his fingertips over the globes of my ass.

I'm fucking dead. Kill me now.

He wondered what I thought of his bed? Well, I want to tell him it's going to have a six-inch-deep puncture in it if he keeps this up.

"What are you doing?" I laugh.

His stomach settles onto my ass, his chest fitting against the small of my back. Trailing his open palm up my ribcage, he whispers, "Making up for lost time," and presses another kiss to the center of my spine.

Fuuuuck.

This is not going to end well… for *me*, but… I want it. It's normal to want something you've never had, right? Freaking extended foreplay. Who knew?

Biting my lip, I bury my face in his pillow. It reeks of Aaron's delicious scent and isn't helping matters, but I let my body go lax like dead weight. I couldn't move if I wanted to right now, save for the urge to rut into his mattress.

His fingertips dust the edge of my nipple as his tongue flicks the space between two of my ribs. I grunt against the urge to shudder.

I was wrong. He's not sweet. He's cruel as shit. How long do I have to lie here like this?

Those fingers move lower again, right to the hollow between my hip and thigh. He finds an opening and takes it. When his weight lifts an inch, I follow like a marionette. As soon as his hand wraps around my cock, he settles back onto me, effectively imprisoning my dick in his grip. My ass bucks backward into the hardness pressing against it. With nowhere for me to go, all that does is leave me gulping for even more air. God, it's like being owned. Owned by Aaron.

Wouldn't you love that? Some depraved, obsessed voice in my head whispers.

He gives me a stroke and I whine, fisting his pillow. Turning my head, I hope for a kiss. Something. Anything to put me out of this fast-building hysteria of arousal. His dick is like an afterthought to him though, leaking against the base of my ass, wasted. My ring flexes, begging, like it wants to grab him and pull him in.

I've messed around plenty of times with my ass. It's always a bit painful, but with enough enthusiasm, and if you get the angle right, you can rock your own world. I've never trusted nor given a damn enough about the guys I hook up with to want that from them. It's on the tip of my tongue, though, to beg Aaron for it right now, to discover what it would feel like to have him inside me. To be *full* of *him*.

He's a bottom, I can just tell, and I think I've made it obvious enough that I'm a top, so I doubt that's going to happen. I just need to try not to lose my mind for a few more minutes until he's ready for me to give it to him. I don't get many complaints, but if he's left disappointed, I'll never forgive myself.

"I was so afraid you'd leave," he mumbles against my cheek, swirling his thumb over my cockhead.

"No," I promise, but it comes out as a groan when his stomach undulates against my ass, forcing my dick through his grip.

Finally, he gives me his mouth. Our kisses are soft and sweet, hungry, and all-consuming. I need air desperately, but my lungs only want his. I can't stop. My toes go rigid and a wave of heat pummels through me, immersing my legs like I'm being dipped in a vat of hot water.

"Wait," I gasp, tearing my mouth away from his. "Stop, I—Shit!"

He stops, but it's too late. I can feel myself pouring over his hand between my stomach and the comforter. Body rigid, I try to think the pleasure overload away.

What a joke. Who can fucking turn off an orgasm like a faucet? It's futile when he gives me a few more languid strokes, making me convulse again.

Shit.

Fucking shit.

I can't believe I came already. That's *never* happened. Nothing like the guy you've been obsessed with for the better part of a decade finding out about it and then premature ejaculating on him the first time he touches your dick.

CHAPTER 23
Aaron

Could that have been any more beautiful? It's just a physiological response, I'm not going to flatter myself, but he did that for *me—because of me*.

Sinking my teeth into my lower lip, I try to get a hold of my breathing as he comes down. When his body finally goes slack, he sighs, burying his face in my pillow. Moving over, I settle down on the bed to free him from my weight. It's my first unfettered view of the back of him. I don't have to look away like that day in his apartment when he dropped his towel. I understand now why he did it, though. The tease.

Reaching out, I trail my fingers down the curve in the small of his back. It feels like such a gift to be touching him after weeks and weeks of becoming addicted to being near him. My entire life outlook just did a one-eighty because of the truth he shared with me. I feel… *good*, so damn good.

Rolling onto his back, his hand is cupped over the glistening spot on his stomach. "Sorry about that," he murmurs, glancing around.

I really don't want him out of this bed yet, so I climb over him and snatch my T-shirt up off the floor. "What's to be sorry about?"

"Thanks," he deflects, taking the shirt and cleaning himself off.

I refuse to give credence to the pink tint on his cheeks. I'm flying too high to let him be embarrassed. The second he looks around like he isn't sure where to put my shirt, I grab it from him and toss it. Leaning over him, I get back to where I left off, exploring new places to put my lips. Each press to his skin is a *thank you* for that astounding revelation that keeps repeating in my head: *Easton wants me.*

Easton. Wants. *Me*. Hoping for it and knowing it are two different things.

I'm practically covering him again now, unable to stay away from his mouth any longer, even though I silently vowed to kiss every inch of his body. With each sweet pass against his tongue, each stroke of his jaw, a delighted voice in my head resounds, *mine. He's mine. This is actually happening.*

His hands slide down my hips, giving me gooseflesh all over. Has it ever felt this good to just be pressed against another body? Those talented fingers of his reach between us, wrapping around me. While my body is fully onboard with the contact, I'm sorry for it at the same time. I could just kiss him for hours. I can't seem to stop myself.

His mouth breaks away from mine, coming up with a breathy chuckle. "Did you think I wasn't going to get you back?"

Grunting, I slide my hips lower; out of his grip. "No. It's not that..." Pinching my eyes closed to fight back the new pang of arousal, I try to get back to kissing, peppering his collarbone. "I could wait for that forever if I get to kiss you like this."

Making a map across his torso, I feel the slide of his fingers into my hair. There's a gentle touch to my arm and then he squeezes my shoulder. It's now that I notice the unsteady rise of his chest.

Glancing up, I'm met with an image a thousand miles deep. Lips parted. Eyes longing, and yet, maybe a little scared. It's the look of an unspoken question, leaving me staring, desperately trying to decipher his silence.

Swallowing, his weighted gaze doesn't stray. The silky skin of his inner thighs slides against my hips. I had hardly noticed my cock slipped down against his ass when I moved. As he raises his knees, however, it nestles me into the hot fold between the globes of his ass. Like a tiny bead of water working its way down a pane of glass, his fingers glide down my back until they come to rest on my hips. They stop, and then... they press more firmly against me.

Time has been suspended. We stare at each other as though he's sharing a secret code.

He doesn't have to say a word.

I've just been extended an invitation.

I'm speechless, so stunned I've forgotten all about mapping him with kisses. I know well enough that he doesn't ask for things. The vulnerable look on his face, however, tells me he doesn't ask for *this—ever*.

Bottoming is about trust. It's about giving yourself over to the sensation of being completely connected and almost at the mercy of another person. It's a unique kind of pleasure—one that requires satisfying emotional needs to get to the physical. You have to be in the right headspace to enjoy it to its fullest. The look on his face says he knows it, and *that...* is what has me humbled beyond words. I could have died happy just kissing him until our lips were both raw, but if Easton Bennick is silently begging me to fuck him, I'm going to do whatever he wants.

I nod, awash with new nerves. It's been years since I topped. I know it's like riding a bike, but not every bike is the same, and not every bike is a precious bicycle that I want to have the best cycling experience of its life.

Leaning in to kiss him, a thought occurs to me. "I don't have anything," I blurt in a panic. "I…haven't needed to have anything…in a while."

"I'm on PrEP," he replies softly, shrugging a shoulder with a little smile like he's back to trying to hide his nerves.

"Oh…good." I nod, but then a nervous laugh bubbles out of my lungs. "Um…we still need something, though. I meant I don't have *anything*. Not even lube."

He pats my arm for me to move and starts getting up. Great. I was just given the sweetest offer of a lifetime and I ruined it.

"I'll be right back."

Watching the shadowed dimples in his ass as he pads out of my room, I silently hold him to that promise. Closing my eyes, I give myself a stroke and blow out a breath. I was ready to go over the edge moments ago, but now anxiety is showing its effects. Remembering all the parts before his request, however, brings my body back online.

"So nice of you to wait."

My eyes flare open to find he's returned. Lying back down on the bed, he tosses a yellow can between us on the mattress. A yellow… *aerosol can* of olive oil.

"Is that…my cooking spray?"

His brows quirk. "You apparently don't know your way around a kitchen."

Oh. My. God.

The things you learn about someone. I wanted to know about what he's been up to since I moved away. This will teach me to be nosy.

Shaking my head, I grab the can, feeling a bit out of sorts, and settle in next to him. How do I even go about this? Picturing myself aiming for his entrance, I doubt that's what he has in mind. "I'm not trying to be a downer, but this doesn't exactly sound mood-inspiring."

"Sure it is. Once you hear this sound, you'll never associate anything else with it."

Taking the can from me, he grabs my hand, and the next thing I know, my palm is being sprayed with cooking oil. The *shhh* noise seems to go on and on as he unloads the oily mist.

"Whoa! Whoa! Okay, that's enough!" I laugh.

Grinning, he guides my hand to his cock and leans up to kiss me. My laughter dies in his mouth, and just like that, we're back to the precarious moment before he stormed my kitchen. Except now, he's slick in my grip, thickening again when I start stroking him.

Jesus, this stuff really does work well.

"I think this is my new favorite recipe."

Groaning, he pinches his eyes closed. "Stop it. Please."

"What?" I chuckle, easing over him, grateful for the distraction. "You planted the seed there. I'll never trust you in my kitchen again."

"You shouldn't, now that I've seen you naked," he snorts, but he must realize what a tell that is because he goes quiet even as my heart flips over the thought of being wanted by him in every room.

Easing my hand lower, his puckered flesh greets my cooking-oil-sprayed fingers. "You're sure?" I whisper.

Turning his head, he grabs up the can and lifts his leg. Sneaking it between us, the *shhh* sound is an elephant in the room, but perhaps only to my aerosol-as-lube virgin ears, because he tosses it and then nods somberly.

God… I will not unsee that. Strangely enough, though, it has its own kind of sex appeal, knowing that he'd resort to uncommon lubricants to be with me.

Circling his rim, I try to ignore the olive oil now dripping from it. Luckily, I'm captivated by the flicker of his pulse in his neck. His breath comes in hot waves on our kisses the more I continue. My reward is his hands introducing themselves to my body in new places—first touches I'll put to memory. Carefully, I slip a finger through his ring, greeted by the fire inside. His fingertips knead my back like a cat flexing its toes in satisfaction. I can tell he's impatient, but if I cause him any pain, I'll never forgive myself.

Easing in another finger, I bite back all the praise I want to shower him with for being in my life, for being so wonderful, and for being the strongest, sexiest man I've ever met. I'll get him to accept those compliments some other day—baby steps.

Grunting, his eyes slip closed, and he shudders when I pass over his gland. Transfixed over the way his mouth falls open, I'm suddenly impatient to be inside of him. I wait, though, slowly working my fingers and watching the beauty of him unfolding before my eyes.

"Okay," he gasps. "Okay. *Now.*"

Raising his knees higher, his eyes dart between my face and where I draw my cockhead over his ring like he can't decide which he'd rather watch. I know what *I* want to watch—him, just him. Nothing has ever been more in focus in my life.

His face looks like he's about to meet his death and yet his hands have slipped to my waist, kneading it sensually. He must finally see something in my expression that gives my nerves away because he reaches up and strokes my cheek with his thumb. I nod for some reason, as though I'm telling us both that it's okay to feel this lost and that it will still be okay afterward. Nothing will ever be the same between us, and I don't want it to be.

Pressing forward, I hold my breath, watching the brave façade on his face. It's mingled with this look of hope, almost like he's watching the sky for a shooting star. His eyes slip shut, and hot gusts of breath hit my cheek. A low moan erupts from his throat. It's a soft, breathy sound that I selfishly wish he could produce to the fullest. He deserves to hear how he feels.

I feel rigid as a board, but my muscles are quaking. My heart is slamming against my ribs from the way his body is cuffing me.

A long sound of relief filters past his lips and the pressure around my cock instantly abates. His eyes flare open, and I know he's seen his shooting star. His gaze flicks to my mouth, and I go happily where his hand directs when he tugs me to his lips. I never knew topping could be just as emotional as it is for the person bottoming. Maybe it's just him. Maybe it's just because it's *him* and *me*. I don't know, but my filter springs a leak.

"I'm so glad you didn't leave." Easing my hips back, my body finds a slow rhythm, encouraged by his moans. "I thought you hated me."

Scoffing, he takes two handfuls of my ass, sending a thrill all the way to my toes as he squeezes. "Thought we cleared that up."

A celebratory whir spins inside my chest, my doubts flying away to a forgotten place. I just… enjoy. And he enjoys. And we watch each other enjoying. I will hear all his sounds in my mind until I'm too old to dream. I'll feel the memory of his heels pressing at my lower back, his hands running over my body as we move like a slowly building chemical reaction.

His head thrashes. I can feel the tension in h s legs and abdomen. I can see it on his face. I can hear it in the way his moans have changed to a sound of sweet agony. He keeps reaching like he wants to either stroke or stop himself. His hand retreats again, and he looks at me like I need to put him out of his misery.

"Fuck," he whispers. "I didn't know it'd feel this good," he grits, baring his teeth.

It's killing me not to pick up the pace. I'm so close, right where he seems to be, too. I don't want it to end. I don't want to unweave my fingers from that wild hair of his. But all good things must end and there's still a higher plane I can take him to.

"I knew it would," I whisper back before capturing his mouth again and reaching between us, making the decision for him.

He groans in protest, like he was determined to hold out longer. God, there's no need. Drawing back, I try not to blink as I come so that I can see his expression. It's like being seen on another level, as though some being appeared in a halo of light the way he looks at me as I pulse inside him and he spills over my hand, clutching onto my wrist.

His voice cracks in a raspy wail. I kept thinking how sad it was that his voice wasn't as perfect as it might've been able to be, but I was so wrong. It's perfect, just as it is. It's the sound of our broken pasts. It's the sound of the man that life made him. It's just as it ought to be.

As our tremors subside, the room goes silent, all but for our winded noises. Droopy-lidded, he smiles up at me part bashful again, but mostly sated. He can say so much without words. Did I ever truly listen? I blink heavily, fighting the sleep that's hunting me. I don't want to look away from the silent heart that just brought me back from the dead.

CHAPTER 24
Easton

Who used to be a highly capable tattoo artist who could finish a design before anyone else in this shop, but now watches the clock, counting the minutes until Aaron gets off work? This fucking idiot... this smitten as fuck...

No. I'm *not* an idiot. I'm...

I'm not going to say it. A giant rock will fall on me, or I'll trip outside and Wolf will accidentally run me over with his van or something. That's what happens when you say it out loud... or think it. Right?

Cleaning my tools from my last job before my next client comes in, I decide there's at least nothing wrong with thinking about *why* I feel how I feel. Yeah. Cool. That's safe.

People fuck all the time. So, why do I keep smiling like I have a secret whenever I think about the other day?

Because you finally got fucked by the only man you ever wanted to fuck you.

Shut up.

Great. Now I'm arguing with myself.

One of me *does* have a point, though. It wasn't exactly fucking. It was... the *other* kind of fucking. The nice kind.

Does Shannon have the heat cranked up in here? The memory of feeling like Aaron was part of my soul while he looked down at me like I was the only thing he wanted to see for the rest of his life sends me into another hot flash. Okay. It's not our furnace.

Snickering, I can't wipe the grin off my face. I'm still too blown away to be embarrassed over daydreaming like a fool.

He's just so… *Aaron*. About *everything*.

When we were done, he looked like he was as tired as I was, but he lay there, fighting it. He just kept staring at me with this dreamy smile.

"You glad I got that out of my system?" I'd snarked, feeling self-conscious.

"Well, I hope once wasn't enough to get it out of your system."

Hearing that he wasn't disappointed brought me way too much joy, but that wasn't even the worst part. He leaned over and pressed a kiss to my chest, just over my heart, and then pulled me against him in his arms. We… cuddled. I'm a fucking cuddler now.

Jesus.

For as much as that sounds like aliens abducted me and replaced my personality with some sappy person who gets attached, the thought of cozying up to him again tonight has my knee bouncing with anticipation for the freaking clock to move faster.

Something stabs me in the back of the shoulder. I turn around and get a face full of mail thrust at me by one agitated-looking Clark Wolverton.

What the fuck? He could have just dropped it on my side table.

Shit. There's a lot here.

"Your mail was falling out of the box. When's the last time you even checked it?"

Flipping through the letters, I spot one from the parole board. My throat closes and I see rage, as usual. They need a way for people to request not to get these damn things. Leonard can rot in there for all I care. Tossing it in the trash can, I hold up my utility bill, check the postmark date, and glance at Wolf.

"Not since last Tuesday, from the looks of it."

"Dude…what is the deal? Are you guys like boyfriends now? You're over there all the time."

Boyfriends…Is Aaron my boyfriend? It's only been a week. And we only did the *nice kind of fucking thing* once. That doesn't make him my boyfriend, does it? The closest thing I've ever had to one was trading handies and blow jobs with Ben when I was a teenager. Mostly, we just hung out. Kind of like I've been hanging out with Aaron for just a little over two months now. Hanging out with Aaron is different, though. I didn't get that strange giddy feeling with Ben the way I do with Aaron.

Wolf is still eyeballing me like he expects me to answer the boyfriend question. Shit. Why do I feel sick at the thought of Aaron being hurt if he heard me deny such a claim in front of him? Or if *I* heard him deny the claim in front of *me*? Oh my God. Do I actually want a boyfriend?

Do not smile. Do not fucking smile right now or he'll give you shit forever.

"Does Melissa have you scrapbooking or something? I didn't know you were including my life events in your memoirs," I snark.

Rolling his eyes, he walks over to my stool and gives it a weak kick. "We're breaking up."

Yeah. I've heard that before. I swear those two do not know how to fight. They don't even yell when they fight.

"Well, there's always next week."

Glowering at me, he stuffs his hands in his black jeans, looking ready to commit murder. "For real this time. I caught her texting with some guy she works with."

Oh, brother. He's always so over-possessive, like he thinks everything will take off on him like his mom did.

"*Like boyfriends*?" I parrot, smugly, trying to show him how ridiculous he's being.

Nostrils flaring, his expression sours further. 'No, like '*Can't wait to see you tomorrow, beautiful.*'"

Oh… shit.

"Damn. I'm sorry." I don't know what else to say, but that must be enough because he nods, fucking with my stool again.

"Guess you're bunking back at your house, then?" I venture.

Snorting, he cards his fingers through his hair roughly, pinching his eyes closed. "No. Mom called. She said she's selling it."

Okay, I liked Melissa well enough. She always championed Wolf and didn't treat him like he was disabled. It's sad his relationship is ending this way, but his mom is selling the house? It's a gut punch. It was like a second home for me for a while. Or… third home, if you count Nancy's. Fourth if you count Hampton Hell. Whatever. Wolf's lived there his entire life, minus the periods of time when he gets serious with a woman and stays at her place. How the fuck can his mom up and sell it on him when it's the only home he's ever known? When she was off galivanting the world with whatever guy she was seeing at the time, it was Wolf's only source of security besides his time with me and Jasper at Jasper's shop. When the gutters went bad, he fixed them. When the furnace went out, he's the one who'd call for repairs. The guy has been doing his own grocery shopping and cooking since he was like twelve all Mac-Caulay Culkin style. The way I see it is that it's his house. No wonder he looks like a black cloud is hanging over him.

"Fuck, man." Standing up, I take a step forward, so he knows he's got my full attention now if he wants it. "That's some bullshit."

Shrugging, he fiddles with my ink display. "It's her house."

Liar. He *so* does not feel that way either.

"What are you going to do?"

"Look for a new place, I guess. She hasn't even gotten an appraiser lined up yet, so I've got a while. I'll start going through my stuff, though."

Giving his arm a soft punch, I flash him a cheerful grin. "You can come be my roommate. I always wanted someone to cook for me."

Snorting, he shoves me before heading out of my stall. "Yeah, right. Get your fucking boyfriend to cook for you."

He does cook for me. And it's damn good.

Shit. Maybe I do have a boyfriend.

For fuck's sake. At least quit smiling about it.

CHAPTER 25
Easton

Panting, Aaron rolls off all fours onto his side. "I didn't think you were ever going to fuck me."

"What? Why?" I laugh, still trying to catch my breath.

"It's been almost two weeks since…since we first did."

It's funny that he thinks we can't talk about my bottoming. I mean, it's not at the top of my conversation list, but… with *him*? I think we could talk about anything.

"What? Are my blow jobs not up to snuff?" I ask, flopping down next to him and snagging the hand towel off the nightstand.

They've become a permanent fixture there these past two weeks of us fooling around and getting each other off in every way except the way we just did. I didn't mind taking things down a notch. It felt… natural. It was like we were getting to know each other in new ways, and I've never laughed so much while just screwing around. Some nights, we didn't even do anything other than curl up on his couch or put more puzzles together. Handing him the clean half of the towel, I watch his brows shoot up the way they do when he's trying to come up with a retort.

"Uh, I'm pretty sure my brother will be getting a noise complaint call from the neighbors about what you did to me last night."

"Just last night, huh?"

"If you want praise, you don't have to ask for it," he says, rolling into me and throwing an arm over my waist.

Why does he always smell so good? And feel so good? And kiss so fucking good?

"I've got plenty of nice things I can think to say if you ever want to hear them," he murmurs sleepily when he breaks away.

"Yeah?" I laugh nervously.

I'd die to know what those things are, but if Aaron was any sweeter, it might kill me, so I'm damned either way. I'm…happy.

Is this really real? It feels like being on the high of my life and waiting for the bottom to drop out at the same time. He left once. What if he leaves again? What if I'm just helping to ease his broken heart?

Rolling his eyes, he smiles and gets out of bed. "Come on, I'll walk you to the door."

My breath catches at the sound of my intuition coming true so quickly, so I cover it with sarcasm. "Damn. Kicking me out that fast?"

"You told me an hour ago that you should head home because you have to open and catch up on bookkeeping tomorrow. I don't want to be responsible for keeping you from your business responsibilities, but if I lie here next to you any longer, I'll fall asleep and not be able to kiss you goodnight."

Well, when he puts it that way. Sitting up, I reach for my pants and shrug into them. "Admit it. You just want to see me on my motorcycle."

The way he clings so tightly to me that I can hardly breathe when we're on it makes me feel needed. I didn't know I'd like to be needed. It does all sorts of possessive things to me that are terrifying—like wanting to ask him if I can spend the night.

It's the first time I fucked him. Usually, the first time is the last time. The thought of a last time with him is like a kick in the gut, though. I've officially obliterated my one-and-done rule. It was… God; I don't even have the words.

"Want you," he'd murmured urgently against my mouth when he pulled me up off his cock in the living room earlier. *"Want you to fuck me."*

We probably looked like a blur racing to his room, ripping off the rest of our clothes. It was the perfect mix of sweet and ravenous. I'm embarrassed over how many times I fantasized about it, only to experience completely different emotions when it actually happened. Wolf was right—this is fucking me up, except I don't know that I mind. For the first time, I wasn't just fucking someone to get off. I was…*present.* I was *us.* I hung onto each of his gasps and moans. Watching his every reaction made my heart feel like it was going to burst, knowing they were because of whatever he felt for me. I'm becoming addicted to the *'nice kind of fucking'.*

Out in the living room, I shrug into my leather jacket by his doorway. He treads out of his room in his stocking-clad feet, tugging a sweatshirt over his head. My skin warms, eyeing the fine dusting of hair on his bare legs up to where his boxer briefs end. The backs of those legs are silky smooth and were just pressed against the front of mine while his body was hugging me like it was claiming my soul.

He's right. I *should* leave, because I want to drag him back in there and pull the blanket over our heads just to fall asleep next to him.

"What?" he laughs self-consciously, smoothing out his hair.

"Nothing. That's a cute look on you."

"Yeah. I'm designer runway material." Cheeks going pink, he gives himself a once over, smoothing out his old sweatshirt before looking back up at me.

Suddenly, I'm no longer ashamed of my youthful infatuation or how long it lasted. How could anyone ever stand a chance at that smile of his?

Reaching out, I trace my thumb along his jaw. I reach to cup the back of his neck and pull him toward me. "I can't help looking when you smile like that all the time."

The kiss was a bad idea. The way his body instantly goes soft against mine when he wraps his arms around my neck has me determined to tell him that there's a murderer on the loose, so it's not safe for me to leave. I don't get the chance, though.

"It's kind of hard not to smile when your boyfriend is so sweet," he murmurs in front of my lips.

The words reverberate in my heart like it's an instrument, and he just strummed a chord on it. I'm frozen, unable to breathe.

"Sorry," he whispers, his eyes scanning my face. "I guess I'm just emotional from the sex and..."

I cut him off, silencing his unnecessary apology with my mouth, pulling him tight against me. My pulse is racing from some ingrained instinct to flee, but I don't want that instinct anymore. I don't want him to take it back.

Boyfriend. Boyfriend. Boyfriend. With each pass of my tongue and lips, I sign the agreement until we have to come up for air.

Beaming, he traces the corner of my mouth and lets out a puff of laughter. "Okay, I'm *not* sorry," he amends. "Because now you're smiling too."

I try to bite it back, but my face isn't cooperating, so I roll my eyes and give his ass a little swat. "Get some sleep," I whisper, giving him a peck on the cheek.

Man, I'm a damn goner.

Opening the door, I try to keep my shit together, but can't fight the urge to glance back when I step out onto his porch. I might have to pull out my old sketch pad and add the image of him leaning in the doorway, all sex rumpled, surrounded by the glow of the light from his living room. Because, yeah---of course, I kept that sketchpad.

"You *did* just want to see me ride off on my motorcycle, didn't you?" I tease.

"I can't help it. You look sexy on it."

As I hop on my bike and start the engine, I can feel my smile behind my helmet shield as he waves to me. I'm a *boyfriend*. A *sexy* boyfriend who's being watched longingly as he pulls away. The title sounds promising, like a future where neither of us moves out of state. The warmth radiating through me accompanies me all the way home, along with the grin on my face.

Parking my bike in the garage behind the shop, I still feel the regret of leaving as I lock the door. He didn't ask me to stay, but I assume it was because I foolishly mentioned I have to open in the morning. I only switched with Shannon so I can get out of here early enough to spend the whole evening with him tomorrow. I'm pretty sure, though, if I'd stayed in his bed, he wouldn't have protested about me sleeping over.

A few days ago, when we were falling asleep on his couch, he murmured, "*You don't have to leave, you know, if…you wanted to stay.*"

It's out of character for me, but I can't find a reason *not to* stay next time. Damn. We're actually doing this. *Me* and *Aaron*. My *boyfriend*. That has a hop in my step as I walk toward the exterior staircase behind the shop that leads up to my apartment.

Something shifts in the shadows of the stairwell enclosure. If the freaking alley cats are pissing in there again, I'm going to be livid. We should really get a door on this thing.

The darkened shape takes more form as I approach hugging my jacket to keep out the night's chill. It's too big to be a cat. Way too big.

My heart thumps as the form of a man manifests in the darkness. Shit. Am I about to be jumped? There's something leaning against the stairs near his feet, though. A bag? Maybe he's homeless and just looking for shelter from the wind.

"Can I help you, buddy?" I call out as best I can, hoping my cordiality is returned in kind.

He steps out of the enclosure entrance and the parking lot flood light illuminates his features. If I got hit by a truck right now, I'd be less shocked. Every muscle in my body is painfully seized by what feels a lot like fear.

"I wondered if you'd ever show up," he drawls, eyeing me up and down. "It's good to see you, *son*."

Son…

No…

I was right. I shouldn't have left Aaron's. There *is* a murderer on the loose.

The next thing I know, I'm nearly on top of him, my fist slamming into his face. Some unholy broken sound comes out of my throat, feeling like it tore it open. I slam him into the frame of the enclosure, rearing my arm back, knowing I'm going to kill him.

I'm going to…*kill* him.

Fuck.

What am I doing?

Gulping, I let go of my hold like he burned me. My legs are like rubber, backpedaling away from the devil reincarnated at my doorstep. My God. If I touch him, I *will* kill him. I don't want to be a killer. I don't want to be anything like him. Mom wouldn't want me to be anything like him. And Aaron…I don't want Aaron to think I'm anything like him. Who could love a guy who kills his own father?

Heartbeat pounding in my head, my back hits something solid. I've retreated so far I ran into the back of the shop without even realizing.

That face—the fucking face I dreamt about pulverizing so many times—it's staring back at me, calm as a tomb. He spits out a mouthful of blood, dabbing at his lip with a knobby knuckle.

"I deserved that," he pants.

My entire body is vibrating, at war with the urge to give him more of what he deserves and trying to talk myself down. I'm basically just standing here having a panic attack. It feels like I'm a kid. *Again*. I fucking grew up and got stronger. I forgot all about him and wrote him out of my life, but being stuck standing a few feet away from him, I can see it was all wishful thinking. I can say a thousand times that he's not my father, but nothing will change that. He'll always be the man who made me. My kin. And the difference between us is that I won't kill my kin. It's not fair. It's like he has some power over me just by birth right. Why else can't I move?

"Is there somewhere we can talk?"

Talk? Even if I could speak right now, I have nothing to say to Leonard Bennick. There's nothing he could possibly have to say that I want to hear.

He killed her. Not directly. I've beat myself up enough times knowing I had a part in Mom's death because of the car accident. Maybe they would have been able to save her if we hadn't crashed. I'll never know, but we wouldn't have been in that car in the middle of a blizzard if it wasn't for the man in front of me.

I don't know whether I shake my head or if it's my silence, but he must realize my answer is no. His bottom lip presses into his top one, accentuating the new age lines on his face. When is he going to start yelling and raging at me? That was always his thing. No doubt he probably blames me for him going to prison. That can be the only reason he turned up here—payback.

"All right," he says softly. "I can respect that."

Cursing myself for not opening any of those damn parole letters, I gape at him. Since when does Leonard respect anyone or anything?

"I know you don't want to see me, but I've got nowhere to go. There's a halfway house over in Dixon County, but the work there is slim for parolees. I think I can get a job at the pallet factory in Siever. I just need somewhere to stay for a few weeks until I can get a place. A guy you did ink on came in a while back." Smiling like he's proud of me or something, he glances at the building. "Told me what a talented tattoo artist you are. I put your address down with the parole board, hoping..."

Hearing him use words like *parole* and *halfway house* is like hearing a foreign language. They're not words I ever heard him use when I was younger, and he was, for all intents and purposes, what appeared to be a steady working man who held his truck-driving job. The thought of him living and working in Siever, just one town over, is unsettling. It's too close to the life I've built here. A life I want him nowhere near.

Why did he have to come here? He had the entire rest of the state to choose from.

Something about him looks... weaker and not just because his lip is split. I don't know if it's the lines in his face, the gray at the temples of his brown hair, or his unassuming posture, which is so vastly different from the man I once knew. The most startling change, though, is that he's clearly sober. His skin, although more weathered, looks healthier. His broad shoulders and arms have more build to them, telling me how he spent his time in prison, but he's aged.

I don't care how much of his miserable life is left; I'm not letting him spend it one town over. I have too much of mine left to share geography with him since murdering him clearly isn't an option. Siever is too close to me. Too close to Aaron. I need some law of Congress to get him farther away. Either that or...

It's an awful idea. A stupid, terrible, awful idea.

I must be out of my fucking mind...

I have no pity for this man. I don't. I keep telling myself that as my shaky legs walk past the sad looking drawstring bag at the foot of the stairs with the *Maine State Penitentiary* logo on it and nod for him to follow. I want him gone so badly, that if sheltering him for a few weeks is the price I have to pay to keep him out of my life for good, I'll deal with it. There'll be no parole letters next time. Not with the ultimatum brewing in my head. It's a solid plan that a convict can't argue with even if it's taking everything in me not to hyperventilate.

Except, with each step I ascend, a voice in my head tells me I'm dishonoring Mom's memory by allowing her killer into my home. I'm dishonoring every dream I had about beating him to a pulp. Maybe I could stop before he takes his last breath, but I don't trust myself. And the thought of a beautiful smile across town is making me not want to go down the path of anger again. I traveled it for so long, I don't want to go back either now that I've found a new course.

Reaching the landing, I wait, watching his slow ascent. He lets out a cough, and I hear the distinct sound of heavy breathing that he never used to have. Adjusting his bag in his grip, he stands humbly, like he's awaiting orders, and looks at me as though he's fully expecting me to recant my unspoken offer. I've never seen him look like he's at some-one's mercy. I blame that for the reason I unlock my door—he's not the same Leonard I knew. Something tells me it wouldn't be fair to knock *this* Leonard down the stairs and watch him break his neck.

As he steps hesitantly inside and I flip on the light, I hate the way my hands are trembling. He has more build to him now, even if he is older. He might be able to take me, but I honestly don't think he would. I think it's *me* I'm afraid of. I don't want to be the me who hated him. Not anymore. I want to be the me who just left Aaron's house with a dopey smile on his face. I won't be able to do that if I have blood on my hands and rage in my heart.

Turning around, he looks at me with an appreciative smile on his face. "Thank you. This means a lot."

I don't want this to mean a damn thing. That's not why I'm doing it. I don't want his thanks. I don't care if he memorized the Bible front and back while he was in prison. I'm not forgiving him. I never will. I'm only doing this for Aaron and for me. He already ruined my life once; I'm not letting him do it again.

"You can use the couch and whatever else you need," I inform him, motioning to it with my chin when he gives me a curious look at the sound of my voice. If I go into detail about why I speak so hoarsely, I might find my hands around his neck. I need to keep my cool. "You can stay long enough to get your shit together to find somewhere else, but then you're gone. And as soon as parole lets you move on, you're going to head as far away from Hampton as possible or you'll regret the day you came looking for me."

He blinks at me. Why the fuck he looks hurt, I don't understand. Does he not think I'm serious?

"That's the fucking deal. The only deal. Do you understand me?"

His face sags, but then he finally nods.

"And I own the shop downstairs, which you apparently already know. I don't want you down there. *Ever.*"

Grimacing, the crow's feet at the corners of his eyes show them-selves. He nods again, though. "I get it. A man's got to work and doesn't need to be—"

"*And* I don't want to *hear you* or *see you*," I cut him off.

It's true. I can't fucking stand the sight of him any longer. I've done my good deed for the year. Turning, I head to my room and shut the door. And then, I lock it and kick myself for leaving the warm bed and the wonderful man that I don't deserve. *Me*—the son of a killer who has murder coursing through his veins.

CHAPTER 26

Aaron

Unlocking the door to the cottage, I'm still floating on the perpetual cloud that is any time spent with Easton. So, it's not exactly embarrassment that has me engaging him. Making up excuses to talk to him has become my new favorite hobby.

"Are you proud of yourself?" I tease, locking up behind him once we're inside.

"About what?" he chuckles, looking genuinely confused.

"That I made a fool of myself at the movie theater? Did you take me just to find out if I yell at movies in public like I do at home?"

"You only got a few dirty looks," he says somberly, walking over and cupping my face. When he plants a kiss on my forehead, strands of worry wrap around me.

He's been subdued lately, and it doesn't seem natural. Our love-making these past three weeks has been on a plane I've never known, more sensual and emotional than I knew was possible. I have zero complaints, but it's… unexpected not hearing his cocky jokes anymore when we're in bed or messing around. His expressions get so serious, almost like he thinks I'm going to disappear.

I realize I haven't known him in eight years and that I'm still learning about him, but if I didn't know any better, I'd say something's troubling him. I don't think it's me or us because he's stayed here every single night since before I can remember. If I was what was troubling him, he wouldn't stay. Right?

Heading toward the couch, he reaches across his chest and cups his hand over his opposite shoulder. I watch the way his head tilts, stretching out the muscles in his neck and upper back. I remember he said that tattooing can take a toll on your body. He has so many strikes against him from his former injuries, too. It hasn't passed my notice the way his gait seems rigid sometimes now that it's getting colder. He probably has more arthritis than a sixty-year-old after what he went through.

"Do you want to watch something and get the rest of it out of your system?" he jests, picking up the remote. "I know you were holding back at the theater."

See? We're fine. He *does* still tease me, even if not as much as at first.

"I have a better idea." Taking the remote from him, I set it down on the coffee table. Turning him by the shoulders, I urge him toward the bedroom door. "Why don't you go soak in the tub while I finish the dishes? It's getting too cold for you to sneak off to that swimming spot you like. Warm water is better for your bones, anyway."

"You could just tell me I stink."

"You don't stink." For good measure, I bury my nose in the back of his shoulder and take a whiff. "I love your stink, actually, but you look tired and stiff."

Arching his brows, he eyes me suspiciously. "Well, that boosted my ego. I'm supposed to be the younger one here."

Rolling my eyes, I give him a playful nudge. "It's not a contest. You work your ass off. Go on. You'll love it. I promise."

"Do I have to light a bunch of candles and play Joni Mitchell?" he calls even as he obliges and walks into my room.

"Go!" I laugh. "You stink!"

Heading to the kitchen, still chuckling, I shake my head at myself. Maybe I overanalyze things. I know it's wise to question things in life. You can't walk through it blindly without doubt, but you can't have so many that you let them ruin something truly good.

Scrubbing the dishes, I stop mid-swipe, the sponge dripping in my hand. *Something truly good.* That defines perfectly what Easton is to me. Maybe in the grand scheme of things, we're unconventional. I work in an office. He's covered in tattoos. I'm eight years older and was once assigned to a professional guidance position over him. I'm afraid of everything. He's afraid of nothing. Well, unless you count him being afraid to let me know he had a crush on me.

The sponge falls from my hand into the sink, splattering water droplets in the air.

I didn't see it then. Why would I have seen it now?

Is he still afraid of us? Maybe that's why he looks at me like I'll disappear. He has to know that I'm right where I want to be. I thought I'd made it terribly obvious.

I feel warm with embarrassment right now, just thinking about how smitten I feel all the time. Have I been holding back, though? Does he need more from me? If so, I am willing and able to give it. Inhaling a deep breath, I dry my hands and start toward my room, determined. Brave. Open.

What I find when I pass through the doorway of the bathroom is a vision—and not just the sensual kind. It's a vision of my future. The man leaning his head back on the tub, eyes closed, inked forearms draped over the sides, is the man I want in every tomorrow for eternity.

It's like a curtain being drawn open, revealing the answer to a mystery. I'm simultaneously grateful for the revelation and feel a fool for all the choices I made prior to this moment in my life. When Jason, with all his initial charm and promises, asked me to marry him and move to Seattle, I remember thinking, why would anyone say no?

Anyone…

How am I just now realizing that I asked myself the wrong question? It didn't matter what *anyone* would have done. I said *yes* because I couldn't find a reason to say *no*.

Easton's eyes peel open and find me, a lazy smile turning up a corner of his mouth. "I scrubbed. I promise."

I tug my sweatshirt over my head because touching him is an urgent necessity. I shuck the rest of my clothes because as I stare at him, I know without a doubt I could never find a reason to say *no* to having him in my life. Everything about him is a resounding *yes* for me.

"I'll be the judge of that," I murmur, stepping into the tub.

"Ah, this was a setup. I knew it," he deadpans, even as he sits up to make room for me. "You just needed someone to wash your back."

Sliding my feet next to his hips as I extend my legs what little I can, I feel home when the tops of his shins slip underneath my thighs. I once morosely mused that I could live in here. Now, it's absolutely true. I felt slightly less lost when I returned to Maine, but I'm truly home when I'm with him.

I stare, just appreciating him until his brows quirk. Even that is endearing. How can someone so beautiful not be used to being looked at?

"You're too far away to wash my back."

Pulling myself forward, the water makes his skin glide like oil against mine as I rise. His lips are cool, but the rest of him is warm and inviting beneath the surface as I finagle my feet underneath his legs. The water level rises when I settle myself onto his lap, lying on him like a human blanket. I can't hold back anything anymore now that I've seen my heart's secret. Maybe I was waiting for permission from myself to fall in love again.

Like the other half of my soul, so in tune with my emotions, he reaches up, cupping my jaw. The searching look he gives me, the expression of awareness over my need to be one with him right now, is all the proof I need that my heart is giving its consent to be given away. A younger version of me might have thought, who could say no to that look?

The version of me today says no one else will have the chance. It's mine. Only mine.

Rocking my hips into his, our cocks glide against each other between our stomachs. I answer his inquiring gaze with a kiss meant to ease all his worries.

"Do you have any idea how happy you make me?" I whisper, trailing a hand possessively down his side. Not groping; just claiming. I want him to know that he's mine, every inch of him.

"How happy?"

The vulnerability in his expression tells me my assumption earlier was right. I want to wipe it from the pages of history. Cupping his face, I press a gentle kiss to his lips and gaze into those mesmerizing eyes.

"A level of happiness that might terrify some people." Another kiss. Another picture of that heartbreaking look. "But I'm not terrified," I assure him.

"No?" he croaks, wetting his lips.

"No. Because I'm never going to lose you again."

His stomach rises against mine. A thick exhale leaves his lips, and his hand palms the back of my head, pulling me to his mouth. He kisses me like I set something free inside him. I kiss him back, letting him know he can have the key forever.

It's not even foreplay, the way my hips are rocking against his now. It's a carnal, possessive act of my body showing his body that I'm his mate. When his hand grips my ass and lifts, my mate instincts answer.

Reaching into the water, I wrap my hand around him, angling him to where we both need him right now. The second I feel his cockhead at my entrance, I thrust myself down on it like a starving savage. Our moans crash into each other's mouths, a feral sound of relief and anguish.

I don't want to tear my lips away, but I have too big of a message to impart with my body. Gripping the sides of the tub, I straighten up. He shifts inside me, slipping in deeper, well past my prostate. I don't care that there are better ways to stimulate it. I just want him there as deep as he can go. I want the fullness during this moment. I want it rooted inside my body like a waypoint for the thickness of the emotions between us. Rising, I descend slowly, holding his gaze as he fills me again.

Teeth bared, he snakes his hand in an *S* down my torso, fingers gripping needily at my flesh. Some people talk dirty in the heat of the moment. Some people say flowery things. For a man whose job it is to get people to speak, there's probably an irony in how much I enjoy his silence when we make love. I don't need words. It's all there in his face, in his little grunts that almost sound like growls. Easton uses his entire body to communicate, a special language just for me. Leaning forward, he grips my neck and pulls me to his mouth, shifting his hips into me as I ride him. I've abandoned my slow, sensual rhythm. It's nothing short of pouncing on his cock at this point, water sloshing over the sides of the tub.

Shifting his legs, he manages to cross them underneath my ass, leaning me back against my end of the tub. I hold on, feeling weightless, but for my arms. It's like fucking on a cloud. His hands grip my hips, my buoyancy allowing him to thrust me easily onto him over and over. I never take my eyes off his. With each yank on my hips that makes me feel wholly at his disposal, I watch. He watches me back, looking completely lost over the symbology of how it says loud and clear that I trust him to do whatever he wants to me, to use me, to have me, to consume me body and soul. That *I'm his*. Completely his.

"Yeah," I concur with that unspoken message. "Yes. Yes."

It might be just wishful thinking or passion, but I can feel his love saturating the room, the air, the water. "Aaron," he pants.

It's not a plea to speed up the climax. It's not a warning that he's near. It's a statement of desperation. It's the weight of suffering an overwhelming love. I know because I can feel it too in my chest, swelling around my heart.

"Come, baby," I beg, saying that silly word I've never called anyone before. "Come."

A low noise in his throat says he was holding back but can't any longer after hearing those three words. He flexes inside me, so I reach for my cock, although it's hardly necessary. He likes to watch. I've learned that much. So, I listen to him yell a broken sound as he shudders and stares at me as I work myself through the water.

It's too much. So much that I have to close my eyes as the waves of pleasure ripple through me—electricity running up my legs, his heat billowing inside me, his flexed muscles brushing against my wet skin. Neither of us has any air left, but I greet his mouth eagerly when his lips crash into mine.

It's not even kissing, just sloppy exchanges of lips. Silent gratitude. Addiction.

I exert what little energy I have left to wrap my arms around his neck as his weight collapses onto me. Closing my eyes, I decide I'm not going to let go until he makes me. The world could end tomorrow, and I wouldn't be bothered right now.

Sometime later, I wake to a chill in the water and a chaste kiss on my lips. Eyelids heavy, they open to the sleepy, smiling face in front of me as his warm body draws back.

"Why don't we move this to the bed?" he suggests.

"Mm," I grunt in disapproval.

I was already home. I don't need to go anywhere else.

Smirking, he rises and eases his way out of the tub, making me sigh until I catch a glimpse of the dimples in his gorgeous, glistening ass. Sated and exhausted, I blink through my drug-like state, watching his simple acts. Grabbing his towel off the wall hook—the one he's claimed weeks ago. Drying himself leisurely with no sense of modesty or flair—a man in his natural habitat. My lungs ache with wistfulness at how age-old it all looks and feels, how permanent, how perfect. He could be across town right now and I think I'd still sense his presence, still feel his effect on my heart.

"Did I ever know what love was?" The mesmerized words leave my lips as a quiet thought, but they're so much more. I realize that as soon as he hears them, but I'm not sorry that what is felt is now spoken.

My breath hitches, worried that claiming it aloud was too much for him, but I want him to know. He looks neither scared nor uncomfortable, though, rather speechless. Smiling, I lift one shoulder from the luke-warm water as if to say, it couldn't be helped.

It couldn't. Falling hopelessly in love with Easton was unavoidable.

In two strides, he reaches me. Bending down, he hooks his fingers under my chin and leans in. The acceptance in his eyes is like a balm, making my eyes slip closed as he presses a soft kiss to my lips and holds it there.

"Come on," he whispers, sounding choked. Slipping his hand underneath my arm, he gives it a gentle tug. "Come to bed."

I rise without a care in the world, a mass of sated dead weight. He wraps a towel around me, but I don't get the chance to take it from him. I stand obediently in my bliss, watching through tired eyes as he dries my body. Tossing the towel to the wet floor, he takes my hand.

I find myself put into bed. The light goes out, and a lean, warm body slides in next to me. I can feel the ridges of the scar tissue on his legs when they slip over mine as he entangles us under the covers, pulling me closer and tighter than he ever has before.

The thump of his heart against my ear lulls me further toward sleep. I sink deeper into the soothing darkness amid periodic kisses to my head and the gentle circling of his thumb over my arm.

No. I never had a clue what love was—until now.

A scratchy whisper dusts my temple. "I'm very happy too."

I used to make him try to speak when what I should have done was listen. I've never been so grateful as witnessing how silent is the heart. It's the loudest, most beautiful sound in the world.

CHAPTER 27
Easton

Happy and terrified.

The words have been running a race in my head since last night. Staring blankly at the cash in my hand and the piles on my desk, I realize I've lost count again. Fuck.

Scooping up the sales from yesterday, I start over. Smiling to myself, I can't fight the newest distraction that's creeping in. I replay the memory of Aaron calling out to me, and then his little declaration that made my heart damn near stop beating. He *loves* me…

I decide I'm mostly happy because why should Aaron loving me be terrifying? That's what you want a crush to do, right?

My elbow knocks my coffee tumbler over, spilling a brown pool onto my desk. Shit. There goes the count again. Scrambling, I right it, set the cash to the side, and grab a roll of paper towels off the shelf behind my desk.

It reminds me of the coffee mug ring I noticed on my living room table when I came home from Aaron's to shower and dress for the day. The quaint mess where Leonard has taken up residence on my couch is an eyesore I can't avoid. Each morning, I come home from Aaron's like I'm living my best life only to have it marred by the snoring lump on my couch, huddled under a blanket with the television murmuring in the background. He fucking better not be ordering anything on my cable account. Why couldn't he find a job working a day shift?

The cynic in me ignored his claim of getting a job at The Siever Pallet Company, just like how I ignore him any time he tries to strike up a friendly conversation. He must have forgotten the *'I-don't-want-to-hear-*

you' rule. The uniforms folded up on my coffee table and the beat-up pickup I've seen pick him up out back in the afternoons, however, make it difficult to believe my doubts. So, maybe he actually did get a job. Good for him. How fucking long is long enough for an ex-con to save up first and last month's rent is what I want to know? It doesn't matter that he basically only occupies a six-by-six area of my apartment, and I only have to see him if I go up there in the morning or to change before I see Aaron in the evenings. He's like an intrusive growth.

I… *want* to be happy, so badly I can taste it. I want to swallow it, drink it down whole, and let it cleanse me of every skeptical thought I've ever had about love. But Aaron was right—*'A level of happiness that might terrify some people.'*

How can you let yourself freefall into the level of happiness he represents for me when there's a bad omen living under my roof? Leonard's done nothing wrong since he's been here, short of several obnoxious attempts to offer me coffee or breakfast in the mornings that break the *no-speaking* rule. I can't explain it, but I won't stop being terrified that my life will implode until he's gone.

Wolf's footsteps make a stomping sound coming through the office door. Tossing a pair of nitrile gloves in the trash can by his desk, he lets out a sigh. Watching the agitated lines in his face as he skulks to the fridge to grab a soda, it's strange to be the happy, coupled one among us for once. I know he's sore over the Melissa ordeal, but my bet is it's the upcoming loss of his house that's the biggest reason behind his glum mood of late. Having that conversation would be like poking a badger, though. No thank you.

Intrusive growth upstairs—Debbie Downer downstairs. I used to *enjoy* coming to work.

Wolf sulks back out to the shop without so much as a glance at me. It'll be a fun day when he moves the last box out of *Chateau de Wolverton*.

Channeling laser focus, I finally finish my count. Gathering up the deposit for tomorrow along with my own personal sales, I head to the file cabinet and open the fake door front, balancing the funds on my knee so I can do the combination.

Jesus, I have four days' worth of deposits sitting in here in front of my emergency fund. I have officially been living in Boyfriend Land.

Whatever. My nest egg far exceeds four days of sales.

It's comical that Aaron keeps insisting he could carpool me back and forth from his place since I keep refusing his offers to return my Suburban. I've got enough stashed in here that I could buy him his own brand-new vehicle, but even I know that would look like overkill. Yeah, it's getting cold as shit out on my bike, but I don't mind when the short destination means I'll have him to keep me warm. He wants to drive around to look at Christmas lights tonight. Are grown men supposed to be so damn cute?

"Hey! Did you leave something running upstairs?" Wolf calls from behind me.

"What?"

I didn't think he could look more pissed off than he already was. What the hell would I have left running upstairs and why is he wiping his forehead off? Is he sweating?

"There's water dripping from the ceiling down into my station."

Water? Why would there be water? The only thing that's up above his stall is the spare room I use as my home gym. I may have had a moment of decency where I considered converting it to a guest room, but remembered I don't have a decent guest. The only reason there would be water coming from up there would be if…

Oh, shit.

It *was* built to be a spare room and so it has a bathroom attached to it, a bathroom that Leonard's been using. Son of a bitch.

Tossing my bundles into the safe, I glance back to tell Wolf to cool his jets, and I'll go take care of it. I don't need him finding out I've been housing Leonard after the way he lectured me when Aaron and I first got together. No way am I telling him about my unwanted visitor now while he's unhinged about being single and soon-to-be houseless.

"Hey," Leonard calls, making every one of my muscles go rigid.

Leonard. Fucking Leonard. In my shop.

It's like watching your most embarrassing dream play out in front of a live audience. What is he doing down here? Wolf gives him a once over, looking confused as Leonard squeezes in the doorway next to him.

"The faucet handle broke off in the shower. I can fix it, though, if you've got a plumber's wrench and tell me where the shut-off valve is."

I should have added *don't touch anything* to my list of rules. Slamming the safe door closed, I get to my feet. I need to just channel some of my hostility to issue him a *get out of my life* rule, but I don't want to become a dick again and have it spill over onto Aaron. Ignoring Wolf's questioning look, I hustle past him, motioning for Leonard to move his ass. I hate how I look like him. I hate that it's probably incredibly obvious to my best friend to see the resemblance. I don't want to deal with this right now.

Racing upstairs, I rush to the bookcase on the far wall of the living room and shove it out of the way. Stupid fucking place to put a bookcase, Easton. I know. Opening the hatch behind it, I turn off the water line to the spare bathroom only to find Wolf has followed us. Wonderful.

Brow furrowed, he glances from me to Leonard who's babbling in that obnoxious new calm of his about how he'll get everything set to right. Did he take a fucking plumber's course in prison? I don't remember him lifting a finger when I was a kid other than to raise a bottle to his mouth or point at me and wield one of his degrading accusations about my weak stature or sexuality.

Shaking my head, it's a silent warning to Wolf. A silent apology too, perhaps. Maybe he'd understand. Maybe he wouldn't. He'd definitely worry about why I let Leonard into my home, though, and I don't need anyone worrying about me. Wolf's got his own shit to deal with, and I've got everything under control.

My spare bathroom is a flood zone. Grinding my teeth, I eye the spurt of water coming out of the faucet base decreasing. It's one of those freestanding tubs with a shower pipe that hangs overhead like the one Aaron and I made love in last night. Leave it to Leonard to further shit on one of my favorite memories in my life.

"You got any tools, son? I can get this fixed up in no time."

Why does he have to call me that? The word makes me feel like a pressure cooker about to blow the way it makes recognition flicker across Wolf's face.

Yanking towels out of the cabinet, I grit between my teeth, "Under the kitchen sink."

Sopping up the pool of water near the baseboard of the wall, I can feel my friend's eyes on me. Can't he just spit it out and get it over with? Sighing, I glance over, hating the indignant look I know is probably on my face.

"Dude…" he whispers. "That…that's *him?*"

I can still remember the day I told him my ugly truth—the one about how Leonard came home drunker than ever and shot my mother. I left out the part about how he was just firing aimlessly at the horizon like he was angry that we were running away scared as he screamed at us in his stupor. Maybe he really didn't mean to actually shoot one of us, but I didn't figure at the time he deserved any grace, considering the end result. He still doesn't, if you ask me.

So, it's no surprise that Wolf asks his next question, "Why?"

"It's just for a little while until he can afford his own place and then get out of my life forever."

I can see from the look on his face that he's thinking the same thing I did. Just give the guy some money to be gone, but the sadist in me wants him to work for it. I want him to feel some of the humility that I did.

Glancing at the doorway, my gaze connects with the man in question. What the hell do I care if he heard? It's nothing different from what I told him when he first showed up on my doorstep. The sickening sensation of guilt heating my face shouldn't exist.

"Here," he says, moving past Wolf. "I can see what the problem is. Looks like someone used PVC pipe for your water valve. It's cracked, so that handle never stood a chance either way. I can follow it through and put a brass valve on. I'll call off work and pop over to the hardware store. They should have everything we need."

I'm going to find and throttle that company of idiots we took a chance on who did the renovation work up here when I moved in. How can a former drunk and convict know more about plumbing than they did? And I fucking paid them. Shifting over on my knees, I ignore his wisdom and continue soaking the water up with the towels and my freaking pant legs.

"Oh, my gosh! What happened here?"

Aaron. No. Oh, God. No.

"Hey." I scramble to my feet. "Um, plumbing problem."

"Oh, my gosh. Look at you," he chuckles, bracing my hips gingerly. "You're soaked."

I love that it's second nature that he leans in and gives me a kiss. I love that it's second nature that I look forward to it each time we say hello and accept. I *don't* love that when I draw back, Leonard is taking in the scene. There's a flicker of surprise on his face that I answer with a molten hot warning, daring him to spout off his old pleasantries that filled my teen years.

"Do you want me to come back after he's finished? Otherwise, I don't mind waiting. I could go pick us up some dinner and bring it here," Aaron offers, rubbing the small of my back.

It's now that I take in Leonard's navy work pants and SPC uniform shirt with his name tag on it, *Leo*. Who the hell ever called him Leo?

I don't know what to say, but am grateful that Aaron hasn't made the connection that Wolf did. Clearly, he thinks Leonard is a service worker. The out for a white lie brings me more relief than it should.

Leonard clears his throat, making me cringe. He doesn't need to fucking speak right now. I can only imagine what will come out of his mouth; ugly shades of his personality from the past likely to rear their heads finally.

"Sir, I should have you fixed up in an hour or two if you want to go get yourself some dinner. No sense ruining your plans over this. Leave it to the professional." He smiles.

Did he seriously just play along… for my sake? Who the fuck is he?

"We were just going to go drive around and look at Christmas lights," Aaron informs him, looking so giddy over it that it eases some of my horror at the sight of him unknowingly engaging my father.

"Oh, that's nice. They've got a good bit up over on Chatham Avenue," he offers.

I'm going to be sick. The panic bubble in my throat is damn near choking me, hearing the friendly chit-chat and watching the way Wolf looks like he's waiting for my head to spin around.

Grabbing Aaron's biceps, I tug him to follow me out into the living room. "I'll…be back later," I call over my shoulder to my 'plumber.'

Behind Aaron, Wolf signs to me emphatically, nodding toward the bathroom. *Should I stay?*

Giving a stern shake of my head before Aaron notices, I hope he gets the hint that I don't need or want him to babysit my convict father. Frowning warily, he nods and says goodbye to Aaron before making his way back downstairs. I'm sure I'll hear more about keeping this from him later. Fantastic.

Running my hands up and down Aaron's arms, I let out a breath, taking in the joy that radiates off him these days. "Just give me a second to get changed. Okay?"

"I think that's a good idea." He chuckles, plucking my soaked sweatshirt away from my stomach. "You're sure you don't need to stay while the plumber's here? I don't mind staying in. Lord knows you've had to drive home from my place enough times."

Ugh. I freaking lied my teeth off to every guy I met before him. Why should this be so difficult? I could just tell him, but hopefully Leonard will be gone soon and there will never be a reason to mention him again. *Soon* will require actually speaking to him to see how close he is to his housing search, but I don't care. I'm not going to chance ruining anything with Aaron by housing someone of questionable nature any longer than I have to. He sees me as his boyfriend. I'm not going back to being seen as a kid with trauma and triggers again that he needs to fix. And maybe a part of me is just…embarrassed. I had enough humility back then; I don't need another dose of it.

"No. It's a mess." Just as I say it, I spot Leonard's uniform stack. Luckily, he moved it to the bottom shelf of the end table by the couch, so it's less noticeable than before, but it sends my pulse racing. "I should probably come back here tonight, though, and get the bathroom cleaned up when he's done. It leaked into Wolf's stall downstairs and he's not too happy about it."

"Oh, crap."

"Yeah," I concur, grabbing his hand and leading him to my room with me past Leonard's campsite area, hoping he doesn't notice. "So, I'll need to go check downstairs too to see if there's any damage I can contain later."

"We don't have to go out. We can do it another night. I could help you with whatever you need to do."

In the privacy of my room, it feels odd to disrobe in front of another man while Leonard is nearby, but I tear my sweatshirt off as a distraction attempt. Running my hand down my chest, I smirk. "You think either of us would get any work done if you were here?"

His gaze follows my hand as I unbutton the fly of my jeans. When he looks back up, his cheeks are pink, and his eyes are filled with the longing I feel. Laughing, he shakes his head. "Fair enough."

There's nothing fair about what I just did. It's completely self-serving because if he knew who the man in my bathroom was, I couldn't stand the possibility of him seeing me as *less*.

CHAPTER 28

Aaron

Sometimes it feels like my past belonged to someone else or was a story written in a book of fiction rather than a reality I lived. Nights like last night and tonight with Easton are to blame for that surreal feeling.

Wiping the smile off my face as Mariah Carey's *'All I Want For Christmas Is You'* plays on the radio of the Suburban, I shake my head at myself. The past creeps in on the happiest moments to remind us that even fairy tales start out bleak. Easton is proof enough of that.

"You're not enjoying this, are you?" I had asked him as we drove around looking at Christmas light displays. "Don't tell me you don't like Christmas lights. Oh, my gosh. Wait. You don't. Do you? I didn't see any up at your apartment or your tattoo stall."

It's true. Shannon has the reception desk decked out with garland and lights and every one of the artists has some kind of decoration in their work areas. Easton's was its usual blank, sterile setting when I was looking for him in the shop earlier.

Scoffing, he shrugged and lifted a shoulder lazily. "We never put up lights when I was growing up." Squinting, he gazed out the window at a ten-foot inflatable snowman in someone's yard like it was a riddle he was trying to decipher. "My mom had one of those tiny little trees she put on our coffee table for a while," he added casually.

The *'for a while'* part made me think something bad happened to the tree, so I didn't ask. He didn't look sad exactly, just indifferent. I think the indifference broke my heart the most.

"I'm sorry. We can go back. I know you've got that mess to deal with and I'm keeping you from it."

"No. It's fine. I told you," he assured me, reaching over and squeezing my hand.

"Easton, you've barely looked at the lights the entire time. It's okay. I can accept when I have a bad idea," I digressed.

"It's because I'm too busy watching you looking at the lights."

I got so lost drinking in the adoring look on his face that I ran over a curb. Nothing says you're careful with the vehicle someone lent you like running over a curb.

"Like a deranged, drunk-driving Christmas elf," he murmured playfully as I righted the vehicle.

His comparison wasn't far off. I love Christmas. And him. God, I am *so* in love with him.

Pulling into my driveway, I sigh at the sight of the cottage. It's been weeks since I slept here alone. I'm a big boy. I can sleep alone. I've done it countless times in the past two years, but my addiction to my boyfriend is strong.

The wind whips a chilly gust that blows my coat open as I unlock the door, giving me goosebumps. The house is warm but quiet and less inviting, knowing it won't be filled with Easton's smooth voice tonight. It's definitely less empty since his surprise furnishing of it, but perhaps it's my sentimentality that has me thinking the empty space between the TV console and the front windows would be perfect for a Christmas tree. I wonder if he ever got to experience picking out his own and chopping it down. I used to just put up a fancy artificial one in Seattle that was pre-lit, but when I was a kid, the entire family would go pick one out and my father would cut it down. If Easton thought it was cute watching me *ooh* and *ahh* over Christmas lights, I'm sure he'd love my excitement over picking out a tree together.

I told my parents last week that I'd met someone. I wonder if Easton could handle picking out trees together with them as a way to meet them for the first time? Mom is certainly anxious to meet him and looked like she's finally given up on worrying about me.

Would meeting them make him more aware of not having his own family? I want to give him everything he doesn't have, but I should try to silence some of my protective instincts. He has Wolf and his friends. They're their own kind of family, in a way. Maybe I'm just excited at the thought of him meeting mine to show him even more how important he is to me.

I get my coat hung up and shoes kicked off, trying to decide how to spend my evening alone. Hot chocolate sounds like a good way to celebrate my Christmas elf spirit, as Easton would say. Heading into the kitchen, I pull a *Swiss Miss* packet out of the box and dump it in a coffee mug, pouring the milk over the top of the powder. While it microwaves, I lean against the counter and smile at the puzzle of a lakeside scene we put together the other day. It reminds me of the day he took me to his lake spot and the moment I hoped for a kiss before he swam away.

I got my kiss eventually, but it's now a memory I'll forever associate with how fragile love can be and how wary a heart can be of it. I know our love is new, but it feels hard-earned, and I'm proud of that. It means nothing should be able to come between us since we've done the hard part already.

The microwave beeps, alerting me my treat is ready. Just as I reach to fetch it, a knock at the door startles me. I never get visitors other than George or Easton, and George certainly never visits past dinner time since he always likes to be home with his family.

Heading toward my front door, my heart does a little skip, wondering if Easton changed his mind. He usually just walks in, but I locked it since I was home for the night and wasn't expecting him. So much for suffering the night without him. I'm not disappointed in the least that he chose me over cleaning up his plumbing mess.

"Well, hello. Oh…" My sexy greeting is cut off when I realize the man at the door is definitely not Easton.

He's an inch or two taller, with wider shoulders under a black peacoat and a black stocking cap on his head that matches his midnight beard. His skin is tan and the brown eyes behind a pair of horn-rimmed glasses are the same chocolate brown as…

"Hello," he says, the sound of his voice jarring the memories inside me loose. Taking a step closer, he pulls his glasses off and flashes a sheepish smile. "It's me, babe. I promise. I'm real."

The blast of cold air that hits me runs a chill down my spine as though someone walked over my grave. My heart wallops against my ribcage as my jaw flaps uselessly without a sound.

"Ja-Ja-Jason?"

"It's good to see you," he whispers, inching toward the threshold.

Am I dreaming? I have to be dreaming. Or I'm being haunted. He looks so real. Completely different with a beard and glasses and tanned, but *real!* And he's coming toward me. He can't be real. I saw remains, remains with his wedding ring on his finger. I buried him. I picked out his casket. I…I…

Backing up, my legs feel like broken toothpicks, wobbling beneath me as he follows, stepping inside and closing the door behind him. Oh, God. He *is* real. There's a mass, an entire living, breathing body in front of me, *in* my house. He's real, whoever or whatever he is. He's not a ghost or a hallucination.

"Jason?" I squawk, unable to conjure any other sensible question.

"Yeah, babe. It's me."

That voice. I know that voice. I remember that voice.

My legs buckle. My knees slam onto the hardwood floor and I catch myself with my palms. The room is spinning. Maybe I'm spinning. I can't seem to get enough air into my lungs. Have I lost my mind?

CHAPTER 29

Aaron

"It's okay, babe. Come on, *Aar*. Breathe. I'm fine. I'm here. Everything's going to be fine."

Gasping, I'm afraid to open my eyes as the familiar voice repeats those words over and over. The body crouched down on the floor next to me, the heavy arm wrapped around my shoulders…it *is* him. He even smells like him.

Tears spill down my face. It feels like my heart is breaking all over again. It's grateful that he didn't experience the agony I imagined so many times that he did. It's sorry for all the pain I went through grieving for him. But it's also confused, so fucking confused.

Raising my head, I summon the courage to open my eyes to this apparition. My God, it *is* him. This is really happening.

"But you…you're…you were… They said you…" I don't even know what to say to convince him that he shouldn't exist. "I *saw your car!* It was…it was destroyed."

"I know. I know," he soothes, pulling me tighter to him and rocking me. It's constricting. I already can barely breathe. This only makes me feel like I'm further suffocating. "I'll tell you everything. I promise."

Rising, he hooks his hand underneath my elbow. It's Jason, or at least some part of my brain is registering that it's Jason, but each touch feels like I'm being mauled by a stranger. I stare up at him stupidly, trembling like I'm looking at a ghost. For all intents and purposes, he should be.

"Come on. Get off the floor. Let's go sit down and I'll tell you everything."

It's like walking in a dream, being hyperaware of the smallest things. The floor creaks under his weight, telling me he does, in fact, have mass. I can hear the scrape of his shoes against the boards. The couch cushion depresses as he sits on it and pats for me to take the place next to him. He looks so foreign sitting here; like a puzzle piece that got thrown into the wrong box. As I sit down and take in his new look, a thick but trimmed beard covering his once impeccably shaved jaw, the bizarre dream is starting to feel like a nightmare. There's only one man I've stared at sitting across from me on this couch, and his name is Easton, the man I'm in love with. It's not his playful, smiling face staring back at me. It's not his wavy brown hair and smooth face. It's a past I worked hard to get over and it's… back. My husband is back. I should be crying with joy.

"What…what happened? *How?* I…"

Sighing, he sets a black gym bag down on the floor I hadn't even registered he was carrying and unbuttons his coat. Each move of his hands is more surreal than the last. Sitting back, he leans his elbow over the back of the couch like it's perfectly natural for him to be lounging in my living room and… *not dead!*

Reaching out, he grabs my hand off my lap and holds it in his, brushing his thumb over the top of my knuckles. It's a hand I tried to remember holding so many times after I thought he died. Right now, it sets off an unusual panic in me as though it's a bear trap and I'll lose fingers or exchange the death I thought he had with my own.

"Do you remember that addition I had put on the clinic a few years ago?"

"Yes."

Why is he talking about his clinic? He should be talking about how he didn't die. I *have to be* dreaming.

"Remember all those problems I had with the contractors screwing me over, changing the estimate and the labor hours repeatedly?"

"Yeah, but…what does that have to do with anything?"

"They were criminals. I didn't tell you, but they kept threatening me, saying I owed them more money, and each time I refused to pay, they added interest."

What does this have to do with him being killed in a car accident? A car accident that didn't happen. Or did it? My head feels like it's going to explode. Easing my hand back, I rub my temples.

"I don't understand. You never said anything. Did you tell your lawyer?"

"No, Aar, you don't." He frowns, shifting. It's the annoyed tone I remember he always used when I couldn't understand something because he wasn't telling me all the details. "They were organized crime. Not the kind of people you can solve disputes with by getting a lawyer."

Like the mafia? Is he telling me the mafia was after him?

Holding up my hands, I try to piece together why being on the wrong side of an organized crime faction would make someone disappear for almost two years and then show up with a beard and glasses.

"Are you in the witness protection program or something?"

My mouth gapes open, watching him laugh. It's a loud, amused sound that has no business in this conversation. "Oh, my God. You still watch one too many movies. No," he adds, leveling me with a coy look. "I'm smarter than that. I played them at their own game. I found out that they were going to come after me."

"Come after you? Like…murder you?"

He traces his fingertip over my shoulder and grimaces. "I'm sorry. I didn't know what to do. I went to the police, but they wanted to put a wire on me and have me meet with them, but I wasn't going to risk losing you if it all went south or have our names all over the news."

I wait for more, but his very real-looking mouth doesn't move again. That's it?

I blink stupidly, trying to wrap my head around the information, but the fingertip tracing anxious circles on my shoulder is distracting; like a spider crawling on me—a dead spider.

"So…so what? You…pretended that you died?" Instantly, a pang of guilt hits me at how accusatory the question comes out. "Or did you really get hurt? Your car…I saw it. It was completely crushed."

Scoffing, he rolls his eyes and stands. "Aaron, enough about the car, okay? I'm a doctor. I know how to get medical records."

I blink, unbelieving, as he stuffs his hands in the pockets of his black slacks and starts to leisurely pace around the room. He… planned to die. Or… planned to *fake* die. Am I really hearing this?

"I had to lie low for a while and wait until you got out of town. I figured you would," he says, glancing over his shoulder at me with a pleased gleam in his eyes. "And you did. Just like I hoped."

Seeing any kind of joy on his face after I was so miserable for so long has me suddenly frustrated. He planned this entire thing down to how he thought I would move on with my life in his absence? It's all just too much.

"You never said a thing to me. You could have told me something."

Sighing, he swoops in, taking a knee in front of me. I flinch when he cups my face, but blame it on the quick movement. Why would someone flinch when their husband touches them?

"Babe, I couldn't. They were watching the house. It wouldn't have been safe for either of us if I'd tried to contact you."

I remember all the nights spent feeling so numb it seemed like I'd been electrocuted; sickening nausea, being unable to eat, and my eyes so puffy I physically couldn't cry anymore. What does he mean he couldn't have ended that misery? He could have sent me a postcard or an anonymous phone call.

"I went to your funeral, Jason! I..." My voice cracks. Liquid heat fills my eyes as I grip two handfuls of his lapels, trying to grasp onto some sense of relief from him not suffering what I thought he had. "I thought you died," I warble, unable to hold my head up any longer.

His arms wrap around me again, pulling me against his chest as I fall apart, lost in a sea of gratitude, confusion, self-pity, and an odd sense of betrayal. I don't know which feeling to cling to. Making soothing sounds, he rubs my back. It's the type of comfort I wanted from him *before* he died and shortly after. Right now, it feels like being held by someone on a blind date whose face I haven't seen yet.

Drawing back, his hands clamp onto my shoulders and give me a gentle shake. "Hey. It's okay. I'm here now. I told you; everything will be fine now. We're safe."

Safe?

It's one more word out of his mouth that doesn't make sense. Each week since he'd '*died*' became a new week of trepidation over my future existence. The unexplained bills. Trying to find out how and where I would live. I haven't felt safe in a long time. At least, not until... Easton.

Oh, God. Easton...

Can I not see him anymore? Should I even be thinking about that? I'm *still* married. I'm a *married man... again.*

A new wave of nausea crashes into me. And then another for feeling nauseous over being married. Am I a horrible person?

Staggering to my feet, I sidle out from between the coffee table and couch. The need for air and space seems tantamount.

"I had to sell the house," I blurt, nonsensically. He's done all the talking so far and likely has no clue about all the things that have happened since he...left. "There were bills. All kinds of bills. Things I had no clue about," I explain, trying to sound more informative than accusatory. "You didn't leave any notes. I even had to sell the cars. That's why I moved back here, but creditors still keep calling. Your mom said..." I stop in my tracks, remembering all the unpleasant calls from Grace. It's one ray of light in this discovery—that Jason is finally here to explain everything to her. "Wait. Does your mother know?"

"My mother?" he parrots, rising from the floor. "Do you think my mother would approve of a scandal like that?"

I'm not sure if he's referring to these criminals who tried to blackmail him or him faking his own death, but either way, he's right. Grace Reider holds her public image highly, making me feel foolish for even asking.

I nod, dumbly trying to take an odd sense of pride in the fact I'm the only one he's appeared to have trusted with the knowledge, even if the information is coming well overdue. I honestly didn't know he held me with more regard than her in the trust department, sometimes feeling like a third wheel in his relationship with his mother.

I find him in front of me suddenly and realize I've just been standing here, staring at the floor, and biting my thumbnail. "Come on," he soothes, turning me toward my room. "Don't worry about any of this anymore. I have a plan, but for now, let's just go to bed. It's been a long day. We can talk more tomorrow."

As my feet move obligatorily from years of following his lead, I stare at my bed through the doorway in horror. The sheets are still rumpled from Easton and me last night. I slept next to Jason for eight years, but the thought of lying next to the man I married right now makes my throat constrict. It feels like it would be a desecration of one of the places I relate to the greatest joy of my life. It's heartbreaking and treacherous all at once. My legs stop moving and he bumps into me.

"I…I can't."

"You're tired. I can see it in your face," he soothes, rubbing the back of my neck over my stiff muscles. "I haven't had much sleep myself lately. Why don't we just crawl into bed and hold each other? Remember how we used to do that?" He smiles, his voice going soft.

I do remember… in the beginning. Years ago. Shortly after we moved to Seattle, though, it was all work, work, work. He'd often come home late and silently move my arm or hand out of the way if I'd drape it over him like it was disturbing his pose or comfort. Even after sex… he wasn't much for holding each other… not the way Easton does. It always made me feel pathetically needy and yet left a chasm of disconnect between us.

"Yeah," I laugh breathlessly and try to smile. "But…I'd rather not."

"What?" He laughs like I'm joking.

Glancing at the bed and then back at him, I try not to squirm under his gaze. "I…it…it's just a little strange. It's a lot to process."

His eyes study me for what feels like an eternity. Can he see through to my soul? Hear the moans I've let out in that bed? The laughter with another man?

I wanted to be what he wanted for so long, and yet it feels like if I walk into that room with him, my life will never be as wonderful as it has been of late. Maybe that makes me a terrible husband. Maybe I was never a good one to begin with.

Straightening, he nods, looking resigned. Stroking my cheek, his smile seems forced, but he leans in and pecks me on the lips. It's a kiss, causing a little flicker inside me because it's a kiss, but it's just skin-to-skin. It's an action with no reaction, leaving me further floundering about why I'm not overjoyed that he's returned.

"All right. Yeah. I'll give you some time. We'll talk soon. Okay?"

He turns back toward the couch and picks up his gym bag. The amount of relief coursing through me that he appears to be leaving is shameful.

"Where are you staying?" I ask. It's such an odd question to voice. "Do you…have somewhere to stay?"

Buttoning his coat, he flashes me a smile and a wink, motioning with his head to the front exterior wall. "Nearby."

What does '*nearby*' mean? How long has he been here, I wonder? And still… why *now,* after almost two years? I have so many questions that I no longer feel guilty for asking him not to stay. I do need to process. With any luck, I'll wake up tomorrow in Easton's arms and this will all have been a horrible nightmare… even if that makes me a horrible husband.

CHAPTER 30
Easton

The sight of your convict father in nothing but an MSP sweatshirt, knee socks, and his boxers, watching your television like he owns your living room is a sore comparison to the vision of Aaron's elated face amid the glow of Christmas lights. Hanging my keys up on the wall inside the door to my apartment, I avoid his gaze by glancing across the room to the open door of the spare bathroom. I can tell from here that he followed through on his promise to make it right again. He clearly replaced both faucet handles with new ones when only one was necessary. I want to roll my eyes. Going above and beyond will get him nowhere with me.

"It's all cleaned up. New pipe's on, too. You shouldn't have that problem again."

Just to be a dick, I walk in and inspect the bathroom, resenting the *Old Spice* toiletries I see littering the sink counter. They're aligned tidily, but I don't want to see or smell Old Spice because I associate it with *him*. The water stain above the baseboard appears to be fading, drying enough that I might not have to worry about a mold problem. I'll go shopping tomorrow to buy new ceiling panels to replace the stained ones I took down from above Wolf's station, however, just to keep things copacetic with my business partner.

"You're not going to get fired for not showing up to work?" I challenge, heading past the couch potato toward the kitchen area.

"No. I explained what happened, and they understood. The parole officer won't have a problem with it either if he finds out. I get some paid time off, so it's not a problem."

Like he's doing me a fucking favor. He's the one who caused the damn leak to begin with. Grabbing a beer out of the fridge, I stare at it in my hand for a second. I've not seen him touch a drop since he arrived. It's probably not wise to even keep alcohol in here with him around to be tempted by it.

Turning around, I watch him bite into a piece of fried chicken straight from a carryout container, flecks of crumbs tumbling down his chest. An episode of *Swamp People* is blaring on my big screen. He's living his best life while I gave up an evening with Aaron to clean up the rest of the mess he caused downstairs.

"You like this show?" he asks, motioning to the TV with his chicken leg. "They're pretty funny."

Stomping over to my recliner, I pop the lid off my beer, no longer giving a fuck about his self-control. If he falls off the wagon, maybe it'll cure me of the lapse in judgment I had by taking pity on him. Swiping up the remote off the end table, I drop into my chair and bring up the menu. Kickboxing—nice. Something violent to express my current mood.

"You finding a place anytime soon?" There. I got to the point of why I chose *Swamp People* over spooning Aaron tonight. Short but sweet.

I can feel him eye me warily. In my peripheral, he drops his chicken leg and sets his Styrofoam container down, swiping up a napkin to clean his hands.

"There's a complex not too far from the factory," he explains in that annoying slow drawl of his. "I heard they're open to admitting parolees, so I got a renter's application from them. I just need another paycheck or two if they accept me."

"Good." I nod, pretending I'm immersed in the fight.

"How was your evening with…your *friend*?" The way he hesitates to say '*friend*' is both telling and grates on my nerves. To top it off, he adds, "I hope I didn't ruin any plans you had."

Should I tell him I can't bring Aaron back here because I don't want him subjected to my homophobic father? Does that constitute ruining plans?

"It was fine," I grumble. "I prefer to stay at his place for now," I add, hoping he'll get the hint. "I don't want him over here until you're gone."

Taking a long draw from my beer, I wait for his reaction. He wants to be nosy? He wants to try to get to know me? Let him choke on that Pride flag and try to hide his true colors.

"He seems like a nice guy. You been together long?"

It's said so passively, I don't know what to think. Where are the sneers? The derision? How is this the same man that called me a *sissy* and *fag* whenever he'd catch me ogling men in my mother's magazines?

"A few months." The words flop out of my mouth with no defense in them, my nerves trembling.

"That's good. I hope he treats you well."

It's too much. I don't know how to receive it. Prison was supposed to be a hell he rotted in, not a place where he turned a leaf and shed his bigotry and alcoholism. They call it reform for a reason, but I can't wrap my head around the change from what I remember of the past.

Tossing the remote on the end table, I push out of the recliner.

"Better than anyone I've ever known," I spout off in the only way I ever remember talking to him and head toward my room.

I tell myself I lock my bedroom door behind me because he's a criminal who killed my mother. It has nothing to do with the conflicted emotions bubbling inside me, threatening to crack the armor I built that helped me hate him for the last decade. Of course, I fucking hate him. I don't care if he found his own boyfriend in prison or whatever the hell it was that has him imparting well wishes to his queer son. Except, I'm really tired of hating. I never realized how exhausting it is. I thought I hated Aaron once for making me think he was the answer to my prayers and then running off to give those prayers to another man. I was wrong about him, but I can't be wrong about Leonard. Still, I can't wait for him to be gone. I don't want hate in my heart anymore now that I found something better to live there.

Shedding my clothes, I step under my shower and focus on better things, happy things. Only one thing, if I'm being honest. One person. Watching the suds circling the drain, I smile at how freely Aaron offered his help to clean up the mess tonight. It doesn't matter whether we're just putting a puzzle together or cleaning up shower water; he seems to be content doing anything as long as it's with me. I certainly owe him one for the gesture and abandoning him tonight. My little Christmas elf.

Ha. I know just how to knock his socks off tomorrow. I have to go to the hardware store anyway to buy more ceiling panels. Shaking my head, I laugh. Someone's going shopping for Christmas lights for the first time in their life tomorrow.

CHAPTER 31

Aaron

Killing the engine of the Suburban outside the cottage, the frazzled mood that accompanied me to work today amps up another level at the sight of the black *Lexus* in my driveway. Florida plates—the car Jason drove away last night when I locked up for the second time.

Is it a rental? If so, how is he able to rent a car without an identity when I can't even get a credit card at the moment?

Glancing around the yard, I don't see a sign of him. It's too frigid and windy to take a stroll in the surrounding woods. An eerie feeling prickles the back of my neck, searching for a sight of him. It adds to the paranoia from the questions that ran through my head all day. How did he even know where to find me?

Fingers going numb, cheeks frozen, I start for the door, deciding that he'll resurface like he did last night. He'd better and soon. Easton's supposed to be coming over. I don't want Jason here when I have to try to explain to him that my husband is no longer dead.

God, I might vomit. How am I going to do this? I don't want to lose him, but it feels like the end of... the beginning.

His playful text messages today left me feeling like a traitor each time I mustered some kind of witty reply. I refuse to tell him something like this over the phone or via text. I'd like to refuse to tell him at all, but how can I? This is what I get for cursing my previous reality before we reconnected. What is he going to think?

Unlocking the door, the smell of herbs assaults my senses. I gape at the movement in my kitchen. Sleeves rolled up to the elbows and a dish towel slung over his shoulder, Jason looks well at home in front of a boiling pot on my stove and a frying pan of grilling meat, scrolling through a phone. He has a phone? Why didn't he leave me his number?

"Hey, there he is!" he calls.

It's such a jarring welcome, as though it's perfectly natural for him to be in my kitchen… and *alive* like nothing has changed. "What are…how did you get in?" I hedge, trying to keep the accusatory tone out of my voice as I tear out of my coat. "Was George here?"

Stirring the steaming pot in front of him, he flashes me a smirk. "I've learned a few things living off the radar."

If that was meant to dissipate my wariness, it did nothing of the kind. Can he pick locks now? Is that what he's been doing for the last two years?

Seeing my last box of pasta open and empty on the counter touches yet another nerve. I was going to cook Easton dinner. Before or after I unloaded my terrible surprise on him, I don't know—I hadn't decided yet which would be best. He texted earlier to inform me he's spoiling me yet again by bringing dinner over, but still. That was *my* pasta. Mine and Easton's. I've been budgeting well, coming up with a payment plan for the remainder of the debt I was able to consolidate into one payment. That includes saving up as much as I can to buy a used vehicle so I can return Easton's before the worst of winter gets here. Every dollar counts, and if Jason is still able to obtain that expensive cologne he always wore, he doesn't need to be using my pasta. I'm glad I asked him to leave last night. The number of peculiar details that jumped out at me today while at work, like remembering that hit of his cologne I got last night, put things into perspective. Something isn't adding up.

"Jason, you can't…I don't think it's a good idea for you to just turn up like this," I begin, inching my way into the kitchen. "I mean, if you're not going to go to the police and you say you have all these people after you…Well, anyone could see you. My family thinks you're dead. This is one of George's rentals. What if he'd been here and seen you? I…I don't even know how to explain to him yet. And if you're worried about people finding you, won't my family be in danger if they find out you're alive?"

"Here. Sit down," he says, completely unfazed, pulling out one of the kitchen chairs. I comply, simply because I'm so baffled that sitting seems like a good idea. He heard me, right?

Turning back from the stove, he wields one of my wooden kitchen spoons, ladled with a helping of the sauce he's cooking. Holding it out, he cups his other hand underneath it and brings it toward my mouth. "Try this."

Dumbly, I part my lips when the spoon gets so close to my mouth that I can't avoid it. My face, however, must say *what-the-actual-fuck* though, because he sighs as I take a sip of the exotic-tasting red liquid.

"I told you. I have a plan." Turning back to his cooking, he carries on like some master chef. "I started a practice in São Paulo."

"*São Paulo?*"

That sounds foreign. Why does that sound foreign? And how could he start a practice when I have to count how much money I have to afford pasta?

"Brazil," he informs me cheerfully.

He'd talked about how he did a few mission trips there early in his career when we first met, charming me with his knowledge of the Portuguese language and culture. It was one of the things that made me think he was so worldly and far beyond my station.

I'm so lost in connecting dots that I barely catch his excited chatter. "We can start over there. Have a new life. You can change your name."

"*Change* my name?"

"I changed mine." He turns around, grinning at me. "I got you a new identity too when I did, and…" Holding up a hand, his frenetic movements are dizzying as he starts out of the room. "Wait here a second. I have a surprise."

I don't want a surprise, pleads some sensible voice in my head that's seen millions of horror movies. I watch him scurry to the sideboard by the door and rifle through that black gym bag he brought with him last night. Is he living out of there?

Hurrying back, he's carrying what looks like a certificate paper in his hands. Beaming proudly, he hands it to me. I can't make heads or tails of the foreign print on it. From what I can tell, though, it's an agreement between two men. I have no idea why he's showing this to me.

"What is this?"

"It's our marriage license for our new lives."

I read the names again. *Tomás* and *Afonso*. Which one am I supposed to be, I vaguely wonder. It's dated eight months ago. *Eight months.* Suddenly, his excitement over his plan and his ease in explaining it, as though it's already in motion, activates a light bulb in my brain. He has a practice there, he said. *'Our new lives.'* He… wants me to move there with him?

The panic that hasn't hit me in months comes in full force like a gale wind. My lips go numb, and my pulse erratic.

"But…my family."

"They can come visit us. I have a beautiful house there. You're going to love it." Squeezing my shoulder, he drops a rough kiss on my forehead and slips the paper from my fingers. "I told you, everything is going to be fine," he calls, returning the document to that now eerie-looking bag that feels like Dora's backpack if Dora the Explorer were someone on the run in a *Lifetime Movie Network* film.

"Honestly," he chuckles, holding his hands out to the sides, "this might have been the best thing that ever happened to us."

How? I want to screech, but my voice comes out in barely a whisper. "But…m-my job." I realize he probably has no clue about the new life I've built while he was out foraging for one for the both of us, thinking he was solving our problems. I also realize what a pleaser I was, the way I bowed to whatever he wanted. It explains why that old suffocating feeling is back. "I'm back at Hampton Hills," I continue, grasping for straws while still locked in that submissive role I never acknowledged I held in our relationship. "I took over Dr. Norton's old position."

Snorting, he shakes the skillet, flipping the meat he has cooking in it. The potent overuse of herbs is starting to turn my stomach.

"I know. I did an internet search. Don't worry. You won't ever have to work at a place like that again. You'll love the clinic. You can head the speech pathology program there. I've already performed quite a few vocal repair surgeries."

His disdain for the place we met is nothing new, but hearing his plans for me makes me feel like livestock that has no say in my fate rather than a considerate action to ease my employment concerns. It's too reticent of all the grand promises he made that were the allure of going to Seattle with him.

When I chose to stay on at Seattle Mercy after finishing my fellowship there instead of joining him at his clinic, it was a point of contention I felt represented a power struggle to him. I thought keeping our work separate would be better for our marriage. At the time, he said he agreed, but I can see my wishes went unheard in the end.

The zeal pouring off him as he anticipates my reaction has my heart in my throat. I can see his excitement over this extension of our love story that he's concocted in his mind, but mine doesn't share the vision. There's already a permanently rooted vision there that looks nothing like him.

"And my…" The word *boyfriend* wants to burst out like a penalty flag to halt his escalating fantasy, but I know I'm technically not allowed to have one of those if I'm still married, so I settle for, "I have friends here."

His shoulders go slack as he blinks at me. "Aaron, it's not like I have many choices," he finally lets out. "I know you probably need some time to process this, but we'll be happy there. I know it."

Could I be happy there with him? Could I be happy with him *anywhere*? I made a promise, *'until death do us part.'* The problem is that I thought the death part came and went, leaving me to put away my hopes for the life I had before in the past.

"Or…don't you want me anymore?" he ventures quietly.

My gaze snaps to his. I must have been sitting here in my own thoughts for too long. How do I answer that question?

Rising from my chair, I go to the kitchen window that overlooks the backyard, hoping a reply will come to me. Do I want the man he was before? No… not exactly. Do I want the man he is now? I don't even know who he is now. I feel like I should want some version of him, but obligation and want are two different things. I wait too long to answer.

"Is there someone else?"

My face burns with shame, and then it burns some more because I'm not ashamed of what I have with Easton. "It…it's new."

From the corner of my eye, I watch his expression turn stony. He sets the cooking spoon down and nods, but more to himself. Sucking in a breath, he stuffs his hands in his pockets and faces me with a tight smile. "I forgive you."

My head might have actually reared back. What is there to forgive? He let me think he was dead.

"Are you in love with him?"

It feels like I've been unfaithful, standing in the line of his narrowed gaze. Technically, I have, but given the circumstances, I'd like to think my actions are forgivable. Maybe it's just the eerie calm about him that has me reluctant to share any details.

"I told you. It's…new.

Stepping forward, slowly, his eyes never leave my face. He doesn't stop until his chest brushes against my shoulder. I want to move, but moving seems like it would give off an indication of guilt.

"Are you fucking him?" His words come out disturbingly low, almost like the thought of it turns him on.

My windpipe seems to have constricted two sizes. I don't like the filthy connotation affixed to his query, nor the derision. Stepping away, I throw my hands up. "I thought you were dead! It's been almost two years."

"That's a long time to wait," he says dryly.

I never get mad. Ever. Right now, though, I hate that I'm being put on trial. I never fully grasped what a passive-aggressive bully he was, but it's glaringly obvious at the moment.

Some bold version of my voice speaks up, one that was grown in love and happiness. "And it's a long time to think your husband's dead."

Even as I say it, though, my breath feels caught in my throat, anticipating repercussions. His shoulders rock on a bitter puff of laughter, though, and he looks down, shaking his head in amusement.

I never knew how to argue, but it feels like I have the upper hand, so I continue with false confidence and frustration. "He's supposed to be coming over here, so I think you should leave. I need to talk to him."

"About us?"

I have so many mixed feelings about hearing *us* as an *us*. What even are we now? What are Easton and I?

"Well, I at least need to tell him you're alive."

I don't know if I'm even *allowed* to do that. If Jason hasn't told his mother and has kept this big secret from me, it seems like no one should know, but I can't *not* tell Easton. Yet, he nods and fetches his coat from where it's slung over one of the chairs. I watch with bated breath, wondering what his sudden compliance means, but then I hear the front door creak open.

"I hope you're still in the Christmas spirit because—"

Easton doesn't finish his sentence, but my heart breaks seeing the boxes of Christmas lights under his arm and bags of takeout slung over his other. Could he be any sweeter? And now I have to deliver hell to him.

"Hi," I call, but barely any sound comes out. It's too bizarre having him and Jason in the same room—my past and my present.

Jason steps in front of me, blocking my view, and leans in, murmuring, "On second thought, maybe it's better you don't tell him."

I don't understand why there's a smirk on his face when he draws back. What's amusing about this? Does he see something in Easton he finds comical, or is it the situation? It's like being suspended in time, watching him walk to fetch his bag mere feet away from Easton.

"It looks like your company's here," he calls back cheerfully to me. "I've got to get going, anyway. It was nice to see you again. We can catch up more another time."

Easton looks confused and subdued, almost like he thinks he just burst in on me having company. I can't move. All I see in front of me is an impossible choice—a life I didn't know I was supposed to live and one that was so close I could almost taste it.

CHAPTER 32
Easton

"I've got to get going, anyway. It was nice to see you again. We can catch up more another time."

I shrunk in on myself when I first walked in, wondering if I'd intruded on Aaron having company. He never said anything about being busy when I texted earlier that I was bringing dinner. The way the dark-haired man in the kitchen stood so close to him a moment ago gave me a sick sensation in my stomach. He was too near something that's mine.

There's something oddly familiar about him, but I thought maybe my eyes were playing tricks on me. Until now.

That voice… that smug-ass voice, I'd remember it anywhere.

It can't be.

As he walks toward me and picks up a gym bag off the sideboard, I have a full view of his face. Thick black hair, cold brown eyes—*Reider.* Why the fuck does he look a hell of a lot like Jason Reider with a beard?

Flashing me a wink, he slaps me on the shoulder. "I don't want to interrupt anything."

It's a hard slap, but that's not why the bag of carryout slips from my grip and crashes to the floor. It *is* him. I swear by all that's holy, it's him. The way he quickly moves his foot out of the way, like he's worried about damaging his shoes, if something from the containers leaked, only convinces me more.

"Whoa. Careful there."

Dropping to my knee, I re-stack the containers inside the bag with shaky hands, reminding myself to breathe. It smells like dinner in here already. Were they cooking together? Does he have a twin brother? What in ever-loving hell is going on?

Aaron rushes over, bending down to help me. He takes the two boxes of Christmas lights from underneath my other arm and sets them down on the sideboard without a second glance at my gift for the night.

"This is Easton," he tells the Reider lookalike. "Easton…this is…"

I don't like how he looks uncertain. I don't like how pale his face is.

"Tomás," the man supplies, squeezing my hand more tightly than necessary. "I heard Aaron moved back to town and thought I'd pay him a visit."

Why am I getting an explanation like he knows I should be here, but he shouldn't? Jesus… he even smells like Reider used to. I nod dumbly, my head full of questions hammering at my skull. The article I found on the internet said Reider died. I didn't imagine that. I want to believe Aaron's confirmation of that was true. I want to believe the tears he cried over being conflicted when I made that pass at him at Pulse were real, but my instinct is telling me I've been lied to.

"You two behave yourselves," the man calls and heads out the door.

I watch Aaron slowly lock it behind him and stare after the man through the glass pane for a moment. He lets out a sound of relief, turning toward me. His gaze satellites from mine to the floor in rapid succession. He looks nothing short of sick. Sick and… guilty.

"Was that…" I swallow against the dryness in my throat, not even wanting to say the words. "That looked a lot like–"

"Jason," he blurts.

It's a gut punch I didn't think him capable of delivering. I know he doesn't just mean it *looked like* Jason.

"He showed up here last night. I nearly had a heart attack."

"But he… You said he was dead."

"He was! At least, I thought he was!" He grips two fistfuls of his hair and starts pacing. I've never seen his eyes look so wild. "A coroner came to see me," he rationalizes frantically. "I planned an entire funeral and went. I sent *Thank You* cards to everyone who paid their respects. I have *a death certificate*. I…I still can't believe it."

Shaking his head, he stares at the floor, looking lost. I can hear my heartbeat in my head. It's not a comfort seeing Aaron as shocked as I am, even though it tells me he was unaware that Jason was still alive.

Still alive… How the fuck is he still alive?

Suddenly, that terrified feeling I've had makes sense. I knew things were too good to be true.

Looking up at me slowly, he flounders for words for a second. A more pitiful expression has never been made. "I didn't want to tell you over the phone. I was going to tell you tonight, but when I got home, he was here again. I don't even know how he got in. I didn't give him a key."

Visions of a ghost walking through walls come to mind, hearing how the man appeared here with Aaron unawares. That's freaking ridiculous. I just saw him in the flesh. My brain feels like it's gone for a spin in a blender.

"I don't understand," I mumble, shell-shocked.

"Here. Sit down. I'll tell you everything I know."

I go with him when he tugs my arm toward the couch. My skin crawls knowing Jason was in here last night and again today. Did *he* sit here? Did he touch Aaron on this couch—*our couch?* For the next twenty minutes, I watch his mouth move, unsure if I'm actually absorbing all the things coming out of it. Something about a building project and an organized crime faction screwing Jason over. Interest. Threats to his life. Faking his death. Fleeing to South America, where he's started a whole new life, complete with a new medical practice.

All I see is the distress on the face of the man I've fallen for. This time it's worse than the last time Jason Reider caused him pain. Where are the answers to those questions?

"What about all those bills you said you have because of him? Did he say anything about that?"

Blinking down at where he's wringing his hands, he shakes his head absently. "I... No... I don't know. Just that...because of these people that were trying to con him, I guess. I still feel like I dreamt the entire thing."

What does that have to do with properties that Jason supposedly owned that Aaron didn't know about? I desperately want to ask, but fear I already know he doesn't have the answers and is too frazzled to even consider my suspicions. Are they suspicions or is it just jealousy? Because why would he come back if not to...

"So...he wants to get back together?"

"He got us new identities and wants me to go to Brazil with him to work at the practice he started there." It looks as painful for him to answer as it was for me to ask. Why does it look painful?

"And...you're going?"

"No. I...I don't know."

What... the fuck?

I'm suddenly back in that white room at Hampton Hills with my leg in traction. Helpless. Worthless. Unable to compete. What the hell did I ever do to Jason Reider that he repeatedly comes to take the only thing I've ever wanted?

Popping up off the couch, I can't sit patiently any longer. I wanted answers. Well, I got them.

"I don't want to," Aaron amends, springing up beside me, "but..."

"But *what?*"

"But...he's my husband."

I gape at the man in front of me, the one who just a few days ago told me he loved me in not so many words. The intelligent man whom I've seen blossom over the past few months, crawling back from the guilt and agony of saying goodbye to a broken marriage.

"He *was* your husband. You're a widower."

"I know. I know, but this…changes everything. I…I don't know what to do. I wish he'd just go to the police. I don't understand why he didn't. Or maybe I understand why he didn't *then*, but now—" he rambles. "I'm sorry. I know this all sounds so…"

My patience is gone. I can't hold back my frustration any longer.

"Like an episode of *Dateline?*"

Gripping his hair again, he lets out a delirious laugh. "Maybe."

Is he not hearing the alarm bells that I am? Fucking Aaron—why does he have to be so understanding to everyone about everything? If I have to lose him to another man, fine. I'll freaking deal with it and not lose my shit like last time, but not to *this* man. Anyone but this man.

"Aaron, he faked his death, shows up two years later, and wants you to move to another country with him under an alias. There's no *maybe* about it. I don't trust the guy. Why all of a sudden? Why now?"

"He said it wasn't safe for either of us," he babbles, looking even more lost, like just having the conversation is taking a toll on him.

No shit, it wasn't safe. There's nothing safe about Jason.

"And me? Does he know about me?"

Some of the color returns to his cheeks and he looks away. What the hell is that about?

"He knows I'm seeing someone."

I remember the creepy gleam in Jason's eyes when he said, "I don't want to interrupt anything." It felt like half dare, half threat. What married man would leave his husband alone in a room with someone his husband has been seeing? Nothing about what this fuck-stick is up to makes any sense. All I have to go on is what Aaron is telling me. Maybe I'm asking the wrong questions.

"*Are you*…still seeing someone?" I ask with my heart in my throat.

"I want to," he replies with tears in his eyes, and then he adds an awful word to that sentence, "but…"

Three letters just killed me. Jason's corpse has been traded with mine. He wants to see me, *but*…he won't.

"I have to figure this out first," he whispers.

I nod because what else can I do? There's nothing for *me* to figure out. I'm not a husband. I'm just a boyfriend… or was. Everything about me has been reduced to three-letter words.

"I'm so sorry, Easton. I know I can't ask you to wait for me, but…"

Maybe it's the evident remorse pouring off him, or how he looks as heartbroken as I feel. Maybe it's that this time the word *'but'* offers me hope.

Pulling him toward me, I wrap my arms around him. He hugs me back, but the embrace is weak and awkward, not nearly as comforting as either of us needs right now. It's not like our hugs that make me feel as though we're two halves completing a whole. There's an invisible canyon wedged between us, and it has Jason Reider's name on it.

Did Jason hug him? God, I can't even stand the thought of Aaron being in the same room as that man. Something foreboding tells me the longer he's around him, the more likely he'll be to slip through my hands.

"If you need me here for moral support when he comes back, just let me know."

"Thank you," he mumbles into my shoulder. "But it's probably better that you aren't. You've done so much for me already, and I think it would just make things more difficult."

Difficult how? Difficult to say goodbye to me? Or difficult for Jason? If it's the latter, I have no fucking problem hanging around to make him uncomfortable.

"Why don't we eat?" he says, trying to sound optimistic, but it's wasted because I can feel him trembling. "I saw you tried spoiling me again."

If the reminder of our normalcy brings him comfort now, I'll attempt it. I follow him to the kitchen after we gather up the now-cold Chinese food I brought over. It seems like a saving grace if he's asking me to stay for dinner, but after we set out our food and sit down, nothing feels salvaged. We eat in silence. At one point, he reaches out and holds my hand, rubbing the top of it anxiously with his thumb.

When I first started sketching years ago, I used to press too hard on the paper. It was a rookie mistake. No matter how much I tried to erase my errors, I could still see the marks from my pencil. Picking at my food, feeling that pitying stroke on my hand, I feel like one of those failed sketches. Kind words, good intentions—no matter what Aaron said, it feels like I'm no longer in the picture.

CHAPTER 33

Aaron

It's only been two days since I last saw Easton, but it seems like an eternity. I thought, for sure, Jason would show up last night, but I waited on pins and needles. The house was so silent and it felt like the apocalypse was coming, but then nothing. I finally fell asleep in the wee hours of the morning, exhausted from being on edge for so long.

The days haven't been much better, trying to think of what to text Easton that doesn't sound like forced pleasantries. Asking how he's doing and relaying silly things from work have lost the appeal they had only days ago. Each time I typed a message, this dirty sensation enveloped me as though I were an adulterer, leading him on. I am, aren't I? If I don't know what in the hell I'm going to do about Jason, then I'm stringing along a good man.

And Jason...

He's my husband, whom I wept over for months on end. Granted, we didn't have the best relationship, but it wasn't all terrible. I grieved in earnest. And now he's alive, but did I give him a warm welcome? I don't think I even hugged him. What is wrong with me? I can't be what either of them needs me to be right now.

When I think about Brazil, I get this mix of happiness for Jason for having a good life awaiting him there and bitterness that he's been living so comfortably while I was miserable. That has to make me the most selfish person to walk the planet.

As I pull out of Hampton Hills for the day, I idle at the first intersection. One direction leads toward home, the other toward downtown. I should go to the cottage and see if Jason will turn up out of thin air again, try to get more answers out of him, and try to talk some sense to him. I should. I really should. I'm grateful, though, that my hand turns the wheel down the street that leads me to a certain tattoo shop.

Shaking the rain off my coat, I hurry inside out of the wind. Shannon greets me like an old friend, giving me a much-needed dose of comfort. I'm not disappointed to learn from her that Easton had to run upstairs. I'd rather talk to him in private. Kiss him in private. Maybe convince him to lock me in his room for the night and tell me th s is all a bad dream.

Bounding up the back staircase, breathless, I knock on the door to his apartment. The sound from the television murmurs inside. With any luck, I caught him on his dinner break.

The knob turns and the hinges creak, giving me a second's notice to brandish a smile full of affection. I have no right to ask him to wait in limbo, but maybe I am selfish because I want him to wait. The face that greets me isn't the handsome one I'm desperate to see. It's older and weathered. While the man oddly looks like he could be an older version of Easton should Easton live an incredibly rough life, I believe it's the plumber from the other day.

Crap. Is he having plumbing issues again?

"Hi. I was just coming to see Easton," I inform him, although I'm not sure why I'm announcing myself to the plumber.

"Oh…um, yeah. Yeah, come on in." Stepping back, he draws the door open wider. "You're, uh, the boyfriend, right?"

Am I still? "Um…yeah."

"He just headed to his room."

"Okay. Thanks."

I'm about to start toward Easton's room, but the man is just standing there with his hands in his pockets, smiling at me. Does he want to shoot the shit? No wonder he's back again. Easton mustn't be getting his money's worth if the guy just stands around like this.

"Aaron…what are you doing here?"

Saved by the sight of a beautiful man. "Hey!" I call, catching him coming out of his room with a zip-up hoodie in his hand. "Shannon said you ran upstairs, so I thought I'd catch you while you weren't busy."

"I was just grabbing a sweatshirt." His gaze darts to the plumber and then back to me. Starting toward me, he guides me by the shoulder toward the door. "It was getting cold downstairs. Let's, um, go outside."

I know things were grim the other day, but I don't even get a semblance of a smile. Maybe I should have called first.

Out in the hallway, I wait for him to head downstairs with me, but after he closes the door, he just stands there. Shit. He probably has to wait for the plumber to finish again. My brain is so useless right now.

"Are you still having problems with the pipes?"

He's just staring at me. Why isn't he saying anything?

Oh, God. Is he giving up on me already?

Shit. Do I blame him?

"Easton?"

"He's not a plumber."

The skittishness and the strange glances, like he was preoccupied by the older man's presence, take on a new meaning. It's not possible, is it? He wouldn't... cheat on me, would he?

What am I saying? Given his fight-or-flight response, after the other night, I should hardly be surprised if he looked for physical comfort to blot out the drama I laid at his feet. Still, the thought pulverizes something inside me.

"He's...my father."

CHAPTER 34
Easton

The look on his face—I can't bear it. This isn't supposed to be easy.
I knew that he'd eventually show up to say goodbye. I also knew that
nothing about him issuing me goodbye was going to be easy, but
this would make recovering from it quicker. Two days alone with my
thoughts while Jason was out there… *not* dead—it's a miracle I didn't
hop on my bike and drive halfway across the country by now in a fit
of madness.

"He got out on parole and had nowhere to go," I explain casually.

"But…he killed your mother."

"More or less."

"Wait…why did you say he was the plumber?"

Because I'm a fucking idiot who's used to lying to every man I sleep
with. Nope. Not responding with that.

Because I love you and didn't want you anywhere near him. Because
that was before I thought you were going to give up on us. No. Not going there either. Stick with the plan, Easton.

Squinting, he stares down the hallway in thought. "Wait… That was a
week ago. How long has he been here?"

Slipping my hoodie on, I shrug like it's no big deal. "A few weeks."

"And you didn't tell me?"

"He said he wouldn't be here long."

"Is that why you always stay at my place and don't want me to come
over here?"

Is he actually hurt by that? I never said I didn't want him to come over here. Fuck. Why didn't I just lie? Leonard looks like a shitty plumber. Maybe Aaron would have believed it.

"I didn't want to be *here*. I wanted to be *there*," I concede, because it's the truth and I don't have it in me to act aloof any longer.

"But…Easton, I don't understand. How can you let him stay here?"

"He's my father."

"He's a murderer!"

I want to believe his concern is for my well-being, but the hike in his confidence over my affairs compared to his own the other day strikes a nerve. I didn't think he'd judge me. Or maybe I did and was hoping he'd prove me wrong. I can see the opening like a sinkhole appearing in the ground, ready to swallow up our relationship. This is what I wanted, isn't it? A way to be pissed off again instead of feeling like I got dumped for Jason.

"*You're* staying with one, aren't you?"

"What?" he balks.

"The man who *killed* your husband," I challenge, stuffing my hands into my pockets.

A blush creeps across his cheeks and his posture deflates. "That's not the same."

This is fucking stupid, says the heartsick part of me that equals ninety-nine percent of my being. Why am I trying to pick a fight? I don't want to fight with him. I just want him to tell me he doesn't give a damn that his husband is still alive or that my father is an ex-convict. I want him to tell me he's come to get us both out of here until the unwanted people in our lives fuck back off to where they came from. I want him to tell me again how he *never knew what love was* until he met me. And I want the chance to tell him back without getting my heart smashed by a boot heel of a plastic surgeon with shitty taste in cologne.

"What are you doing here?" I murmur, picking at a splinter on the doorframe.

"I just…wanted to check on you and see how you were doing."

To *check on me…*

To *see how I'm doing…*

Oh, God, doesn't that sound familiar? And it's a far cry from the way he usually greets me, distant. We're back to day one again when he first showed up at my apartment with his electrolarynx. I saw this coming like a drunk staggering into the shop wanting their partner's name tattooed over.

An ugly sound comes out of my throat. It doesn't quite feel the way laughter has recently.

"Well, I'm living with a murderer and my boyfriend has a husband who isn't dead. I'm fine. How are you?"

His little puff of air twists something in my heart. "I've been better."

I can't do this awkward pleasantries thing anymore. I need to know, and I need to know now.

"Have you figured out what you need to figure out?"

"No. I don't think I've figured out anything." He grimaces, scrubbing his hands down his face.

The foolish part of me that would do anything for him is pitying, but something is glaringly obvious. He freaking figured out that he *hasn't figured out* where *I* stand with him. He *did* come to tell me goodbye. Maybe not today. Maybe tomorrow or in a few weeks or months, but I can see it.

I see all his smiles and images of his laughing profile flash before my eyes as I stare at him. I can hear all his aroused breaths, his sleepy ones, and feel the touches of his hand. I'm almost embarrassed to ask, dreading the answer, but it's just too damn hard to let all that go.

"Did you need somewhere to stay?" I venture, hating how hopeful it sounds, almost like a plea.

His wary gaze travels to my apartment door as if he can see Leonard wielding a chainsaw through it. "No. Um, Jason's making dinner tonight. I have to get home."

Jason's. Making. Dinner.

How fucking quaint. If I could scream, I would.

"South America—I'm sure you'll like it there."

Frowning, his brow wrinkles. "I never said I was going with him. We just have a lot to work through."

But you never said you weren't…

I can't fucking do this. Turning, I start back toward my apartment. If I head downstairs, he could follow me. At least this door locks, and if I want to hit something, there'll be a deserving target inside my apartment.

"Yeah, well, call me when he gets into another car accident."

"Easton…that's not fair."

That's life, I tell him with my hands.

"Don't do that. Please. Don't close up on me."

Him and his freaking projects. I'm not a damn crossword puzzle. If he wants something to fix, he can go home and find plenty to do there.

It's full circle, the way I open the door and see him standing in my hallway looking befuddled, just like he did the first day he showed up. It's some creepy-ass déjà vu shit that feels like there was a brief inter-mission in an alternate universe where I discovered what being a boy-friend for the first time was like. I don't understand what the point was, but I'm not going to waste another eight years dwelling on it.

"Why don't you worry about the other man in your life? I did just fine without you."

CHAPTER 35

Aaron

The glow of the candles on my kitchen table makes my home look like a séance. The plated food with settings next to them does the opposite of rousing hunger in me. I feel like I'm going to be sick. I think I just lost him.

"You're late," Jason calls, pouring red wine into a glass on the table.

I don't have wine glasses. I sold most of my kitchenware at a pawnshop in Seattle before I left. Where did he get wine glasses?

"I had to take care of some things," I mumble, hanging my coat up by the door.

Arching a brow, he studies me as I make my way to the kitchen. I don't have the energy to hide anything, and for once, I honestly don't care. If I have to accept the changes in him, he's going to have to accept that I had a life while he was… dead.

"Your tattooed friend?" he ventures, arching a brow.

I don't know how to respond, but a part of me doesn't want to say Easton's name in front of him. Not because Easton's mad at me, but because he's *mine*. Even if he's no longer mine, he's still *mine*. He's not someone I want to be casual conversation with Jason.

"Didn't figure that'd be your thing," he murmurs, looking amused. Sliding a chair out, he gestures for me to sit. "I kept it warm for you."

I take a seat and go through the motions of eating without tasting. It all feels so formal, not like the haphazard meals Easton and I would share, as though food was always an afterthought to each other's company.

Jason talks about all the things we can do in Brazil. Hiking. Museums. A theater. When he mentions camping, I do a double take. I can't remember how many times I asked him to go camping, but he always dismissed it. Would he finally make time for me, or is it an empty promise? A tinge of guilt flickers through me for even thinking so. I never doubted anything he did years ago. Is it him who's changed or me? Or is it both of us?

My gaze catches on something that seems out of place. My mail is piled on top of my puzzle boxes on the bay ledge below the kitchen window that overlooks the backyard. I spot the puzzle Easton and I last finished canted sideways and upside down. The picture on the box will get scratched like that.

Who sets a puzzle box upside down? My heart sinks, seeing it stowed away so carelessly. I had left it put together on the table as a vigil of sorts, a comfort that made me feel Easton was still here.

"Dessert?" Jason asks. I hardly noticed him clearing my plate and standing.

"Um, no. I had a big lunch. Thank you, though. That…that was good."

Clasping my hands together, I blow out a breath to try to be present. Except it doesn't help. This *is* the present, the wounds of my argument with Easton still fresh.

Why did he lash out like that? It felt almost… calculated. It reminds me of that first day at his apartment and his closed-off demeanor. He was posturing then, I've since realized, because he was hurt. The tension in my body eases, considering that information.

I know Easton. I know him now. Today, that wasn't Easton. Not the one who is *'very happy too.'* Of course, he's hurt. I'm here with a husband.

Soft music interrupts my thoughts. Watching Jason set his phone down on the counter with a playlist pulled up, I get a flicker of agitation. He still hasn't given me his number. I could ask, but I shouldn't have to ask. Why didn't he give it to me the first day he showed up?

Walking over, he holds his hand out. I take it, realizing I've been just sitting here for however many minutes while he rinsed the dishes. I turn to head toward the living room, wondering if talking will be less awkward with the television playing in the background. I don't get but a step, however, when his hands alight on my hips.

His beard tickles my ear, and his chest presses against my back. "You look good," he murmurs.

I don't feel like I look good at all, so the compliment falls flat. "Thanks."

My heartbeat skips in alarm when his arms wrap around my waist. I should be happy. I should welcome the embrace. I should be grateful that my husband isn't dead and wasn't murdered by criminals. Happy people don't stand like terrified statues, though, when their loved one holds them.

"I missed you," he breathes into my neck.

I close my eyes and say the words I feel owe him, "I…missed you, too."

It's not a lie. I did…once. As he starts kissing my neck, a tear tracks down my cheek. I missed what I thought I knew of him. Maybe if *that man* had walked through my door, and sooner, I might have fallen down, crying tears of relief. I close my eyes in shame knowing these are tears over the death of a fairy tale I'm starting to think only lived in my youthful dreams.

"Do you remember the night we drove out to that drive-in theater not far from here when we first met?"

God, that was a lifetime ago. He'd never been to one, and the way he looked so out of his element was endearing. We were so happy then, laughing at everything. I was just floored that someone like him even thought to look my way, let alone wanted to spend an evening doing something antiquated with me.

"Yeah. They just opened for the season, but it was still freezing."

Chuckling, he turns me around. "And you kicked my horn when we climbed into the backseat."

Groaning, I drop my head as my face heats. "I was mortified. Thankfully, there weren't very many people there."

His fingers hook under my chin. When I look up, his beard tickles my jaw. For a second, I see the man I fell in love with leaning in to kiss me. I can't find a reason to say no when his lips touch mine. He's my husband. I'm supposed to kiss him. I'm supposed to at least give him a chance.

It's soft and delicate. I wait for some life-changing moment, some flicker that will right all the confusion in my brain and my heart. And I wait…

When the tip of his tongue slips past my lips and his fingers cup the back of my head, it's like kissing a stranger. Worse than that, it's like *not kissing* Easton. I can find a thousand reasons to say no, and they're all because of him and the betrayal I feel I'm committing coursing through my rigid body.

Breaking away, his mouth travels to the side of mine. He peppers me with another round of kisses there as his hand moves to the small of my back, swaying us to the music. "I can't wait to see you in our bed when the sun from the coast comes through the windows in the morning," he croons, while my fingers grip in panic at the front of his sweater. "You don't have to cook. I hired a chef, and the cantinas there are out of this world."

I can't breathe. It's like I'm paralyzed in fear. His words are like prison bars wrapping around me. His hand tugs, drawing my hips into his. The hard bulge that presses into me shouldn't be the shock it is. For so long, I wanted for him to want me more often than he did, not just our random perfunctory sex that often left me feeling like my emotional needs weren't satisfied. Maybe I should be glad I still turn him on, but something like revulsion flows through my petrified body. I want something to wish me away.

Swaying our hips as he grinds into me, he whispers, "I'll take you out dancing."

Dancing… Visions of Easton. Memories of how *Easton* made me feel even before I knew I was falling for him. That's how talk of dancing should make someone feel. Not this horrifying paralysis that has bile rising up my throat.

The death grip knots I've made in the front of Jasons's sweater finally loosen and my palms flatten against his chest. "I can't." I push, breaking free of that suffocating breath on my neck. "I'm sorry, I can't."

"Hey, it's okay," he soothes, releasing his hold on my hips to run his hands up my arms. "We don't have to. I know it's been a while. It probably feels like we have to get to know each other again." He smiles and leans in like he's going to kiss me again. "But we can look forward to that," he adds with a smile.

"No." My voice comes out firmer this time as I dodge my head to the side. "I don't think I can go to Brazil."

I don't *think* I can't. I *know* I can't. Nothing in me wants to go.

"You just need time." He smiles, that laughing look that always made me feel unheard.

Drawing away, I take a step back and shake my head. On this, I need to be heard.

"No. I know it all sounds wonderful, but…I just can't."

My message finally registers on his face, his playful look sagging. I'm almost grateful that his nostrils flare. At least it means he knows I'm serious.

"Is this about that guy?"

Hugging myself, I wish it was Easton's arms wrapped around me instead of my own. I bite my lip, knowing that not replying must look guilty. Easton's not just *'that guy,'* though. Not to me.

"You think you're in love with him?" It's rhetorical and full of disgust. Snorting, he shakes his head and glances skyward.

"I love you too," I assure him in a rush. At least, I think I did once, but I don't want to end things with him on bad terms. "I want to help you Jason, and I will, but…I'm sorry. Everything's changed." An odd sense of peace settles over me now that the words are out. They're not quite true, so I amend them with more clarity. "*I've* changed."

He studies me for a long time like a newly discovered blemish on a neglected family heirloom. Nodding, he stuffs his hands into his pockets. "So…one little mishap, and that's that, then?"

A *little mishap?* He cannot possibly see disappearing for two years as a little mishap. I walked myself into an argument with Easton earlier. I'm not going to make the same mistake now. That will get us nowhere.

"I think we should go talk to a lawyer."

"About what?" he asks like it's the dumbest idea I've ever had, as he shuts the music off on his phone.

"About what happened to you. About all of it. We could get advice on what's best to do."

"I don't need a lawyer. They'll want to go to court, and then I'll be right back where I started being exposed to those criminals. Did you listen to anything I said to you?"

"Yes, but I could talk to one on your behalf while you…lie low or something. I won't tell them where you are, and we can get it worked out so you can go back to Seattle. You could be able to see your mother again. I know this hit her hard."

Pinching his eyes shut like I'm daft, he shakes his head. "She doesn't—" Sighing, he holds a hand out. "Forget it. It's fine. I'm happy in Brazil. Happier even." He shrugs, rubbing that dig in. "Just…I thought maybe *my husband* might be happy there with me."

I'm not even uncomfortable over his clear bitterness. Maybe he did love me once, or maybe he thinks he still does. Maybe he doesn't know what love is and can't see that I'm just a possession to him. He'll never know what love is, though, if I go with him. And I'll never feel it again if I do.

"He might have been," I digress, gently. "Maybe if he'd had a choice, but…you know things weren't always perfect between us. We can't pretend they were."

Some of the wounded pomp leaves his posture. "I thought they were pretty perfect."

That does make me feel bad—if he truly felt that way. Still, I can't change that I saw things differently. Moving to a new country isn't going to change that.

Stepping forward, he adds sagely, "Nothing's perfect, Aaron. You're not so naïve that you think so, do you? That's what marriage is—it's work—and I know this might seem like more work than average, but I didn't ask for this. I know you didn't either, but it's what we've been dealt. Are you really going to give up on us when we have another chance?"

I know he's struggling to process this, but his words seem so unfair. As I stare at him, all I can think is that *I* never gave up.

He must read something in my silence because he scoffs. "Or you must really be in love with this guy." Shaking his head, he paces to the window, hands on his hips. "Lucky him. He must be pretty perfect not to have any baggage. You always said I cared too much about what people think. Well, apparently living with a husband who's down on his luck is too much for you."

How can he put his decision to disappear for two years on me? I've tried to save him his pride through all of this, but my decision has nothing to do with a shallowness he must think I possess.

"That's not true. *Everyone* has baggage. His father killed his mother, and now he's out on parole, staying with him. He has plenty of baggage."

Whirling around, his eyes are wide. "What?"

Why did I say that? It clearly didn't help my case, and I don't feel any better spilling Easton's secrets. "It's not about our pasts," I explain. "We barely dated before we moved in together, and then we got married shortly after that. If we're being honest with ourselves, we hardly knew one another."

"And you know this guy so well?"

This time, I know exactly what to say. I only hold back a second to soften the blow.

"I do."

The words fill me with warmth, knowing they're true. I *do* know Easton. I know he's just hurt and feeling betrayed. I can fix things with him; I'm sure of it, just as long as I stick to my guns for the rest of this conversation with Jason. Easton is my future. Jason isn't.

I watch the way his teeth seem to be grinding. I've never seen him look so humbled or… humiliated.

"I have some things to take care of before I leave," he mutters off-handedly, stepping closer, but then looks me in the eye. "Maybe we didn't know each other, but we had a life together. It meant something, didn't it?"

Jesus, this is not how I thought my marriage would end up when I said 'I do.' It's so damn heartbreaking, but I can't see any alternative, even if Easton wasn't in the picture. We're not… right for each other.

My voice comes out choked with emotions over our shared loss of shattered dreams from long ago. "Of course it did."

That seems to appease something in him. He lets out a long exhale and walks to the door, pulling his coat off the hook. "I'll come see you in a few days—before I go," he says, picking up his bag.

The unspoken message is clear—*to see if you changed your mind.* I don't want to have this painful conversation again, but maybe it will sit better with him if he sees my answer hasn't changed in a few days.

Hand on the doorknob, he steadies his gaze on me. "We have our whole lives ahead of us to make it better, *Aar*. We'll never know if it could be if we don't try again. Try to remember that."

The cold air gusts inside as he exits, washing away the tension in the room and thinning the lingering scent of his cologne. My lungs stop aching instantly. I don't need a few days. I dig down deep, trying to feel guilty about that, but the guilt never comes.

CHAPTER 36
Easton

Another night hanging out with Leonard while creepy-ass *not-dead* Reider is doing God knows what with or to Aaron. Yahoo! I love my fucking life.

Taking another draw off my beer, I glare at the episode of *Farmhouse Fixer* playing on my living room TV. Leonard's affinity for modern television shows is astounding. Did they not have cable in prison?

It decides to speak because it doesn't remember the rules. "You know, burying yourself in a bottle isn't going to fix our disagreements."

Where in the hell did that come from? Can't a guy just sit here and contemplate if the man he hates most in the world is considering buying goats and renovating a colonial building?

"Not everything's about you."

He must miss the sincerity in my warning because he follows up with an open-minded, "Then try me."

Am I drunk or did Leonard actually just offer to be my therapy couch? He's been camped out on that thing for too long if he's taken on the persona of one now.

Holding up a hand, he adds, "I've fucked up enough stuff in my life, I've gotten pretty good at fixing things."

Oh, please. Why can't they just show some goats so he can return his attention to the TV? *Fixing things?* What, pray tell, would he have gotten good at fixing in prison?

"*Most* things," he digresses more humbly. "Things that are forgivable."

Ugh. If he even goes there, I'm going to lose my shit. He's not going to stop talking, is he? Whatever. I can only listen to this shit in my head for so long.

"You ever meet any con men?" I ask off-handedly, like I couldn't care less if he replies.

What the hell is the snort for?

"Prison's full of con men."

Oh. Well, I walked into that one.

Good talk, Leonard. Good talk.

"Your guy? He pull something on you?"

My guy? I wait for the disparaging remarks, remembering he saw Aaron and I kiss when he broke my shower. Side-eyeing him, I find him waiting curiously for an answer, not an ounce of derision on his face.

"Someone's conning *him*, and I don't know what to do about it," I mumble just so he'll quit looking at me.

"The old fear of God is a good way to start."

Yeah, because Jason looks like a bible-toting man. And, uh, is that what Leonard tried to do to me and Mom back in his tirade days? What a wonderful source of advice I chose.

"It's his husband. I don't think I've got the right to put the fear of God in him, even if I want to."

Good. He finally shut up.

Where are the fucking goats? I couldn't care less about wall colors.

"You sure you're not the one being conned by both of them?"

"I'm not as fucking stupid as you think I am."

"I'm just saying…your mother and I had our problems, but not once did either of us ever stray."

Oh, the fuck he didn't. Springing out of my recliner like an ejection seat, I level my index finger at him over my beer bottle.

"You don't get to fucking talk about *her!*" Just in case his brain does that thing where it tells him to speak when he shouldn't, I add, "*Ever!*"

Tromping to the kitchen, I polish off the rest of my beer, trying not to let his moment of stupidity push me over the edge. They had their problems? He freaking caused her death. How can he honestly think I'd be receptive to him claiming he loved her once? That's all null and void once you contribute to someone's demise. The fucking idiot.

"Easton…"

Ugh… it's speaking again. Of course, it is.

"I can't take it back. I *know* that, but I'd do anything to take back what I did. *Everything* I did."

Gripping the handles of the refrigerator, I suck in a deep breath and lean my forehead against the cool stainless steel. "Stop," I warn. "I don't want to hear it."

I don't open my eyes until I'm convinced he's finally shut up for good. Sighing, I wrench open the door and grab another bottle from the twelve-pack I bought earlier. If Leonard doesn't like it, he can go to a meeting. Maybe he'll find someone there who wants to adopt him as their recovery houseplant. Just set him next to your couch in front of the television. He'll love it there.

My ass barely lands back in the recliner when that rough, old voice floats across the room again.

"Your guy…he's off with this husband of his, I take it? Is that why you look like a dog's ass?"

I spare him an unimpressed look as I kick my boots off with my feet and let them *thunk* to the floor. If we're going to start exchanging compliments, I've got a few in mind for him that make a dog's ass sound like a beauty title.

"He was dead." I laugh at the absurdity of using the past tense. "A car accident. Faked his own death. Now, he's back almost two years later, out of the blue, like nothing ever happened. Who does that?"

I'm getting better at shutting him up. I bet they don't even hear stories like this in prison very often.

"And your guy?" he finally asks.

"*Aaron*. His name is Aaron. Okay? And he's obviously not *my guy* if he has a fucking husband again now."

"Is he…okay with this?"

I wish shaking my head would bleach my brain of the entire ordeal and this conversation. "No," I mutter, because Aaron clearly wasn't okay with it. "I don't know," I add just as quickly. Because some dumbass lost his cool the other day and probably drove him to be okay with it. "But he's not like us. He's…*good*. He's *too good,* and I can't stop him from being too good." I don't know why I'm still talking other than I want it out of me and I don't know how else to purge the pain. "I don't want to. It's what I…"

'*Love about him*' gets stuck in my throat, and my voice starts to sound wrecked. Leonard doesn't need to know that. He didn't need to know any of it. Jesus, I've lost my mind.

Scoffing at myself, my laugh sounds like it belongs to *Snidely Whiplash's* dog, *Muttley*. "Why the fuck am I telling you?"

That was meant to be rhetorical, so naturally, the world's shittiest plumber pipes in. "Sometimes it's good to let things out. You can't keep everything bottled up or—"

"Save it," I cut him off, heaving myself out of the recliner.

Family time is officially over. I need to go burn some damn sage now. If I have to hear him preach to me after I just spewed all that crap, I might light more than sage to cleanse my apartment.

A good cleanse… that's exactly what I need. No wonder I can't even be content being miserable in my own place.

"And you need to leave," I inform him on my way to my room. "I can't have you here. Not now. Not like you gave me much of a choice in the first place."

"I'll sign into the Siever halfway house tomorrow. I'll be gone in the morning."

There's no saltiness to his tone. It's so agreeable, it just pisses me off even more.

"Whatever."

CHAPTER 37

Aaron

"Thank you for coming." The greeting sounds so formal as I click my front door shut behind Easton.

Head downcast, he's like a dead man walking, completely closed off with his hands jammed in his jeans' pockets. Toeing some nonexistent mark on the floor with his boot, he doesn't even look up at me. Please tell me I haven't done too much damage.

I don't know if he's receded so far inside himself that I can't reach him, but I can't wait another second to set my news free. No way was I telling him over the phone and having it come off as a throwaway comment.

Skipping right to the point, I blurt, "I'm not going to Brazil."

Whatever blanket of invisibility he'd thrown over me falls to the floor. Those gorgeous eyes of his, filled with surprise, snap to mine. Was he that convinced that I would?

"Is Jason…gone?"

"No." I should probably be ashamed of how disappointed I feel to have to tell him that, but mostly I'm heartsick that I can't say otherwise. "I told him, though. Last night. I told him I can't go."

That seems to assuage his worry, his features softening. A bloom of hope unfurls in my chest.

"What did he say?"

"He said he'd give me a few days to think about it."

"And *that's* why you asked me to come over?"

I used to think he was the one who had problems communicating, the way he held everything inside. Watching his expression crumple, however, I'm starting to realize *I'm* the weak link in the explaining department.

"No! No. I asked you to come over because I needed to see you." Does he really not know? "I told him I can't go because I'm in love with you."

I've put my heart in his hands, back where it was in the first place. I want him to close his fingers around it and keep it forever. The disbelief on his face has me stepping forward, hoping it means he never actually gave it back to me.

I beg so hard it's a whisper. "Do you still want me?"

I'm only in agony for a split second. Something elemental answers for the both of us, our bodies colliding like two boulders careening down opposite mountainsides and crashing into each other. Kissing him is my salvation, making me realize how Jason never stood a chance, and I was just going through the motions. I could have lost Easton by trying to conform to formalities that no longer apply to me.

I grip onto him like he'll disappear if I let go. With each slant of my mouth, I accept and deliver the longing. It's a battle of desperation to show the other how lost we were at the thought of being separated. That only adds fuel to the fire.

I slip my hands under his shirt, needing his skin against mine. I need his warmth melded with my own, any way to join us together. Spinning me around, he presses me against the wall, panting with the same urgency. We must look like a blur, flinging clothing, yanking down zippers, and grabbing at each other.

His hand dives into my boxer briefs, taking hold of me. It's a gesture of ownership that doesn't suffocate me, especially when his hand makes a languid stroke up to my tip and swirls around my cockhead. It's wanton and ravenous, yet sensual. Jerking into his grip, I moan into his mouth, slipping my hands into the back of his boxers to grip that perfect ass of his.

He grunts and bucks against me, telling me I'm not the only one who's lost. I'm about to pull him out, but he drops to his knees, yanking my underwear down when he goes. His lips are around my cock before I can even focus. Hot, wet, and dire, he works me with his mouth like a starving man.

Shit. There will never *not* be an inferno of passion between us.

I am not letting this chaotic reunion end like this. For all his teasing and false airs, he's such a giver. Well, I've got news for him. He's not leaving this house without me giving back as good as I'm getting.

Gripping his shoulder, I push him back. It's nothing short of tackling him to the floor the way I land on top of him. He lets out an *oof* sound and smiles, but I cover it with my mouth before it's fully formed. Drawing him out, I sigh at the feel of his heated thickness against me. Groaning, his eyes slip shut, and he rocks his hips into the grip I have around us.

The floor is cold and hard under my forearm. I'm sure this wouldn't be comfortable for him if it were just another day. Today, though, we're on another plane, neither of us caring where we are as long as where we are is *together*.

His palms slide over the globes of my ass. The sensation of a part of my body being covered by a part of his feels like being home. Dipping his finger into his mouth, it comes out wet, and he stares into my eyes, reaching back around me. Yes. God, yes.

I spread my thighs as much as the constraints of my lowered pants will allow and make a meal of his mouth as he circles my pucker. *Now...* I'm home. *Him... in me.* Any part of him.

My keening against his cheek is answered by a throaty rumble. Pinching my eyes closed to hold off the pleasure overload, I snake my hand further down and cup his balls. Arching my hips back into the tortuous stroking inside me, I grind my stomach into his, the damp frotting between us sending tingles up my legs.

"I missed you. I missed you so much," I babble between kisses. The words are easy to say this time, and they're attached firmly to the organ deep inside my chest.

"I told Leonard to get the fuck out. I couldn't be miserable *and* have him there at the same time."

"I was so worried about you. I didn't want to leave you there with him."

Slipping his fingers into my hair, with a loving gaze, he drags me back to his mouth. All our concerns are conveyed through the physical after that as we fuck into each other and I ride back on his fingers when he slips another inside me. Damn him. He's not going to do this to me. I know he loves seeing me get off, but I love watching him just as much.

Slipping my fingers below his sac, I stroke his taint and his hole. His throat makes a strained grumbling noise that lights my body up. He's got that tense look on his face when our kiss breaks. I love the furrow he gets in his brow right before he comes. Just the thought of it has me spilling between us, but soon, I feel the return of his wet heat basting my stomach, too.

My hole is slightly sore from the lack of proper lube, but it's a welcome sore. Laying my head on his shoulder, our chests battle to breathe against each other as we come down. My body has spent the bulk of the turmoil that was living in my stomach like poison since Easton first showed up after Jason arrived. It feels like something sacred has just been preserved by this purge of worry. As the last of our post-haze begins to fade and he slips his arms around me, the safety net of our feral reunion starts cracking. I can feel it in the tension of his body underneath me, an unspoken understanding that nothing will be well until Jason is gone.

It's not perfect again yet, but I take comfort that we're here, together. That's all that matters right now.

"Will you stay?" I whisper, tracing my finger over his heart.

Capturing my hand, he brings it to his lips and presses a kiss to my knuckle. "I'm not going anywhere."

CHAPTER 38
Easton

Are people supposed to fit this well against your body? Opening my eyes to the soft glow of dusk filtering in around the curtains in Aaron's bedroom, his peaceful face has me laughing silently. He's such a fucking cuddler, even in his sleep. I was never able to get comfortable when a guy would tangle himself around me like this. I guess they were just doing it wrong. Reaching out, I stroke his cheek with the back of my hand, wishing I could keep his serene expression in place. It only took an all-day fuck fest to put it there yesterday. Granted, there were a few short naps in between. I don't know how he's going to work in a few hours when I could fall right back to sleep.

Nestling my head deeper into the pillow, I shut my eyes again. No sooner do they close than my phone lets out its horrendously loud, blaring ringtone. Rolling away, I scramble to fetch it off the nightstand, hoping I don't wake the other half of my pretzel. It's five in the morning—why is Wolf calling me?

"Dude…where are you?"

"I'm at Aaron's. What's wrong?"

"What?"

Fucking hell. I'm not raising my voice loud enough for him to hear me. Hanging up, I shoot off a text.

I'm at Aaron's. What's wrong?

Robbed? Who would rob a tattoo shop and what would they even have taken? It's not like it would be difficult for the cops to keep an eye out at pawn shops for tattoo guns. And, no, I wouldn't hear my alarm because I live there, so I didn't bother setting up the app portion of it that Wolf went on about when we got the thing installed. I figured hearing the device screeching in my apartment would be alert enough.

The safe… Oh, shit.
Shit!
Slipping my legs free of Aaron's, he lets out a little moan. I'm not waking him up only to worry him. I have a feeling of where to look for who did this. Aaron doesn't need to see me finally lose it when I pummel the bastard's face in.

I stop my bike so fast outside the Siever halfway house that I have to grip the handlebars tighter to keep from lurching over. My boot skids against the pavement to help bring me to a standstill, probably shaving off a layer of the sole. Fucking Leonard.

Aaron's reaction to discovering him the other day was on point. I should have never let him under my roof. And all that father-of-the-year wisdom—ugh! I'm so mad I could throw him through a damn wall. Some part of me thought maybe Mom, in her kind and forgiving nature, would be pleased I gave him a chance. He killed her—I must have had a lapse in sanity to think he actually regretted it. The man has no soul if he could do that and then turn around and steal from his only son.

Shoving through the doors, I try to appear like I'm not about to commit assault as I ask the receptionist if I can see *'my father.'* He must check some list to make sure my name isn't flagged as a no-contact party. Mistake number two, Leonard.

"He's in wing B. I'll call down there to let him know."

"Thanks." Nodding, I bypass the desk to the right hallway as soon as he turns to pick up the phone. I'm not waiting for an invitation.

"Sir…wait. You can't go back there!"

His call is cut short when the door closes behind me and I storm down the hallway, scanning the names on the occupied doors. It smells of *Simple Green* and body odor, making me fume even more. Was it his plan all along to rob me, or was he pouting after I kicked him out, knowing he had to come here?

It would have been simple to tell the police who I suspected, but then I wouldn't get the satisfaction of hearing it firsthand when I choke the life out of him. If he's still breathing after I'm done with him, I can give Hampton PD a call that something jogged my memory. And now I owe Wolf yet another favor for not saying anything. I could see it all over his face that he knew it was Leonard too. Maybe he just didn't want to humiliate me.

The sight of my name on the scratched brown door makes me cringe, knowing it could have been Mom and me behind it years ago if we'd made it through the car accident. Who in the hell knows where we would have ended up or what I'd have become, but we'd have been together.

Turning the knob, it won't give. I guess if you have a safe's worth of cash in your possession, locking the door seems wise.

I pound on the wood, not caring how many people I disturb in the process. "Leonard! Open the fucking door!"

It swings open, revealing the culprit in his half-button Siever Pallet Company uniform shirt. Right. Go to work today to look like you weren't up to fuckery last night.

Taking two fistfuls of his collar, I drag him and the stupid look of surprise all the way across the room until the wall stops his back. Some gangly-looking guy around my age hops off the other bed and scrambles around the frame toward the door.

"Shit, man," he gasps.

"Easton, easy boy," Leonard cautions. His vise grip on my wrists is the only thing saving him from a lack of air.

Go *easy?* I've not even started.

"It wasn't enough? You fucking killed her, and that wasn't enough?" The volume I want won't happen, nearly hitting its mark before my voice breaks.

"What are you talking about? What did I do? I left. You told me to leave."

Jerking him forward and then back again, his head makes a satisfying *thunk* against the concrete wall… so I do it a few more times as I unload on him. "*Months!* I was in some shithole rehab place for months, trying to learn how to speak again after a fucking coma just because I tried to drive her to the hospital to save her from what you did. I can't even fucking scream at you! You took *everything* from me, but that wasn't enough?"

He blinks at me, looking a shade paler. I refuse to think it's shock or remorse. Maybe he just finally realizes now how much I hate him and that if I find him in an alley without witnesses, he won't get out alive.

"I worked my ass off for that money. I gave you a place to stay even though I wanted to hold a pillow over your fucking head every night, and you fucking steal from me?" I'm so hoarse and gravelly, it brings back all my old frustrations. I'm supposed to be kicking his ass, not on the verge of tears.

"What money? What are you talking about?"

God, I hate him. I fucking hate him with every fiber of my being.

Jamming my knee into his gut, I ram my elbow into his throat a second later and press all my weight against his windpipe. He sputters, locking one of his rough meat hooks over my fist. The next thing I know, his other hand is on my elbow, torquing it up enough that it's painful trying to keep the pressure I have on him. The bastard is strong for his age.

"You know exactly what I'm talking about," I rasp. "You couldn't just pry open the safe? You had to trash the fucking office, too, like it was some random thief? Like I wouldn't fucking know it was you the second I saw it. I know you saw the safe the other day. You just sat there waiting for your moment, spouting all your '*I'm-a-reformed-man*' bullshit."

His leverage increases, making my arm slip from his throat if I don't want to dislocate my shoulder. He doesn't let go of my fist, though, dragging it downward instead. Before I can push him away, he throws his other arm around the back of my neck, hugging me to his chest in a headlock.

"I told you, boy," he growls as I writhe against him and knee the fuck out of his thighs. "I'm a lot of things, but I'm not a thief. I'm not the same man I was. You're all I got left," he adds, giving me a shake. "Why would

I steal from you when you put a roof over my head? I've got to check in with parole. What could I do with that kind of money?"

Buy some fucking goats, go on Barn Builders, and find some new wife he can beat? How the fuck should I know?

"Skip fucking town?" I growl, deciding I just want out of his hold instead of wasting my energy battering him with my knee. Tugging at his arm, I get free with little effort, almost like he let me go.

"Well, I ain't," he pants, holding his hands out to the sides. "I'm *here*."

"Sir, you can't be in here," a man calls from the doorway. "You'll need to come with me."

"It's all right," Leonard assures him, waving a hand but not taking his eyes off me.

"Mr. Bennick, are you sure?"

"Yeah. Just a disagreement with my son."

Glancing around the sparsely furnished room, I can see an indent in the pillow on his bed. Rumpled sheets. His work boots are neatly aligned at the end of his bed. There's a wall locker open with his uniforms hanging up in it. His meager collection of sweatshirts, pants, and underwear is stacked in the cubbies. The duffel bag he showed up to my apartment with is lying listless and empty at the bottom of the cabinet. It doesn't look like someone who just absconded with tens of thousands of dollars.

What's really baffling, though, is the old photograph taped to the inside of the door. Him, Mom, and me. I look like I was about eight years old. We're all smiling—a rare moment before his drinking got too out of control.

"Use your head, son," his voice cuts through the torrent of confusion inside me.

Glancing behind me, I can see that the wolves have stood down. It's just me and Leonard. I look back at him, wondering what in the hell he's talking about.

Exhaling like he's frustrated, he adds cryptically, "Who *else* do you know that could play you?"

For once, I don't disregard his words. A taste of bile creeps up my throat at the image that manifests. Wolf isn't even a consideration. There's only one other person in my life in a position where they could play me—Aaron. No. He wouldn't. There's no way he'd be behind something like this. The only way would be if Jason—

Jason... the guy Aaron threw me on the fence for just days ago before our miraculous make-up.

CHAPTER 39

Aaron

I knew something was wrong when I woke up alone. He's never gone off and left without saying goodbye.

The radio in the Suburban repeats what I heard earlier on my lunch break. S&H Tattoo *robbed.* I still can't believe it. This is the last thing he needs after everything I've put him through lately.

When I stopped by the shop, Wolf said he took off as soon as the police were done getting a statement from him early this morning. I checked my house, thinking he might be waiting for me there like he used to. Except he wasn't. He hasn't answered any of my messages or calls either. There's only one other place he could be...

Turning off the road onto the gravel drive that leads to the water's edge, I spot his bike parked next to the ivy-covered pump house. He's here. At *his spot.*

I can't believe he drove his bike in this rain. Give it another ten-degree drop, and it'd be sleet. This is ridiculous. He's taking his SUV back, whether he likes it or not.

Scanning the shoreline, I can't find him anywhere. There's no shelter out here unless he snuck into the old pump house, but it looks like it's been boarded up for decades.

Rounding the corner of it, my shoes splash against the wood decking that overlooks the shore. I'm ready to give up hope, finding nothing but the drab backdrop of the dormant ivy that blends in with the worn dock under the dreary light of the overcast sky. Squinting through the rain, I blink when something moves, assuming it's a trick from the droplets in my eyes. I blink again when I see skin, tatted sk n that nearly blends in with his scenery.

He's soaked to the bone, literally. Elbows res:ing on his bare knees, his fingers are steepled under his chin. My God, why is he in nothing but his boxers? It's freezing out.

Eyes closed, it almost looks like he's sleeping, sitting upright with his back to the ivy. His hands move, sliding up over his lips like someone lost in prayer, and he opens his eyes to the sky. I don't know how big of a hit this robbery was to him, but this can't be how he goes about '*thinking*' in his spot. This isn't healthy. Peeling off my coat, I rush toward him.

"Easton? What are you doing out here? You'll freeze to death."

"Did you play me?" he calls in a strange tone I've never heard him use. "Was it all a game?"

"What?"

"The money."

I don't understand. Is he panicking about finances now that he's been robbed? "I told you…I didn't want to accept the things you brought over. I could have done without all that furniture."

Snickering an ugly sound, he shakes his head.

"You've seen my office. You know where my safe is."

What? Oh, God. He can't possibly think it was me.

"Is that what you think?"

"I don't know what to think," he mumbles, closing his eyes and burying his face in his arm like he's exhausted. "You needed money. Jason shows up—*not* dead. You fuck with my head about opening up. You get me to fall in love with you. Was that your plan all along?"

It's the first time he's said the actual words, declaring his feelings for me. What I would have done to have prevented it from being like this.

"You can't possibly think that," I choke out around a painful lump in my throat. "Please tell me you don't think that."

Scrubbing his face, he shakes his head like he's battling demons. "It doesn't matter. It's just money."

"What did the police say?"

"They interviewed the most likely suspect."

"Your father?"

His bitter laugh has me regretting how quickly I came up with that assumption. "Yeah. I guess his parole officer saw the news and remembered where he was staying—*my* father. The '*murderer.*' That one, remember?"

I'm shocked he almost sounds defensive about him after all the hatred he had inside years ago. I didn't think he'd ever be able to forgive the man.

"I'm sorry I said that the other day. I was just worried about you. I know what a hard time you had with it when you were at Hampton."

"Don't," he snaps.

First, I accuse his father, then I say one of his trigger words, '*Hampton.*' This is going fantastic.

"Is he still at the station?"

"They let him go. He checked into a halfway house just like he said he would after I kicked him out the other day."

"That's good," I offer supportively, but he levels me with an appalled look.

"How is it good?"

"It's good that he didn't do it after you already had trust issues with him. I couldn't imagine dealing with that if he had."

Grimacing, he seems to sit in that for a moment. I hope it means he believes I have no ill will toward his father and that my only concern is for him. Clearly, he's conflicted about the man. I'm honestly so proud of him for being brave and strong enough to take him in. Not many people could do that.

"I went to see him," he says absently. "He had a theory about who might have done it."

I wait, hoping there's some lead that can help him restore what he's lost. I keep waiting when he glances over at me until I feel the suspicion in his gaze. I think it cracks my heart in half, imagining how he must feel right now if he believes what he's accusing me of.

"Easton…I told you. I would never."

"Maybe not you," he adds gravely. "Maybe someone who knows your boyfriend does all right financially. Where is old Jason, by the way?"

Jason? Why would he think Jason had anything to do with the robbery?

"I haven't seen him since…like Thursday." I try to wrap my head around the possibility, but I never even told him what Easton does for a living. "He wouldn't," I assure him. "He's not a thief. And besides, how would he have even known that was your shop? I never told him where you worked."

He rises rigidly like he can't deny the effects of the cold. "How did he know where to find you?" he asks, sounding tired, almost like he's figured something out that I haven't. "And don't you think it's odd that he took two years to contact you?"

I want to argue and tell him he's just spun up over everything and drawing wild conclusions. I don't know how Jason found me, though. He said he found out I was working back at Hampton Hills from the internet, but that doesn't explain how he knew where I was staying. George didn't own the cottage I'm staying in when Jason and I first started dating.

"I'll ask him," I mumble, my stomach churning, wondering what the new Jason was capable of. He picked my lock, after all.

"It doesn't matter."

"It definitely matters. If he stole from you, he needs to admit it and return whatever he took."

"No. It doesn't matter," he grumbles again, picking up his leather jacket to reveal his clothes protected underneath it. I try to make sense of why he was so clearly upset about the robbery, only to sound like he doesn't care now.

"*What* doesn't matter?"

"Any of it," he huffs, stuffing his wet legs into his jeans. "I'm the son of a criminal. You're married. It's never going to work."

"Easton, I know things seem so screwed up right now—more screwed up than I could ever think possible—but I love you. None of this changes how I feel about you."

"What the fuck is love?" he rasps, his voice sounding more worn than I've ever heard it. Bending down, he grabs his jacket. "You were depressed, and I had a crush. And then our realities came back to us. If you don't see the wake-up call, your head's in the clouds. It'd never work. We were fooling ourselves."

I think I like it better when he holds things in. His logic cuts me to the bone.

"Easton, you don't mean that. I know you don't."

Shoving his bare feet into his boots, he levels a look at me. "I told you. I'm not the marrying type."

I could cry and tell him how much it hurts me to see him put that bullshit armor of his back on, but I'm part of the shitshow that caused it. Maybe not by choice—I didn't ask for Jason to show back up in my life, but I could have done a better job of letting Easton know he wouldn't be a part of my future. When he stomps past me, I grab a hold of his arm.

"Easton, stop. Please. You're just hurting. You don't mean this."

I find myself backed up against the soaked ivy as he pivots and steps toward me. He hasn't laid a hand on me, but the wild look in his eyes is a side of him I've never seen.

"Do you know the thoughts that went through my head?" he whispers, only inches away from my face. I can see how red his eyes are now and the sad lines on his face. He's shivering, his lips tinted purple. "How I thought about you and him sitting there laughing and plotting the whole thing?" he continues. "How I thought about him fucking you? You moaning and smiling under him? How I thought about what it would feel like to have my hands around his neck?"

It's a disturbing picture, but even more so because of the self-hatred I can see all over his face as he grimaces and chokes up. "Because I did. You know why?" he steps back, panting, and spreads his arms out wide. "Because I'm the son of a criminal. It's in my blood. I'm no good. Is *that* love?"

He lets out a broken sound that mirrors the sob that falls from my lips and then swipes the rain from his face, shaking his head. "I don't know what the fuck love is, but if it's *that*, I don't want it—and you shouldn't either."

CHAPTER 40

Aaron

The way the couch cushion is bulging around me is like my own personal little nest. The blanket I've swaddled myself in adds an extra shield from reality, feeling like a cocoon. I could just live here—here on this couch, under this blanket.

The news recycles again to its headline wrap-up for viewers who've missed the top of the hour. I stare at the screen as numb as the first time I heard it, as numb as when the police came to my door this morning as I was about to leave for work.

'The body of an unidentified man was found on Maranacook Lake today, discovered by two fishermen.'

I'm sure once the police release the details of how the unidentified man was already presumed dead once two years ago, the press will have a field day. I should finally tell my family now. There's no excuse not to. There's nothing left for Jason to hide from.

Maybe I should have asked him what he was doing when he wasn't with me at the cottage. He spent more time away from here than he did here. *'Taking care of some things,'* he'd said. What things? Things that got him killed?

Before I can deal with my parents and George, it seems only right to tell someone else first. Digging for my phone from underneath the blanket, I palm it and stare at Easton's contact picture. It can't go any worse than the last phone call I made, but I don't have the energy to speak right now after my day at the police station.

> **Jason's dead. They found his body in Lake Maranacook.**

I hit *Send*, knowing it's the most messed up text message in history. At least this way, he'll have time to process it. I think our draw to be near each other conflicted with our need to process things lately, causing us more problems than necessary.

My phone rings seconds after I set it down. So much for processing.

"What?" he gasps.

"He's dead." Pinching my eyes shut, I shake my head, knowing I've said those words before. "For real this time. I saw the body."

"What... How... What happened?"

"I don't know. They said he drowned. He had a head injury, but they don't know if it was foul play. They found my name and address in his wallet. That's why they came to ask me if I knew him."

"Jesus. I... I'm sorry."

"For what?"

"For your loss."

I grieved Jason once already. I'm sorry he met his end like this, but it feels like a different man than the one I buried two years ago. Maybe I never knew that man either. Or maybe I'm just too spent on grief to grieve again.

"It... wasn't me," he adds.

I had wondered briefly today when I had to go to the morgue if Easton would be capable of such a thing out of jealousy after his proclamations yesterday. Does that mean he was right? That we shouldn't want love if I could consider such a thing, even if only for a moment?

I hear a puff of breath over the line. "You don't believe me," he says, almost like he's thinking aloud.

"No. I do."

"You don't. I can hear it in your voice. I promise you. I would never have done something like that."

I can feel a smile on my face, which is at odds with the events of the day. I'm smiling, though, because he just confirmed for me that he didn't mean anything he said the other day.

"I called his mother and told her," I digress, hoping once he has more of the picture, he'll understand why I don't doubt him. "She broke down crying and screaming, asking me what I did to him."

"Why would she think it was you?"

"She must have known he didn't die in a car accident. There was something in the way she reacted…it was like she was in shock, but not about him turning up. It was more shock like he'd died for the first time. Then she started screaming at me. She didn't even mention the accident, so that's how I realized it meant she knew all along. They must have…I think she may have been helping him the entire time."

He swears under his breath. I can practically hear him pacing from here. "Are you okay?"

"I will be."

Closing my eyes, I know it to be true. Even with silence on the other end of the line, just knowing he's there and that the nightmare is over is the solace I needed this evening. I can move forward now and live my life. I can finish whatever healing I hadn't done yet and right all my remaining missteps.

"I'm going to go buy a car tomorrow after I get Jason's arrangements taken care of," I inform him. "I'll drop yours off after I do."

"That's not necessary."

"No, I'm going to. It's too cold out to be riding your bike, and it's the right thing to do."

"Do you…want me to come over?"

He's seen me as a mess enough already and lifted me up the last time I fell. I won't lean on him this time.

"No, but thank you. I have to tell my family what's been going on and make arrangements to send Jason's body back to Seattle."

After he wishes me a goodnight, I glance back at the TV, which has fortunately moved on to other news. I think I sat here waiting for the last few hours to see if I would feel anything other than numbness. Hearing Easton's voice and telling him what happened settled an air of calm over me.

I'm arranging to send my husband's body back to his mother tomorrow—and I'm not even crying about it. Maybe I'm no good either, as Easton suggested about himself the other day. I'm less concerned about being 'good' than I am about hoping my husband stays buried this time.

CHAPTER 41
Easton

I'm grateful for the detail of the sleeve I'm working on for this customer. It's a lot of line work that requires focus and has kept me engaged for the last two hours. It still hasn't stopped me from glancing at the door each time I hear it open, but at least my mind is more devoted to work than it has been of late.

It's barely after lunch, so I shouldn't even be expecting Aaron to bring the SUV by yet. I don't know how long it takes to make arrangements to have a dead person transported across state lines, but I doubt it's a speedy process. I want to believe that he's simply worried about me freezing my ass off on my motorcycle, but after the shit I said the other day, paranoia is kicking my ass.

He was so subdued on the phone yesterday, almost vacant. Maybe it was just the shock over what happened to Jason, but returning my vehicle the day after doesn't bode well. It feels like it would be a loss of connection to him. I don't revel in him needing anything from me, but I would really appreciate excuses to see him in the near future. Was he just being polite yesterday on the phone? Will I represent memories of Jason for him now that Jason's actually gone for real this time?

Worse yet, maybe he could only deal with so much in one day. Yesterday was to process that his husband was found dead—again. Today is for returning the vehicle to the unstable boyfriend he wants to get rid of to reduce the rest of the drama in his life.

I didn't mean it... Any of it.

Well, I believe the part I said about me being no good, but I didn't mean the rest of what I told him when he found me the other day. I'll never love anyone but him. If there is such a thing as love, Aaron is it for me.

Two quick knocks resound on the wall of my station. I look up to find Wolf not looking like a crab ass for once. He's left me a wide berth since the robbery. Right now, though, he looks like he's about to tell me someone died.

"What?"

"Aaron asked me to give these to you."

Watching his arm extend, I stare at the keys to my Suburban in his hand. Why would he give them to Wolf? Excusing myself with the customer, I rise and take them from him, glancing around the shop.

"Where is he?"

"He pulled in out back when I was getting out of my van. He got in a truck with some guy and just asked me if I could give these to you."

He didn't even come in to talk to me. Something tells me I won't need to worry about glancing at the door anymore. I blew it. It's over.

I'm not sure what this sleeve looks like by the time I finish, but the man doesn't complain. Hopefully, there was some sense of autopilot engaged in my brain from years of tatting that allowed me to create something presentable for him. I try to sound cordial, explaining the aftercare process to him and about making arrangements with Shannon to schedule his color work, but it all sounds like a monotone mumble.

My phone rings, making my pulse jolt, so I excuse myself quickly. Please be Aaron. Please.

It's some number I've never seen, sending my heart right back into the pit of my stomach.

"Hello?"

"Is this Easton Bennick?"

"Yes."

"Hi, this is parole officer Dobbs. I'm looking for Leonard Bennick, and he had you as his point of contact for his last known address."

Like I needed another reminder of Leonard right now. Sighing, I rub the bridge of my nose. "Yeah. Well, I *was* when he was staying here, but he checked into the Siever Halfway House a few days ago."

"Well, that's the problem. He didn't show up for work yesterday or today, and I checked with Siever halfway. He hasn't been there since yesterday afternoon according to their sign-in logs. I was wondering if he might have gotten in contact with you since then."

'I'm a lot of things, but I'm not a thief.' The adamant declaration doesn't sit the same with me now as when I left that tired building full of men with broken dreams. Did he put that picture up on the wall locker just to throw me for a loop? More of his father of the year façade? Because he had to have known he would be the first person I came looking for once I found out my safe had been emptied.

"No," I try not to laugh. "I haven't seen him." And now I doubt I ever will again.

"You sure you're all right here? I don't mind closing," Wolf says, sounding as tired as I feel.

"I'm fine. Go on. You've got enough shit to deal with. You done packing up the house yet?"

Frowning, he shakes his head and fidgets with the business card display on the reception counter while I zero out the register. "I got sidetracked."

Oh, boy. Here we go again. It's good, honestly. I need something to distract myself from what's going through my mind.

"What's her name?" I tease.

The frown becomes a full-on scowl. "Nothing. Her name is nothing."

"Hm. Sounds foreign. Is she exotic?"

Rolling his eyes, he flicks a business card at me. It lands inside one of the money slots in the drawer. Sighing, he stuffs his hands in his pockets and stares out the front of the shop.

"*His* name…is Jasper," he grumbles. "And he's back, apparently."

"Wait…Jasper's back in town? That's awesome!"

Isn't it? He was the coolest boss I ever had, one of only two, but still the coolest. Wolf looked up to him like a big brother. Why the hell doesn't he look pleased about this?

"He *moved back* three months ago."

"Really? Well, that's cool, man. I know how much you missed him. I bet he was happy to see you. Tell him to stop in sometime. We can all go out for drinks."

I don't feel like going out anywhere, but for Jasper, I might make an exception. He's a friendly face from one of the better parts of my past and reminds me of Nancy.

"Yeah. Sure," he grumps. "If he's not too preoccupied."

What the fuck is that about?

I don't get a chance to ask. He tells me goodnight and heads out the door. Fucking hell. When it rains, it pours.

Now that I'm alone, I don't have to worry about getting a side eye from him for checking my phone for the millionth time tonight. Drawing it out of my pocket, my last message still has no reply.

I feel like a puppy who bit its owner's hand one too many times. My words are sad puppy dog eyes that have no impact on getting me petted.

A rapid succession of thump sounds echoes softly through the shop. I turn in the direction of the noise and squint through the darkened room toward the lit exit sign above the back door. The thumping grows louder, although it's soft and muffled by the exterior wall. I know that distinct sound. It's the sound my feet have made hundreds of times padding down the stairs from my apartment.

I saw Wolf pull away out front. It wouldn't be him. He knows I'm still in the shop. The lovesick part of me wants it to be Aaron, but lovesick me has shit judgment. Hurrying to the back door, I wrench it open to the frigid night just in time to see a figure hop inside the passenger side of a beat-up old pickup truck. It's a figure that looks a lot like the shape of one Leonard Bennick.

What the fuck now?

The driver, another male figure from the looks of it, spins out quickly, but I don't think they even saw me. It's like they planned on leaving in a hurry ahead of time. That can only mean one thing, and it's *not* a good thing.

I curse under my breath and book it up the stairwell. Bursting into my apartment, I flick on the lights, expecting the worst. I don't know why I'm panicking; it's not like I have much up here that's worth stealing in one go. There was nothing in the pickup's bed. What the hell did he take now?

My gaze lands on the coffee table in the living room, and my blood runs cold. There's nothing missing. Just the opposite. The new addition to my apartment sends gooseflesh over my skin. Why does that look just like the sports bag Jason had?

Hedging forward, I swallow hard, as if the boogeyman will pop out of it. If Aaron were here, he'd probably tell me that if I touch it, I'll be dead. I have no choice, though. There's a note folded on top of it with my name on it. What does the horror movie code say about that?

Son,

We both know I was no good. I'd really have liked the chance to show you I'd changed that.
I can never make up for what I did to you and your mother. God knows I don't deserve your—or His—forgiveness. I had eight years to try to forgive myself, and I still can't.
This won't forgive me either, it only adds another black mark to my soul, but you're worth it. Con men know con men...
I can live the rest of my life, at least knowing you and your fella have the chance you deserve at happiness, and that's enough for me. If he is who you say he is, then you can sleep now, knowing he's safe and what's yours is yours again.

All my love,
Leonard Bennick

PS - Be mindful of your neighbors in the future.

I have no idea what he's talking about. With a shaky hand, I pull the zipper tab back and peel the flap open. The bag is filled with money, *my* money. I know because it's bundled the way I bundled it and some even have my deposit slips still affixed to them.

Reaching inside, I draw out a manilla folder and scan the documents inside. There's a passport with Jason's face on it, but not his name.

It says Tomás, the name he gave me when I first saw him at Aaron's. There's another with Aaron's face on it, looking a bit younger than he does now. The signature on it doesn't look like his. I've seen it.

The next document doesn't make much sense to me because it looks like it's in Spanish, but the longer I study it, I'm certain it's a marriage certificate. It was dated eight months ago. I'm not even going to entertain that Aaron knew about this. I already doubted him once. He wouldn't have been in contact with Jason for that long and not told me. He wouldn't have gotten married again in another country and not told me.

The next document convinces me I'm right. It also makes my knees go so weak, I drop to the floor. It's an insurance policy for a one-million-dollar payout—an insurance policy on Aaron's alias. Hand rattling, I flip to the last paper in the folder. Nothing can be worse than what I just saw.

I stare at a lease. I know for certain that it is because this one is in English. It's a month-to-month lease for an apartment across the street, above the liquor store. The tenant listed on it is Jason's alias name.

I read Leonard's cryptic letter again, and it all hits me like a left hook out of nowhere.

'Another black mark to my soul.'

'Be mindful of your neighbors in the future.'

A tear falls onto the letter as I gasp for air. There's only one reason Leonard would have Jason's bag, a man he'd never even met.

Con men know con men… He figured out what I couldn't and saved the person I love because I was too blind to see what was happening.

CHAPTER 42

Aaron

George's phone pings again with another text message alert. Reading the message, he sighs. Pacing past him on the couch, I give him a sympathetic look as I confirm the details the lawyer on the phone repeats back to me. I'm so grateful that he's here and how supportive he's been since I told him and my parents everything yesterday morning. He even went to the funeral home in town with me to help arrange Jason's transport back to Seattle. Right now, he's running defense to our worried mother and doing an admirable job of keeping her at bay. Rolling his eyes at me, he shakes his head and rattles off another text message to her.

Doing another lap around the couch, I rub the tense muscles in my neck as Sam Hodges, the pro bono lawyer we found, goes over all the information I gave him. He's going to help me navigate through the unexpected debt that Jason racked up and even thinks he can get some of it waived, considering the circumstances.

I don't think Grace Reider will be very happy that he has questions for her, but my sympathy level for my former mother-in-law has severely decreased since I found out she knew all along that her son hadn't been killed in a car accident. I was the one they drained dry and had debts put upon while she and Jason went on living their best lives. While I don't wish anyone ill, Sam is convinced that he should be able to prove some kind of money movement between the two of them. If that gets me further out of the red, I don't mind sharing a little bit of my misery with Grace, after all the unkind phone calls she's given me over the past two years.

There's a knock at the door and my first instinct is that it's more trouble. That seems to be the only thing that's found my door lately. Exchanging glances with George, I shrug, but then I notice the Suburban parked out front.

Smiling, I tell Sam that I'll have to call him back. When I open the door, Easton's expression is dire. I don't understand why until he looks down and angles a black gym bag forward from behind his back. Jason's black gym bag.

"I…found this on my coffee table last night."

"Is that…Jason's?"

Wincing, he nods. Reaching into his coat, he pulls out a folded sheet of paper and hands it to me. "There was a note attached to it."

My hands tremble as I take it from him. What in God's name does this mean? Moving back, I find the sense to let him in and close the door. I don't like how grave his face looks right now. He gives George a nod, looking weary.

I've overburdened my brother and my parents with enough information. Something tells me I'm not going to like what this surprise is, so I'd rather find out before I decide if I want to share it with George just yet.

"George…could you give us some privacy, please? You've done so much already. I don't know how to thank you."

It was nothing, he signs, casting a curious glance at Easton. *Are you sure? I don't mind staying if you need me.*

I want to weep over having my brother back. His quick call to action, when I didn't even know I needed someone, will forever leave an imprint on my heart.

"Yeah. This is Easton," I inform him. "I'll be fine. I'll text you later."

Nodding, he steps forward and shakes Easton's hand. The introduction was something I was hoping for under different circumstances, but it warms my heart that they've finally met. Still, the sight of the bag in Easton's hand has my pulse pumping erratically, anxious for the moment George leaves.

I'll deal with Mom, he signs, giving my shoulder a squeeze before he heads to the door.

"Thank you."

Alone now with Easton, the eerie bag, and a note with his name on it, I cast him a questioning look, but he says nothing. Setting the bag down on the back of the couch, he unzips it, revealing bundles of cash. His throat undulates like it's difficult to swallow, and his gaze shifts from mine to the note, telling me that's where he wants me to find my answers.

Unfolding it, I read it. And then… I read it again, trembling harder the second time.

The message is between the lines, but my brain puts together the meaning of the new black mark on Leonard's soul and why he'd have Jason's bag.

"Did you know?" I wheeze.

"No," he chokes out. "No, I swear."

Gaping at the contents of the bag, it feels like a subway train flashing through my mind. The whir of mental images and the questions speed through my brain in a blur.

I set the note on the back of the couch, no longer able to hold what feels like a murder weapon. There's a folder inside the bag, and my stomach churns upon seeing it. Jason pulled a marriage certificate out of here one day. I can only imagine what Easton must have thought if he saw it.

It's inside, making my face flame, but there are other documents, too. A lease for an apartment in Hampton, with Jason's alias on it.

"What is this? When did he get this?"

He stays quiet, looking grim and pitiful. Why does he look pitiful?

I read on, registering what I missed on my first perusal. The address is the same street that Easton is on.

"Oh, God," I whisper. "He…he was watching you."

"*Us*. I think he was watching *us*," he says sympathetically.

Disgust erupts inside me. I thought it was odd how Jason suggested that maybe not telling Easton about him was the better choice. Did he fucking plan to whisk me off to Brazil, where we'd live off Easton's money? My body is shaking violently on the verge of vomiting, but I'm too angry to stop my discovery. I fan to the next paper, and it just fills me with more questions.

"Why would he have life insurance on me? I never even agreed to go with him."

"It was dated eight months ago," Easton explains and then turns an unsettling look on me that's full of pity. "You need to have it for a year before it's payable."

Payable… Payable, as in…*if I died*. Except, a part of me knows it's more likely for *when* I died.

My grip goes slack and the documents flutter to the floor. A gurgle of bile burns my throat, choking me. My body convulses so hard that I stagger back. It feels like I have no control over my functions.

"Oh, God," I garble, a wave of tears springing to my eyes. "I'm sorry! I…this is all my fault."

"No," he chokes out, inching forward. "It's my fault. I could have protected you."

'*Protected me?*' What is he talking about? How could he have known? "He broke into your building and stole your money!"

Shaking his head, his eyes are red and glossy. His lower lip trembles, and he sputters, "He…could have killed you," he whispers.

I'm aware of that horrifying fact. It's why I don't understand the pity he's exhibiting for me when I've brought nothing but grief to his door until he drops to his knees in front of me. His hands cling to my hips, and his head falls forward against my stomach. A heartbreaking sob pierces the room.

"The things I said…You could have gone with him and…and he would have killed you! All because I was scared and hurt," he croaks. "I know I ruined everything, but I'm sorry. I'm so sorry. I'd have fucking died if he'd done anything to you."

The unsettling sensation from Jason's apparent motives crumbles and falls away. It's replaced with gratitude, so much gratitude it brings me to my knees and the man pouring his agony out at my feet.

"It's over," I whisper, wrapping my arms around him. "It's over now. I'm fine. *We're* fine."

Squeezing me tight, his head rattles back and forth. "It's not," he weeps. "My *father* killed your *husband*." Swiping underneath his nose, his eye color appears electric behind his tears. "And the fucked-up thing is that I'm glad he did because if he hadn't, you'd have ended up dead. I'd have lost you either way. I didn't…I didn't protect you. I fucking closed up, just like you say I do, and I could have stopped it all."

How can he think that? Gripping his shoulders, I give them a squeeze. "It wasn't your job to save me."

His head shakes adamantly. "No. I should have."

Cupping his face, I can't get him to look at me. What I can do, though, is pepper kisses over his tears for loving me so deeply.

"And that's just one reason why I love you so much," I whisper against his lips.

"How…how can you love me?"

"Easily, and whenever you let me."

"But I…I've been complete shit to you," he babbles, shaking his head again. "First, when you found me, and then when I was out of my mind when Jason turned up, and again over the robbery. The things I said…" Grimacing, he rubs the fabric of my sweater anxiously in between his fingers. "I knew it wasn't you. *I knew it*, but I still said it." He looks so lost, it's breaking my heart to see him torturing himself like this. "I'm no good," he rasps. "It's in my fucking DNA. I never will be. I'm…broken."

My God, is that what he thinks? What human being could go through the unknowns we have over the past week without doubts?

"No. You're not," I insist, making sure to look him in the eye as I say it.

Exhaling, his shoulders sag. He hangs his head like my words freed him of some of the weight. I've never witnessed anyone rely so hard on my approval. I didn't know it was possible to love as fiercely as he does.

"What are you going to do now?" he asks, sounding a little calmer.

There are a million things to do, but there's only one thing that I want to do right now. "Go to bed," I reply. "I'm exhausted."

Nodding, he rises to his feet and swipes at his tears. "I'll leave you be."

He's still not looking at me, his head hung like a scolded child. He turns like he's going to head to the door. It's astounding. Not a word I said has sunk in. Grabbing a hold of his arm, I stop him.

"I'm going to go to bed," I say again, but add with emphasis, "whichever of *ours* you're planning on sleeping in."

Lips parting, his gaze scans my face. How could I end up with one man who cared about nothing but himself and another who would walk through fire for me?

Taking his hand, I bring his knuckles to my lips and give them a kiss. "And I'll do the same thing tomorrow," I whisper. "And again the day after that, and for all the ones after that, until you can't stand me anymore."

His tears spill over his eyes. Shaking his head in disbelief, he lets out a ragged breath. God, I can't take it anymore.

Stepping forward, I pull him into my arms and murmur against his hair. "Sometimes being broken just means you're missing your other piece. I don't fit anywhere better than with you, Easton. I don't care how tattered our edges are."

The sob that racks out of him reverberates against my chest. Sputtering, he clenches me in an embrace that I can tell is as strong as the love he has in his heart for me. He was wrong. I *am* protected. I wouldn't have gotten through this without a love like his.

CHAPTER 43
Easton

I'm a fucking mess. A complete and utter mess. I still don't understand how he can so easily dismiss what I did, what Leonard did, or what Jason would have done to him. For the first time in my life, I think I actually want to seek therapy. I know you're supposed to do that kind of thing for yourself, but I'd do it for Aaron. I'd do anything to make sure I'm a solid human being who won't lose his shit and misconstrue things in the future.

My father killed someone I loved. Then he killed someone I despised because he was trying to show me he loved me. How the fuck is a person supposed to feel about that?

If I tell the police my money was returned, they'll go looking for him. I know it's the right thing to do, but it seems like a lousy way to repay someone for saving the man I'm over the moon for. Right now, I just revel in the ability to be able to breathe with ease again. I revel in hearing that Aaron wants to be my missing puzzle piece. A puzzle metaphor—he's such a dork. God, I love him. He's right, though. I know it's the reason I never fit anywhere with anyone else. No one is a fit for me the way he is.

Un-burrowing my snotty face from the front of his sweater, I cup his face. "I love you," I rasp. It's not enough though. I don't know if it's possible to even convey how much I love him. I kiss his cheekbone, the corner of his mouth, his forehead. "I always have, and I always will. If I ever say I don't, I'm lying."

Smiling, he rubs his thumb over my jaw and whispers, "I know."

He says it so matter-of-factly and with such confidence that a puff of laughter leaves my lips. More tears spill down my face. I must have done something right in my life if I found the one man who knows me better than I know myself.

Snaking my arms around him, I just hold him, grateful that he's here. Grateful he's all right. And grateful he exists. We stand there like that for a while. Whether he's just humoring me or he needs it as much as I do, I don't know.

When he finally draws back, I've stopped bawling my eyes out at least. The papers of Jason's hideous plot are scattered all over the floor. The bag of money is open like we just robbed a bank. Aaron's living room essentially looks like a damn crime scene. I bend down to retrieve the mess, but he stops me.

Taking the papers, he tosses them in the bag. "Just leave it," he whispers, shaking his head.

Tugging my hand, he gives me this tender smile like nothing but us matters right now. When he starts toward his room, I go where I'm led. I'm so drained from the mind fuck that was the past few days that I'm grateful for the assistance.

Releasing my hand, he makes no great affair of undressing. He doesn't even face me as he lets his shirt and pants fall to the floor. Bending down, he starts on my boots while I'm still working on getting my pants undone. Smiling up at me, he even waits for me to lift my feet so he can pull them off. Kicking my pants away, I'm about to reach for my socks when he pulls the comforter back and tugs my arm for me to crawl into bed.

My side no sooner hits the mattress, and he's drawing the blanket over us and pulling me into his arms. I was starting to wonder if he was hoping for intimacy, but the kiss he gives me is chaste and sweet. It's like a healing seal over a wound. He places another on my forehead and then sighs, closing his eyes. I stare at his peaceful yet exhausted-looking face for a few moments. My eyes are growing heavy just from the comfort of his soft bed and from being warm in his arms. The sound of his breathing evens out into a slow stream.

He's asleep. He just wanted to sleep next to me… to hold me.

I give up the fight and let my eyes slip closed. I suddenly understand the path to his serenity. We love each other. We know it, and that's all that matters.

I awake to moonlight spilling through the bedroom windows. Blinking, I squint at the stars over the woods outside, remembering the last time I was here. We had the curtains drawn tight for fear that Jason could be out there watching. Aaron must have opened them at some point. It's an inspiring nod to his unflinching attitude in the face of everything. Defeat or be defeated.

Glancing down, I zone in on the soft stroking sensation over my ribs. Aaron's gaze is fixed nowhere, a peaceful look on his face as his thumb traces little paths along my skin. Running my fingers through his hair, I cover his hand with my other one. We must have slept for hours on end.

"How long have you been awake?"

His shoulder rises, and he hums a sleepy sound. "A little while."

"You could have gotten up."

"I was happy where I was." Leaning up, he dusts his lips over mine. "Did you sleep okay?" he asks, drawing back like he's going to sit up.

I go with him, but turn and plant a hand on either side of his hips. Leaning in, I give him another kiss, deepening it on purpose until his head rests on his pillow.

"Yes," I whisper in front of his mouth.

Looping his arms around my neck, he treats me to that beautiful smile of his. I'll never get over his All-American, poster-child-for-handsomeness thing. Bending down, I trail kisses along the underside of his jaw. We've been in this bed dozens of times, but for some reason, everything feels new. Each touch. Each kiss.

It reminds me of the first night we were together and the way he garnished my body with a series of delicate caresses and touches of his lips. It seems fitting to return the gesture now. Moving lower, I work my mouth across his collarbone and around one dark nipple.

There's this sense of freedom in the air and maybe even around my soul, like the burdens of the past are far behind me. I don't exactly want the past to be gone—there were so many moments of it I'll cherish. However, it feels as though it's finally been sorted, a two-thousand-piece puzzle that's last piece has finally been placed.

Trailing my cheekbone along his side, I breathe him in and trace the cords in his arm with my fingertips. His hands stroke my hair lazily, and his stomach rises and falls on a contented sigh.

"I guess you had a good dream," he teases.

Smiling against his happy trail, I press a kiss below his belly button and slide my hand up the leg of his shorts. "No, but I woke up next to one."

He barks out a laugh, shaking against my jaw. "Good one."

Reaching into the other leg of his boxer briefs, I slide my hands underneath him, grip the elastic, and slide them down. When I glance up, he lifts his hips and has that dreamy look on his face that I love. It always makes me feel like I can do no wrong, which is far from the truth.

But, in Aaron's eyes, I don't think I can. It's an unexplained mystery for the ages.

Making up for a lifetime of neglecting foreplay, I paint his body with my palms and brush my lips across the delicate skin at his hips. I work my way down to his knees, which has him producing a giggle when I skirt to the back of his knee. Ticklish spot—noted.

His hands grip my shoulders and he tugs at me to move back up, but I resist. I'm far from finished. Kneading the muscles in his legs, I do my best to give him some kind of massage as I place little kisses and brushes of my tongue on the insides of his thighs.

"Am I going to get to participate in this?" he asks, his voice sounding strained.

I have to look around the obstruction standing in my view when I peer up at him. "It looks like you already are."

Snorting, he reaches down and gives himself a stroke. The sight of him touching himself has my balls drawing up tighter.

"It didn't require much effort on my part," he snarks and then bites his lower lip when he sees the tent in my boxers.

"Good," I concur, crawling higher and sliding my underwear down. "There's something sexy about a lazy, horny man."

His laughter dies out when I slide my lips over the head of his cock until they kiss his hand. Grunting, he releases his grip to cup the underside of my jaw. His fingers slide down my neck, stroking it as I take him deeper.

I swear I appreciate everything from before this mess happened, but everything feels different now. I thought I was more in tune with him than anyone I'd ever been with before, but now…now it's like discovering a new drug. I'm not rushing for a finale, hopped up on pheromones or lust. Don't get me wrong, I still want to see that look on his face when he cums, but just the act of having him in my mouth is a moment not to go unappreciated.

Rolling my palm gently over his sac, I glide my tongue up the thick vein on the underside of his cock. Sighing, he scoots his feet closer to his ass, inviting. I slip my fingers down his crease and then back up. It's nothing to write home about, just a light pet, but it feels more intimate than the times I've slipped my fingers inside him.

"Okay, okay," he lets out in a rush. "I give up now. Come here."

I go where I'm yanked, his fingers digging into the meat underneath my armpits. Landing on his chest with an *oof*, my amusement is stifled by the urgency of his mouth. His legs do some kind of contortionist thing, flicking my boxers off from around my ankles with his feet. Gripping my back with one hand, he stretches his other arm toward his nightstand and fumbles for the bottle of lube. Does he think I'm going to go somewhere if he lets go?

Bending his knees, he widens his legs around me and flicks the bottle open, leaning up to attack my mouth the entire time. I hear a *squelch* sound and then feel him flinch. His hand brushes against my balls, telling me he's smearing his cold deposit over his hole.

Someone's eager. Three cheers for foreplay.

"Impatient much?" I tease.

His slathered hand grips and coats me, stealing my breath. "Overdue," he murmurs, nipping my lower lip. "Just overdue."

I feel like a sex doll the way he guides my tip to his entrance. For the record, I have no problem being his sex doll. The look in his eyes isn't the carnal one I've seen before at times. It's wanting, but wanting for something far beyond the realm of physical touch. It's soul-deep because I can feel it in my own as I stare back at him.

Moving my hand over his, I take hold of myself, stilling his movements. The first time I topped with him was an urgent flurry of insatiability that neither of us could stop. This feels like another first again, but I want to do it differently. He must register something because he draws his hand away and slides it up to the pillow. Gripping it, he waits patiently, like he's just committed himself to a penalty box.

Leaning down, I swipe my tongue against his, a slow carving of his mouth. "I love you," I whisper. The hairs on my arms spike as though they're as aware as I am of how fragile that four-letter word can be. And then I press against his heated ring.

With a mewl, he opens immediately, drawing me in. His breath vents against my lips. His gaze drinks me in. God, all I ever did before was just fuck. Stroking his cheek, I return the smile he gives to me and feather a kiss over his lips.

As I learn the art of making love, I feather dozens more on the mouth that owns the words that give me purpose. His voice sings beautiful sounds that mine will never be able to with each undulation of our hips. For once, I feel no humility in not being able to mirror the exquisite noise. Every time I rasp or my throat makes a growl that should be a groan, it spurs him on. Somehow, I give him what he needs just as much as he does me.

Just when I think he's close and I should push lovemaking to the wayside, he grips my ass, holding me deep inside him. Drawing his legs up around my back, he locks his ankles together. Carding his fingers into my hair, he sweeps his tongue around the inside of my mouth until I come up breathless.

"You don't ever get to leave me, Easton Bennick. I love you too much to lose you."

The words pull a painful sound from my throat. Reaching between us, I grip the end of his cock tight and stroke him. "I never will."

His body squeezes me, unleashing the maddening build in my balls. A wave of heat engulfs my legs. I bury my groan into his kiss, feeling his release crest my grasp as I pulse inside him. His fingerprints are going to be indented on my back like a badge of honor. We shudder and convulse against each other, a battle of two blissed-out bodies.

Blinking through my haze, I slip free when I can no longer stand the torment to my sensitized flesh. For some reason, I want to name the feeling coursing through my veins as he smiles up at me lazily. Happy and terrified. Happy and terrified. Maybe that's what having the love of your life is supposed to feel like. The terrified part is no longer over the thought of him up and leaving or me screwing something up. It's a terrified I can make peace with, one that I hope is years down the road.

Pulling my head down, he kisses me one last time. I peel myself away and stagger toward his bathroom on wobbly legs to fetch him something to clean up with. Once I'm back in bed, I bite back a smile when he pretzels himself around me.

A strong gust of wind rattles the windows. It pulls my mind to a dark place that I don't want to go—a vision of Jason lying dead on the shore of Lake Maranacook. It's in the next county. I'll never know whether it was Leonard's intention, but a morbid part of me is grateful he spared us from having the foul memory in our hometown by doing it away from Hampton.

Aaron's brother must know everything by now, judging by the mood when I arrived earlier. I can't imagine what their parents must think. Recalling all Aaron's stories about them, I don't suspect it was an easy thing for him to tell his family. There will probably still be legal questions or inquiries from the police as they dig into Jason's past. Will this be a dark cloud over us forever? Right now, everything seems like nothing could disrupt the bubble of joy we created tonight, but Aaron has a lot to go through still.

A fingertip taps my forehead, and I find him smirking at me. "There's a question in there. I can almost see it."

"I was just wondering—" Thinking better of it, I shake my head. "What?"

Grimacing, I don't want to ruin his post-coital bliss, but I more or less promised not to hold things in anymore. "I was wondering…what do we do now?"

"Find something to eat," he groans. "Because I'm starving."

Chuckling, I press a kiss to his nose and glide my palm over his stomach. He must see something in my expression, however, because the playful twinkle in his eyes dies.

"That's not what you meant, is it?" he murmurs, tracing my jaw.

"Forget it. I'm being…emotional." I can't believe I'm even using that word.

Intertwining our fingers, he brings my hand to his mouth and kisses my knuckles. "No. It's a good question."

Fuck. The last thing I wanted to do was to make him sad or wary of the future.

"I have a suggestion if you want to hear it."

"Yeah," I agree, although I want to strike my question from the record. *'What do we do now?'*

"Live," he says with this calm sort of wisdom in his eyes. Smiling, he moves his hand over my heart. "And love. Everything else is just background noise."

Live and *love*. It's a two-step life plan I can't find holes in. I think this is the moment I'll officially quit worrying about what-ifs.

"You're pretty smart for a sexy guy. You know that?"

Whipping off the covers, I get up, intent on feeding him. Intent on living and loving, no matter what comes.

Aaron
Easton
LATER

EPILOGUE

Ten months later

"Manicki?"

Looking up from the counter where I'm talking to Shannon, I find Easton leaning against his stall with a smirk on his face. So, he wants to do the customer/tattoo artist thing, huh?

"Good luck," Shannon says, flashing me a wink.

Smiling, I walk toward my man with butterflies in my stomach. He looks positively predatory right now. He'd better not look at all his clients like that.

Leaning in for a kiss, I'm met with a hand held up between us. "Ah, ah! Hands to yourself, please. We don't want other customers getting the wrong idea."

Oh, my gosh. He's enjoying this way too much. Snickering, I roll my eyes and take a seat in the chair I've seen dozens of customers in, but have never once sat in myself. I never thought I'd want a tattoo. I can't say that I even really do now, but I want *what* it will mean. I want it with every breath in my body. It's just a huge bonus that I'm going to get to experience firsthand the sight of Easton at work from this perspective.

"I was thinking," he says off-handedly, pulling on a pair of nitrile gloves. "Why don't we take a vacation?"

I guess this means we're dispensing with the customer/tattoo artist dynamic now. Good. I think I prefer the special treatment of knowing it's my boyfriend who's giving me my first tattoo.

"You just bought a house. Why don't we wait a while?"

"*We* bought a house," he corrects, raising a challenging brow.

This again… I know he wants me to feel like I contributed equally to the down payment, but we both know the truth is that I didn't. And his claim that him staying at my place for the better part of the past year after Wolf moved into his old apartment was payment enough holds no water is this debate. I would have settled for the home he referred to as the seventies drug house, but when he saw how much I loved the craftsman we looked at, he called the realtor when I wasn't around. The rat… the sweet, spoils-me-rotten rat.

"I barely contributed anything," I mutter, my face heating.

I get an eye roll for that remark, but it has no effect on me. I make sure to hold my own these days and put my foot down, knowing there won't be repercussions. I know I won't ever feel beholden or beneath him the way Jason sometimes made me feel; Easton would never let me. While it's a wonderful feeling to have such a caring and compassionate partner, I'm still looking forward to the end of next year when my strict budgeting plan will have allowed me to pay off the few remaining debts that Sam wasn't able to get cleared. Grace was none too happy about having to take over several of them, but in the end, she decided it was preferable to jail.

"So…you *won't* take me on a vacation?" he tries to pout.

"Of course, I will. Just give me a few more paychecks, maybe. Why? Is there somewhere in particular you want to go?"

Leaning in, his lips give mine a sweet kiss. "Anywhere," he whispers with a smile.

Oh. My. Word. I'd get a tattoo every week if it made him this lovable.

"You're way too happy about this." I laugh.

Smirking, he grabs his sketch pad and holds it out in front of me. I've seen some of the other artists put their designs on stencils that they can transfer to a customer's skin, essentially using it as a pattern. I'd be wary about getting it done freehand if it was anyone else but Easton. I know that's why he's showing me the sketch—my last opportunity to change my mind or request any changes. The way I deliberate over little things, it's almost comical that I have zero doubts about this. It's absolutely beautiful just as he's drafted—two halves of a heart that can join like puzzle pieces. His name is on one of them, mine on the other.

"It looks just as good as it did the other day," I tell him proudly, giving him a thumbs up.

Lifting my T-shirt, I draw it over my head and hang it over the armrest. Settling back in the chair, I try to relax my muscles and take in the view of the shop from this vantage point.

"It's going to hurt," he cautions, tracing his gloved fingertip over the center of my chest. "You know that, right?"

I can see in his eyes that he's really asking if I'm sure I want to do this for him. It's as much for me as it is for him, though. He's already permanently engraved on the organ inside my chest. I figured having it on the outside, too, might make me not feel like I'm going to burst with the overload of affection I feel for him every second of the day.

"And then it won't." I smile. "Because that's what love does. It heals."

His features soften, and he closes his eyes for a moment. Leaning forward, he rests his forehead against mine. "Don't talk like that right now, or you'll leave here with half a tattoo."

"It's okay. I know where you live."

Chuckling, he brushes his nose against mine. I love the look he gets on his face whenever we talk about how we've officially moved in together. He gets this gloat about him like he's absconded with sought-after treasure.

Reaching over to his supplies, he grabs his bottle of skin disinfectant and applies it to my chest. My heartbeat seems stronger under the touch, knowing what's coming. Sitting back, he looks serious again. Eyeing my exposed chest, he blows out a breath.

Is he… nervous? This better not be about his whole tattoo lore speech of how it's a bad omen to tattoo a couples' names on each other. We went over this, and I told him I don't believe that. I'm not letting a superstition break us up after all we've been through.

"What's with the jitters? *I'm* the one getting their first tattoo."

"*First?*"

"*Last*," I correct.

Smirking, he swings his plastic-wrapped worktable over and unwraps a new needle. "Oh, I think I can find some other places I wouldn't mind seeing my name."

"What? Where?"

Grinning with the devil in his eyes, he inserts the needle into his gun and sets it to the desired tip depth. Glancing at my chest again, there's this haze in his eyes that looks a lot like pride. Grinning, he traces the shape of a heart over my skin and murmurs, "Just here is fine."

"Yeah?" I venture hopefully. He's asked me if I was sure dozens of times over the past few days. Well, it's not just my name going over my heart.

"Yeah." He nods.

"Does that mean you're *not* going to look for other places to put one?" I tease.

"No," he scoffs. "I've already thought about that hundreds of times."

Well, *that's* interesting! I will now fear for my flesh each time he stares at me when I'm naked. "Oh, really? Care to share?"

"No."

"Come on."

"It's not important."

"It is to me. What did *Fantasy Aaron* have? An ass tat?"

I kind of love that I can still make him blush sometimes. Checking his ink, he shakes his head and murmurs, "That was before I knew what love was."

He's not going to have to tattoo a heart over my chest at this rate. The one beneath my ribcage is about to beat itself to the surface.

When he looks up, his gaze travels to the place where I want my ink. Blowing out another breath, he scrubs his forearm down his face, mindful of his sanitized glove.

I had no idea this was going to be such a big ordeal for him. I knew he was happy about it when I first asked—minus the whole superstition thing—but *this*… this is a whole other level of something. Is he worried he's going to mar me for life?

"*I* should be nervous. Not you. Do you want me to have Wolf do it instead?"

Those green eyes flick to mine with a warning in them. I hear the *click* of a switch and the tattoo gun buzzes to life as he holds that heated look on me. Oh, my word—someone just went total caveman on me.

I burst out laughing. For the next hour, there are plenty of moments when I have to try to keep from cracking up at his antics and comments so I can hold still. I'm a little sore and numb by the end of it, but I can't stop smiling. I used to yearn to know what his laughter sounded like. I never realized I'd discover the sound of my own along the way. I don't know if I'll ever get used to it, but I'd better. It's the sound of my future with him.

DEAR READER

Thank you for reading my story and for getting this paperback copy. I hope you enjoyed where the characters took me. These things pop into my head and I have to get them out.

If you'd like to connect with me you can find me here:

www.diannaroman.com
or over on Patreon